ATONEMENT FOR THE ALPHA KING

THE ALPHA KING'S BREEDER
BOOK TWELVE

BELLA MOONDRAGON

For Larry

CONTENTS

1

———

AN OPEN DOOR

Misty

SOME DAYS I DON'T THINK ABOUT THE WAR.

Some mornings I wake to sunshine and Cole's arms around me while I cradle Adrian in my arms and don't think about how the three of us came to be. I think of clean sheets that smell like lavender, not the smell of Richard's bloody war room where I'd healed that cursed wolf. I sip coffee while watching my mate–my husband–the love of my life rush around the kitchen packing his bag for another long shift at the hospital instead of watching him don that black cloak.

We have a house instead of shared spaces. Our home is safe and full of love instead of constant stress and the crushing weight that, at any moment, our safety will end.

But some days I have to remind myself that we made it out. That we're here, and whole, and together.

Today is one of those days.

Mom peeks into the massive library at the castle of Crescent Falls. Her wine-red hair is tied back in a neat bun, but otherwise, she's covered in finger-paint and wearing an exhausted, but utterly happy, expression as she asks, "Hungry? I can bring you up some lunch, maybe?"

"I'm nearly done," I reply, glancing over my shoulder with a smile. "Don't worry about it. I'll come down soon. How's Addy?"

"He's fine," she smiles, giving me a little shrug. "Trying to resist a nap. He's very interested in everything Blake and Liam are up to today."

"He wants to be a big boy so bad already." My smile weakens. Adrian, who we call Addy most of the time these days, is three months old and growing fast. He's a healthy, happy baby. An easy baby. But I look at him sometimes and see our past—how this little soul came into this world, and how different his life could be right now had my grandmother Isla not sacrificed herself for us.

I swallow past the growing lump in my throat, turning back to my laptop.

I hear Mom's footsteps coming up behind me and smell her sweet perfume as she leans in to look over the top of my head at the screen. "You've been working so hard on this, sweetheart."

"Dad thinks it's important," I reply with a sigh. "So do I."

She squeezes my shoulder. "Make sure you take a break, all right?"

I nod but can't look into her eyes. She'll see the pain in mine, I'm sure. The nightmares, the memories I pray fade into ash.

I wait to continue typing until her footsteps recede, and the library door snaps shut, then turn back to my project.

Cataloging every wolf who went to battle that fateful day.

Anders Evermore was only fourteen when he followed his two older brothers and their father into battle. He snuck away from his mother and traveled for two days, alone, to reach the battlefield outside of Serpentia. He was one of the first "deaths," having perished jumping in front of one of Richard's monsters to save his brother. Marianne Clemson was twenty-three, mated, and had a baby at home when she and several of her friends left their village in the Roguelands to follow their mates into battle after deciding they weren't going to let them die.

I smile at this tidbit of information, even though the memory of the four of us–Sarah, Kenna, Aviva, and me–doing the same thing stings a bit.

I continue down the list I compiled recently when I had the opportunity to interview a group of soldiers from Crescent Falls. It's been easy to tell their stories, especially since all of them have phones and email addresses, but gathering the stories from those in Eastonia has been damn near impossible.

I only know about Anders and Marianne because of those who served beside them, who remembered them from battle and the war camps after the end of the battle. Kenna sent me her list from the infirmary she set up in Serpentia in the days following the war, giving me a better idea of who fought, but still, I'm missing so much information.

The weight of knowing I need to return to Eastonia to complete this catalog–this written history of the war that changed our world–presses heavily on my shoulders when I finally decide to close my laptop and head downstairs to the de-facto playroom slash war zone Mom has set up for the boys.

Sarah's business designing parks and gardens across the capital is booming. She's been leaving her boys with Mom or Cosette during the day while she hops around, elbows deep in dirt. She keeps herself busy enough to forget, I'm sure.

Just like I'm trying to do.

I turn into the playroom at the back of the castle just as Liam jumps off a couch right onto Blake, who squeals and rolls with Liam on his back, a fight ensuing.

"All right, nap time for everyone," Mom says, clapping her hands.

"Where's Cosette today?" I ask, scooping a very sleepy Addy out of his bouncer seat.

Mom separates Blake and Liam, giving them a sharp look I remember clearly from my childhood. "Artyom had a meeting today, and Cosette went with him. She seemed anxious, which is unlike her."

I furrow my brows. Artyom, Cosette's mate and husband, is a retired commander who used to work for my uncle Ryatt in his massive army. Artyom commanded the Ghost army for many years before Evander took over and has been living in a little cottage in Shadowcrest near my brother's house for the better part of four years.

"What was the meeting about?" I ask, a prickle of unease creeping through my body.

"I have no idea. Your dad is in Eastonia, you know, and he took Artyom and Cosette with him. Something about the Ghost army, I'm sure."

"Okay," I whisper, praying silently that's all this is about, and we're not already facing another daunting threat. "Well, I'm done for the day, I guess. I'm going to take Addy home. I think he'll sleep in the car."

"He'll fall asleep immediately," she replies, walking over to kiss her youngest grandson on the cheek. "If you need to get out of the house tomorrow, just come back here. I'll have the boys again."

Thirty minutes later, I pull my car into the driveway of the stunning house we designed last winter. It's a perfect square with two stories and beautiful windows facing south that light up nearly every room. The front yard is perfectly manicured, but the garage is still a mess. We've been taking our time unpacking, seeing as we have a baby and moved in a week after he was born, but it feels good to have a place to land, finally. A place that's ours. A place we made ours.

Cole's car is in the driveway, however, which makes me crinkle my nose in confusion. He wasn't supposed to be off from the hospital until later tonight.

I lug Addy's car seat through the garage door into the kitchen and find my mate leaning against the kitchen island nursing what I assume is his fifth cup of coffee today.

Cole bursts into silent action, taking the car seat from me and saying into my mind, '*I'll put him in his crib.*'

'*If he wakes up, you're getting him back down again,*' I reply, giving him a look. '*He didn't sleep at all at the castle.*'

Cole smiles softly, nodding as he disappears around the corner and into the depths of the house, giving me a moment of quiet I'm not sure I want right now.

I pour myself a cup of coffee and turn, looking out the windows that give me a view of the wooded backyard. Through the trees, I can see the beginnings of another house being built. I let my mind wander over the possibilities that another family like ours will move in, that they'll have a baby boy who will grow to be Addy's best friend, and as the years pass, they'll run through the woods separating our yards, playing endlessly.

Living sweetly, peacefully, in safety.

My heart lurches at the same moment Cole returns. "How'd it go today?"

"I got a few hours of work done," I reply, setting my coffee mug down to stir more sugar into the already pale, sweet liquid. "Why are you back so early?"

Cole sighs, running his fingers through his blond curls. His pale gray eyes meet mine as he motions to the breakfast table. "Can we sit down for a minute?"

"What happened?" My blood runs cold, but Cole shakes his head.

"Nothing, Misty. Everything's fine. I just have something I want to run past you."

I slowly sink into one of the chairs, throwing him an uneasy look. Cole purses his lips as he sits beside me, bringing our cups of coffee with him. "I had lunch with Sydney a few days ago, remember?"

"Yeah." I turn my mug in a circle out of nerves.

"Well, he mentioned something to me that I've been thinking about. How the families here... they still lean toward more traditional shifter medicine. Healing, you know. I have the opportunity to learn more about that side of things."

"Oh," I reply, feeling a little bit better.

"With the new clinic opening in Shadowcrest soon, I feel like it's imperative I take this opportunity now...." He trails off, his eyes holding mine. "Misty, I'd be going back to Eastonia for a few weeks. Two months, at the most."

I stiffen. Neither of us have been back to Eastonia since we settled in Crescent Falls, in Shadowcrest, Sydney's territory. "You can't learn those things here?"

He shakes his head. "Moonrise has an incredible hospital, and

Ryan recently took on a healer in Silverhide from the tribal packs...."
He leans forward, cupping my hands. "When Ryan visited two weeks
ago, he offered to set us up in a cabin near his place if we ever wanted
to visit. You love Silverhide, Misty. We could stay there for the rest of
the summer. You could be with Aviva and her sister, her friends. They
all have babies Addy's age."

I lick my lips, my entire body going numb. The sounds and colors
of that battlefield flash before my eyes. I wonder if I'm the only one
who feels this way... haunted. Even my powers have shied away over
the past several months, simmering just out of reach, like they don't
want to be summoned again, either. Cole is happy and... just
wonderful all the time.

I feel empty constantly.

"Misty," he whispers, lifting his hand to my cheek. "I won't go if
you don't want to go."

"It's not that," I whisper, closing my eyes and leaning into his
touch. "I'm just tired."

I open my eyes to find him looking at me, a sad expression
sweeping behind his eyes. I know he's worried about me. I know he
takes shorter shifts at the hospital and checks in on me constantly
because he's concerned. I know he talks to my parents often. I know
that's likely the reason Mom insists I do my work as record keeper for
the kingdom at the castle, where there's familiar voices and activity to
keep me company while Cole's at work.

Sometimes I wonder if he trusts me to be alone with Addy, and
that breaks my heart.

"I think you need this," he whispers, his thumb coasting over my
chin. "I think you need to be with Aviva."

I pull away from him, hiding the motion by bringing my coffee
mug to my lips. Cole waits for my answer. I already know he won't
push me to reply until I'm ready. It's one of the reasons I love him. I'm
not sure I deserve his patience.

Addy's soft cry echoes from the baby monitor on the kitchen
island. Cole rises, leaning down to press a kiss to my temple. "I love
you, Misty."

I lean into the kiss until he pulls away to fetch our son.

I stare out the window at the sun-lit yard, at the green grass and flowers in full bloom.

I want to feel better. I desperately want to move on. But I have this sinking feeling that returning to Eastonia will just open another door to the war, chaos, and hurt I'm trying to leave behind.

But Cole has done so much for me. So much for our family.

I can do this for him.

Can't I?

2

RETURN OF THE ALPHA

Aviva

It's just after dawn when I slide Lexa into her sling and head out of the house into another warm, later summer morning. The sun stretches across the pastures, casting golden light as far as the eye can see. Lexa–who I've taken to carrying on my back lately–coos softly as she uses my hair as reins, her chubby fingers tangled in the sloppy braid I managed to throw together just after I woke up, alone in bed, in a quiet house.

I stare at the road leading into the forest–out of the valley of Silverhide. It's empty. No wolves trot in my direction. I grind my teeth as the crippling unease that's been coasting through my body for days nearly chokes me, but I turn toward Freya and Andrew's house.

Andrew built Freya a shopfront earlier this spring while they waited for their son, Samuel, to make his arrival. It's cozied up beside his blacksmith shop, and her gorgeous tapestries and woven clothing hang in the sun-glazed windows.

It's not like we have money like in Crescent Falls and the larger

Rogueland cities, but we do trade and barter here in the Deadlands, and so far, Freya's been living like a queen.

I step inside her shop and follow the lifted female laughter and softer chatter to a back room where several looms are currently creaking and groaning over the conversations being had by at least six women and girls.

"I didn't think you'd make it this morning," Freya says excitedly, rushing up to me and kissing me on each cheek. "I thought Ryan was supposed to get back last night?"

"He's held up in Endova," I tell her, biting back my displeasure. He's been gone for two weeks, which is killing me. It's honestly hard to believe there was ever a time I didn't know him, that I lived without him. Now, he's practically the air I breathe and... I'm also desperate for a break.

Lexa presses her mouth against my back, blowing raspberries against my skin. Freya beams, clapping her hands at Lexa's new little trick.

"Where's Sam?" I ask, glancing around while Freya scoops Lexa out of her sling and cradles her against her shoulder.

"He's with... someone...." She looks around until she spots her son fast asleep in the arms of an elderly woman whose fingers are busy knitting what looks like a new sweater.

Out of the three babies–Lexa, Samuel, and Mercy's son, Reuben–I've noticed the boys tend to get more attention than Lexa. It's not that she's not loved and cherished by our pack, but the boys are just... easier to hold. Lexa is a brute, like her father. She's big, strong, exceedingly heavy for an almost four-month-old, and tends to be a bit wiggling.

Even Freya's arms flex as she readjusts Lexa on her shoulder, grunting a bit. "What are you feeding her, Aviva? I feel like she's gained three pounds since I held her yesterday!"

"Just my milk." I motion to my breasts with a sigh. "Blame Ryan. I do, every day. She's already grown out of the clothes I made for her after she grew out of all the clothes Maddy brought when she visited earlier this summer."

"Well, we'll just have to make some more today, won't we? Our little warrior princess." She nuzzles Lexa's cheek before turning to the gathering of women and looking for a lap that's not occupied with a sleeping infant or toddler while I shrug out of the sling and move toward a loom on the far side of the room.

I never used to come to these things. Not until two weeks ago, when Ryan and I returned from the hunting trip where we ran into the hunters from Teshka. With the harvest season approaching, the fall hunts nearing, and the harvest festival on the horizon, our pack has an incredible amount of work to do.

But as it stands, my mate is on a long trip, making his way back from Teshka where he planned to meet the strange boy who was apparently swept in from the furthest reaches of the sea.

So, I've been milling about, helping where I can. I'm still getting used to this whole "Luna" thing, but I've never, and will likely never, consider myself a domestic goddess who finds fulfillment in staying at home.

I wanted to go with him.

It crushed me knowing I couldn't. I just couldn't imagine putting Lexa through that kind of journey, nor putting her in danger.

I knit a very terrible sweater for my daughter while she naps in one of my pack member's arms, blissfully rocked into a deep sleep on the waves of conversation and the rhythmic scraping of the looms.

But I feel a tug deep in my chest that sets my body in a frenzy. I go completely still as the feeling washes over me like a wave before it settles. Then, I'm leaping up, walking steadily to the woman holding my sleeping daughter.

"Thank you for holding her," I whisper, scooping Lexa into my arms.

I don't bother with her sling. Her cheek rests against my shoulder while I walk as fast as my feet can carry me but not fast enough to jostle my daughter back into awareness.

I reach the road just as the sunlight highlights the figures moving through the woods—wolves. Wolves, and a few men, one of which belongs to me.

I bite back the desire to scream his name and fling myself into his arms. I can't let him get a big head over the idea that I missed him this much. That I laid awake every night near to tears over the fact he wasn't here, and I couldn't sleep soundly without him. The last time we were separated like this was because of the war, but even then, we'd been able to travel together, to rest together more often than not.

Ryan comes into full view with the biggest grin on his face. He breaks into a run just as the wolves rush past me to their homes to greet their families.

"Ryan," I whisper as he catches us in his arms, careful of the baby between us.

Lexa wakes with a whine, but calms when she senses Ryan's presence, turning her head to look up at him.

He presses a kiss to my lips–long, and slow. He smells like the forest, like the rivers and creeks running through the Deadlands. He smells like home.

"I missed you," he says into my hair, holding me close. "Goddess, Aviva. I missed you so much."

"That was too long of a trip," I say into his chest. Lexa coos her agreement, and he pulls away and runs his hand over her soft, golden-red curls that are just starting to come in.

"My girls," he whispers, his eyes the deepest blue as he meets mine.

A few minutes later, we're tucked inside our house. Ryan wears the sling this time with Lexa fast asleep against his chest as he unpacks his bag, setting a variety of weapons on the kitchen table. He pulls out a parcel wrapped in cloth, handing it to me.

"What's this?" I ask, furrowing my brow.

"A gift," he replies, watching as I carefully unfold the fabric.

I look down at the gold, turquoise, and salt-water pearl bangles, shocked. "Ryan–"

"You deserve them. You deserve more, Aviva," he says with a heavy sigh, "for carrying our daughter for nine months, for going to war while you were pregnant and while ruling Silverhide in my stead but... I'm just an Alpha."

"Just an Alpha," I echo with a smirk, rolling the bangles onto my arms. They catch the faint sunlight coming through the windows as he steps toward me, brushing my hair out of my face.

"I thought they'd be perfect for you... and I also imagined you wearing them and nothing else, and I couldn't think about leaving them behind in Teshka."

I arch a brow as he steps closer, but we're instantly reminded of the baby between us when she sighs loudly, nestling deeper against Ryan's shirt.

"And also... because I'm leaving again soon."

I frown. "No, you're not–"

"But I'm taking you with me."

A blast of relief echoes over my body, but I still narrow my eyes at my mate. "Where?"

"When I was in Endova, I was visited by my uncle, who is apparently on his way to meet the boy from the sea himself. It sounds like Ryatt plans to bring the boy to Moonrise, and he mentioned that he needed to speak to you, as well."

"About what?"

Ryan shrugs. "He didn't say, only that he required our presence. We'll make a weekend out of it and...." He runs his fingers through his hair.

He seems stressed, which makes me feel uncertain, especially given the odd expression on his face. "What is it, Ryan?"

"I think Ryatt's serious about making you a commander, Aviva."

A rush of excitement blurs my senses, but my stomach hollows out, my feelings conflicting on a major level. We knew this was a possibility. It had been in the talks before the war–before there was even a threat of war.

But things are different now. We have a daughter. We have a thriving pack that's getting bigger by the second.

Being a commander in Ryatt's army could take me away from Silverhide... often.

"Do I have a choice?"

"Of course," Ryan says, stepping toward me and bracing his hands on my upper arms. "We're just going to go and hear him out. That's all. Kenna and her kids will be there, too. She hasn't seen Lexa since she was born."

I smile softly. "It could be fun."

"Just a weekend away, and then we'll return here, and it'll be business as usual. Oh, and, Misty and Cole are possibly moving here for the summer.... We need to prepare for that, too." He turns from me, making a vocal checklist of all the things he needs to do before we leave for Moonrise tomorrow, and I watch him walk away with Lexa still sleeping soundly in her sling.

The rest of the day passes in quiet peace. Lexa is pretty easy for a baby. She's happy and calm and has started being okay with being held by others and not just me. We have dinner in the pack house with everyone and return to our home after dark where we spend a good thirty minutes trying to get Lexa to sleep in her crib to no avail.

I lie snuggled next to Ryan with Lexa sprawled out between us. It's a clear, calm night. The stars hang heavy in the sky. I've gotten used to peace. I haven't seen those white wolves–those angels of the Goddess–in months.

So why do I have the feeling something is still amiss? That something is coming... and we have to stop it?

I slip out of bed, unable to fall back asleep, and walk out on the deck. It's a warm night. Heavy clouds block the stars as I squint into the darkness. Sometimes, I wish I had powers like Sarah and Sydney. I'd be reading the stars all night, seeing and manipulating the future. I'd ensure nothing like the war ever happened again.

I turn to look over my shoulder through one of the windows into our living room where Ryan built a special hanger for my golden bow. It glints in the soft light of a lamp we left on, shimmering against the warm woods of the rest of the room.

I often wonder how the bow was made–who crafted it and gave it its magic.

And why.

And, lastly, why did it choose me?

3

—————

COMMANDER NUMBER FOUR

Aviva

The last time we were in Moonrise was for Lexa's birth. Four months have passed in a blur, which I assume is normal when you have a baby for the first time. Pile on our responsibilities as Alpha and Luna of Silverhide, let alone the rulers of all the Deadlands, and time is merely a construct in our lives that I'm keen to ignore as long as possible.

Still, when Kenna arrived yesterday morning, chipper and excited to see us and Lexa, I felt a weight begin to press into my chest. Whatever Ryatt wants with me comes with a cost—which will be the end of our somewhat quiet, cozy life.

I spent the entire day in Kenna's company while she made her rounds checking on every baby and mother in Silverhide. Ryan went off to do Alpha duties, like making sure James, his Beta, had what he needed to take over for a few days in our absence. His mate, Dahlia, is pregnant again—with twins this time—but Kenna seemed happy with her progress, telling me it's likely Dahlia will deliver in early winter if she goes full term.

Just as night fell, Kenna dosed me and Lexa with herbs to make our journey a little easier on our bodies, and once that took effect, we were whisked into empty, cold nothingness for several seconds before landing on our feet in the familiar, gilded castle overlooking the turquoise lake of Moonrise.

Now, it's morning. I braid my hair in the mirror over the vanity in the little apartment I share with Ryan in the castle–a room that holds memories that are as sweet as they are damning. Months ago, I laid in this bed alone and sobbed while Ryan went to war, not knowing if I'd ever see him again. Now, he's asleep beside our daughter, both of them in the exact same position–like starfish–taking up the entire bed.

I smooth the fabric of the sage green sundress I chose for today's meeting and stare at my reflection. I twist a few of the curls around my face until they somewhat behave and really look at myself, internally reflecting on who I am and what I'm capable of... right now... which is not commanding Ryatt's impressive army or serving beside Evander as a Ghost.

I'm a mother now. I'm a Luna. I'm a wife in a happy marriage. Everything I thought I was before is gone, replaced by this new version of myself... someone softer, someone more empathetic and kinder than the old Aviva.

I credit Ryan for that change.

I left that broken, angry side of myself on the battlefield in Eastonia.

I look over my shoulder at my mate and our daughter. She looks like him, has started to make the same cocky facial expressions and that boyish smile that I love. Her eyes are made in his image–a deep, endless blue. But her curls are from me. Red and wild, they've grown out enough that they're starting to coil around her forehead and ears, turning a pale copper gold as the sun begins to creep over her face.

I move to the windows with caution and silently pull the curtains closed against the sun before creeping out of the bedroom, shutting the door behind me with a wince. I have about an hour before I see them again–when Lexa wakes up and realizes I'm gone, panics, and

Ryan finds me to show our angel that I haven't abandoned her forever.

It's an hour I have to spend with Ryatt and his head commanders.

My only consolation is that Evander will be with me, and as a fellow in-law in one ring of our enormous family, he understands my pain.

"They're serving coffee and a light breakfast in Ryatt's office," Evander says when I meet him in the hallway just beyond the wing where the family apartments are kept. "It's casual."

"Casual," I chuckle sardonically, glancing up at the tall, coppery-blond hybrid shifter mated to Kenna. I've always liked Evander. He's steely and cold, yes, but he's the glue between the two sides of the family. I know for a fact he spent his time in the hours after the war ensuring Sydney and Ryan didn't beat the ever-living fuck out of Cole, which I know Misty is grateful for, as well. He's wicked smart and kind but wears a mask that screams violence and death if anyone were to cross him, or Goddess forbid, threaten his mate in any way, shape, or form.

"I think you're getting a medal or something."

"Oh," I breathe, rolling my shoulders as he leads me up a staircase. "Well, I was hoping for a trophy, but I guess that'll do."

His mouth ticks into the briefest of smiles before returning to a tight line. The air in the hallway becomes extraordinarily thin as we near Ryatt's office, but I'm sure I'm imagining it. I know I'm not imagining the way my heart begins to beat erratically, however. I'm sweating with nerves when Evander raps on the door, then opens it, stepping into the coffee-scented office of Ryatt, the most powerful man in our kingdom.

Ryatt glances away from the conversation he's engaged in with two unfamiliar men and gives me a tight nod in acknowledgment before Evander turns me toward a nearby table filled with steaming porcelain carafes and silver platters full of meats, cheeses, eggs, and other breakfast foods. I eye one of the pastries in particular while Evander pours me a cup of coffee, which I accept gratefully, but my stomach is in too tight of a knot to eat.

Instead, I stand beside Evander in the back of the room and glance from face to face. This isn't a formal meeting by any means. The head Alphas of the Rogueland's strongest packs are here, as are the three commanders at the head of Ryatt's army. Somehow, these men are leaning on chairs and talking casually to each other instead of fighting over a map, which is what I imaged this scene would look like in my mind. Instead, they sip coffee, eat pastries, and... laugh with each other.

My gaze sweeps across the room and lands on a man I almost mistake for Ryatt at first glance. He's just as tall, just as broad in the shoulders, and just as terrifying to look directly in the eyes. A cutting silver gaze holds mine as a man in his late seventies lifts his coffee mug to his lips.

'That's Westfall,' Evander says through the mind-link, raising his mug just a touch in the man's direction. 'Ryatt's dad... my... grandfather-in-law?'

'I can see the resemblance,' I reply, swallowing hard as Westfall's gaze sizes me up. I've heard about him. He's a Shadowsynger, like Ryatt and Kenna. He was the lost prince of Veiled Valley when Eastonia fell to Kane's leadership. I met Ryatt's mother, Cressendra, a while ago but only briefly, at Isla and Maddox's memorial service and the luncheon that followed.

They split their time between Maatua and Veiled Valley from what I understand, but now, I'm wondering why the infamous retired commander is here right now for this... breakfast party.

Before I can process this, Ryatt and his commanders begin to move toward a door off the far wall of his office, and the Alphas follow, everyone carrying on their conversations. I stay close to Evander and notice Westfall falling in line behind us as we enter a large, open room with a circular table at its center.

"So, you're the famed warrior from the tribal packs," Westfall says in a voice that sounds so familiar I have to double check that Ryatt's not the one speaking.

"This is Aviva," Evander says as we come to stop near the door while everyone else slowly takes their seats. "Ryan's mate, you know."

"It's nice to finally meet you," Westfall says with a nod before walking to a chair against the wall, where he promptly sits and drinks from his mug, ignoring the conversation at the table.

I stand dumbly beside Evander, wondering if I'm supposed to sit at the table, but Evander isn't making any moves toward it. In fact, he checks his watch, sighing under his breath, "I'm sure the kids are awake by now."

"What time is it?"

"Close to eight. Ryatt said he wouldn't keep us long."

"What exactly is this meeting about–"

"The highway project is moving forward in both the Roguelands and Tarsian," Ryatt says over the hum coming from the table. He shoots a sharp look at one of the Alphas. "It'll be a good thing for your territories, and you know it."

"So we can have Crescent Falls riffraff spilling into the Roguelands? I think not," one of the Alphas shoots back, crossing his arms over his chest. "We're strapped for warriors as it stands, giving how many men we've had to send to Tarsian over the past six month to help smooth their transition into three kingdoms, three new Alpha Kings–"

"And your warriors will return to you before the snow falls, that's a promise," Ryatt says curtly, but then his gaze flicks to where Evander and I are still standing, waiting for an invitation to the table. "Commander Evander's Ghost army will be overseeing the security during the construct of the road between Crescent Falls and Eastonia, through the border of the Roguelands."

"And what are we going to do to join the two territories? Blast a hole through the mountains?" One of the other Alphas laughs as he leans back in his chair.

"My nephew, Sydney, the Alpha of Shadowcrest and the future Alpha King of Crescent Falls, has some ideas. A railway is the first, bridging the gap between our kingdoms for trade. The road would be built at the same time. Eastonia has lived in the dark for far too long. We need Crescent Falls to bring us into the future."

"So our people can play on their phones and online... shop?" The third Alpha chuckles, leaning toward his companion, "Is that what's it called?"

But I'm watching Ryatt as he glances at his father, then at me. Kenna told me about this–how her father's powers literally make it possible for the Roguelands and Moonrise, and beyond, to have light in their homes. His power protects Eastonia through the use of shields and wards… and he's getting older. Kenna, as a Shadowsynger, has some of those gifts but not at his magnitude.

I stiffen a bit as Ryatt steers the conversation forward, motioning to me. "Aviva of Endova, everyone."

The men at the table turn like they just realized I'm here. I pale.

"She's going to be working with Commander Evander, under his direction, during the construction of the road into the Deadlands."

"The Deadlands? There can't be a logical reason why we'd need a connection to the Deadlands. What on Goddess's green earth could they possibly offer us?"

A pinch of anger ripples through me as I turn toward the Alpha who just spoke. "We saved your asses during the war, if I remember correctly, but then again… I was on the frontlines while the warriors of the Roguelands were running and screaming in the back, looking for anywhere to hide."

The room goes completely, utterly silent.

Then, Westfall chuckles nearby.

I find it impossible to swallow, but somehow I manage it.

Ryatt smiles at me. "Aviva, I'd like you to meet my commanders. Come, take a seat beside them."

"Why?" I ask. Stupidly, I might add. My heart races, but my feet stay firmly planted.

I already know what he's about to say, and I don't know if I'm ready for it because I can't say no.

"Because you're the Commander of the Deadlands, now. Welcome to the table, Aviva."

4

EVERYONE NEEDS A BREAK

Ryan

"Come on, girl. You liked me yesterday." I hike Lexa up and set her on my shoulder so her legs are around the back of my neck, my arm bent and extended so I press my hand against her back. She immediately fists my hair and stops wailing, her sad sniffling turning to quiet excitement. A small giggle leaves her lips as we pass one of the ceiling height windows in the hallway I've been walking her up and down for the past thirty minutes.

Aviva would tell me this is dangerous to do with her at only four months old, but I can't help it. Tossing this baby around is getting her ready to wrestle, which is what I often tell my wife before she stops my fun, but right now, we're completely alone.

I turn a corner, find another hallway, and walk down it with no plan nor destination in sight. In fact, I'm not entirely sure what I'm supposed to be doing right now other than keeping Lexa happy, and currently, the only thing that's going to make her happy is Aviva.

We pass a huge mirror, and I backtrack, turning so Lexa can see our reflection. She stares owl-eyed at herself, her deep-blue eyes round and wondrous and her mouth forming a perfect O, but then she looks down at me and remembers I'm not her mother.

Her tiny, perfect face twists with grief, giant tears falling from her eyes. She wails, the sound bouncing from one end of the hallway to the other, and I have no choice but to swing her back against my chest to try to comfort her.

"She's not gone forever, I promise. It's just a meeting," I grumble, patting her back. Lexa thinks otherwise, but thankfully a familiar face pokes her head out of a door at the end of the hallway and relief rushes through me. "Thank the Goddess."

"What are you doing to that poor baby?" Kenna laughs, beckoning me toward her.

"I'm just not Aviva," I reply matter-of-factly, following Kenna into one of the numerous sitting rooms scattered around the castle. This space, however, seems to have been totally dedicated to her kids.

The walls are a soft yellow against the spray of morning sunlight drifting through the curtains. A mural of a rainbow and mountains made of crystals spreads across the far wall. Pictures painted by Brie and Aris hang from the walls with pieces of tape, and between two couches, a sea of toys and books fans out.

I carefully pick my way across the carpet while Brie and Aris squeal, running between my legs. Kenna scoops Lexa out of my arms and sits on one of the couches, skillfully cradling my daughter and soothing her. "Is she hungry, maybe?"

"No," I sigh, picking up Aris and tossing him into a giant pile of pillows and cushions in the corner of the room. I wait for him to roll out of the way before tossing Brie in the same fashion. "Aviva left some milk. I gave her a bottle, but she wasn't happy it was me feeding her, not her mom. I think she just doesn't like me very much."

"Oh, Ryan, don't be ridiculous." Kenna gives Lexa a loving smile, wiping the baby's tears away with her thumb. "I'm sure she loves you."

"You don't sound so convinced, either," I grumble, glancing at the kids–who've already grown bored of our game and moved onto something else–before sitting down.

"Look, it's perfectly normal for a baby to favor their mother's at this age. She's just a little thing, and she was in Aviva's belly longer than she's been out here, with us. As she gets older, she'll... start enjoying your company more."

I stare at Kenna for a moment before rolling my eyes.

"What?" she laughs as Maeve toddles over to us, sucking her thumb. Maeve looks between us and narrows her eyes at Lexa, obviously upset about the fact there's another baby in her mom's lap.

Maeve is a... strange little thing, honestly. I call Kenna and Evander's kids my nieces and nephews even though, technically, they're my cousins. I'm Uncle Ryan regardless in their eyes, and while Brie and Aris are easy to read and excitable, there's something different about Maeve. It's like a wise old owl took the body of an almost two-year-old toddler.

Maeve doesn't laugh much. She glares–like a cat. She watches, and waits, and tends to bully her siblings. Kenna says it's normal toddler behavior to want to be the boss, to wreck toys and topple carefully built towers but Maeve... nah, she's weird. I like her, but she scares me a little.

I pat the couch anyway, saying, "Get over here, Maeve. I haven't seen you in ages."

Maeve rolls her eyes and walks away.

I glance at Kenna, who purses her lips and watches her youngest child kneel in front of a stack of children's books.

"So, two kids want nothing to do with me," I try to joke, but I notice the unease in Kenna's eyes. "Kenna?"

"Don't take it personally. Maeve has been... she's been a little unpredictable lately."

"She still pulling disappearing acts on you guys?" I ask, leaning back.

Kenna shakes her head, "No, thank the Goddess, she hasn't. Her flames haven't been an issue, either, but we have help in Veiled Valley now. Two witches, actually, who act as her nannies." Kenna sighs. "I know you're going through it with Lexa favoring Aviva over you right now, but Maeve doesn't like any of us."

"That's not true," I laugh. "Come on, Ken–"

"She's different, Ryan. You know that. She's full-blooded Firestone. She's not a shifter. She's a witch but, even then… she's not. I know that doesn't make sense, but the Firestone people were something else entirely, and she's the only one like her. I think she's starting to understand that, and it breaks my heart."

"She's not even two," I remind her. "She can't be going through an existential crisis already."

"It's gotta be some new power emerging." Kenna sighs, shaking her head. "Just like we can sense things–sense things about our mates, our family… she can sense that she's alone, and it's killing us. She loves being in my mom's presence, and for some reason, does remarkably well with Maddy–your mom. With Evander being gone more, and me being needed in Veiled Valley more often… we're not in Moonrise very much lately and it… it's hard on Maeve. I don't know how to help her."

Maeve appears at my side, climbing onto the couch. She sits beside me and opens a book but doesn't thrust it into my lap, wanting me to read it. She just sits there, sucking her thumb.

"I'm… I'm in the position where I need to give up my midwifery practice here in Moonrise," Kenna says under her breath, rising with Lexa in her arms. She lays my daughter in my lap before settling on the opposite couch, neatly crossing her legs.

"Why would you stop practicing midwifery?" I ask, snuggling an almost asleep Lexa close.

"Because I'm the Alpha of Veiled Valley, and my mate is one of my father's most dedicated commanders… and the war showed my dad and your dad the cracks in the foundation of our allied kingdoms. They can't allow something like that to happen again which means more paws on the ground–more outposts, more training… bigger armies in general. Evander is going to be traveling often over the next year, based on what Dad has planned, and I… I have to go home, to our people, to our territory. I'm just a princess in Moonrise. I have to go be an Alpha now."

She looks down at her lap, picking at her freshly manicured nails. She does look the part of an Alpha all of the sudden. Normally,

Kenna's dressed well but somewhat plainly. Her fingers are scrubbed clean and raw from countless hours acting as a midwife, her hair always braided back and away from her face. Now, she's dressed in the typical free-flowing fashions of Veiled Valley and her hair is loose and shining as it falls over her shoulders. Her nails are painted, and she's wearing makeup.

I realize where the conversation is about to go without her needing to confirm it. I reach over to Maeve, gently patting the top of her head. "You're going to leave her here, aren't you?"

Kenna's on the verge of tears. "We don't know what else to do. She's alive here. I don't know how else to explain it. In Veiled Valley she's... a shell of the girl we know and love. She's sad, closed off, sometimes inconsolable. Here in Moonrise, she's... she's whole. It's where she's supposed to be, but I'm supposed to be somewhere else–"

"But you're also the heir to your mother's title," I cut in, my heart rate quickening.

Kenna, to my surprise, shakes her head. "No, I'm not. Maeve is. She was born to be the next queen. I'll never sit on my mother's throne, and I'm okay with that, for Maeve's sake."

"You can't just leave your kid behind–"

"That's not what this is at all," Kenna says, but she's on the verge of breaking.

Maeve's watching Kenna, though. She notices her mom's glimmering eyes and twisted expression and slides off the couch, walking over her. She climbs into Kenna's lap, and it's Kenna's undoing. Silent tears fall from her lashes.

"Ryan, I don't know what else to do for her. I don't want her to be miserable. It's not fair."

"I think you all need a break," I say as sharply as I can without alerting the kids to the adult conversation taking place. Brie is a little snitch, as much as I love her, and I don't want her babbling to Liam and Blake about this when she sees them next. "I think whatever Ryatt needs Evander for can wait a while, at least until the end of the summer, right? What if you came to Silverhide with us? Hell, Cole and Misty are going to spend a few months in the Deadlands. We have room for everybody."

Kenna wipes her eyes on the back of her hands. "I'll talk to Evander about it."

"He's not going to say no."

"Well, my dad might!"

"Ryatt is still Ryatt," I grind out. "Your dad, my uncle. Same guy. He's all tough on the outside, but if anyone gets how important taking a fucking–sorry–freakin' breather is, it's him. Remember the story your mom told us when we were kids about how he didn't leave Veiled Valley for two years after you were born? After they went through hell and back? Well, we've all been to hell recently, and we could use some rest. If you're serious about having to separate your family, you need this time with her, Kenna. You need to know for sure it's the right move."

Kenna gives me a weak smile. Maeve leans against her chest, giving me a strange look as I watch the two of them. I feel like the kid can see right through me, into the deepest, darkest parts of my soul. It sends a shiver up my spine, but I ignore it.

"I'll talk to Evander," Kenna echoes, giving me a watery smile. "It might be fun."

"It will be fun." I smile, but my eyes land on Maeve again, who smiles back at me, to my surprise.

Evander rather suddenly appears, huffing out a breath as he storms through the doorway. He spots me and breathlessly motions toward me, saying, "Hand me the baby."

I rise, uneasy gripping my senses. "What?"

"Hand me the baby, and go find your mate," he says slowly, glancing at Kenna.

"What happened?" Kenna rasps, narrowing her eyes.

I slowly hand Lexa to Evander who cradles her with expert skill, being a father of three, and all. "She's just been named a commander in your father's army and… didn't take it very well."

"Oh, fuck me," I groan under my breath. "Where did she go, exactly?"

"Out. Out of the castle, I presume. She said she needed some air and shifted before she could stop herself."

I look between Kenna and Evander. "I'll be back. If she gets hungry–"

"She'll be fine," Kenna assures me.

I turn toward the door and break into a run.

5

THE ALPHA QUEEN

Aviva

I'M THE BIGGEST BABY IN THE ENTIRE WORLD.

Not only did I freeze the moment Ryatt announced he was making me a commander, but I went so pale that the excited look on his face–his eyes shining with pride–shattered with concern. He took one step in my direction, and I burst into tears... in front of every man in the room.

I ran. There wasn't anything else I could do, honestly. The only man I've ever cried in front of is Ryan, and even then, I hate it.

I'm supposed to be tough. Hard. Unbreakable.

I skirt around the lake in my wolf form, my paws beating the rocky shore. Morning sunlight breaks over the mountains, splitting the sky with ribbons of pure gold. The pretty sage dress I fussed over this morning is caught around my neck and in shambles, which only adds fuel to the fire of my despair and desperation.

I can't untangle the dress, just like I can't untangle my thoughts.

A year ago, I would have been honored to be given this position. I would have jumped at the opportunity.

Now, I have no idea why I can't get my brain to wrap itself around the idea I'm meant for more than being Lexa's mom and Ryan's mate.

What's wrong with me?

I keep running until my lungs give out–at least an hour, based on the position of the sun, and then reality hits me like an arrow to the chest.

I just ran out on a meeting with the Alpha King of the Rogue-lands–the Shadow King of Eastonia… My uncle-in-law, who is likely wondering what the hell my problem is.

And, I ran away from the castle where Ryan and Lexa are probably eating breakfast and wondering where I went–and why.

I slink back in the direction of the city. I get glances, of course. I probably look like a mess, which is exactly how I feel. I limp around the back of the castle, where a quartet of guards let me through the gate without a word, and find Ryan sitting on the steps leading to the winding, exterior staircases that climb up the back of the castle where the private apartments are located.

He sighs heavily as I approach with his elbows resting on his knees. He tilts his head, giving me a sad sort of smile, then groans as he rises, sauntering over to me–wordlessly–and untangles the mangled dress I've been dragging around for over an hour.

"Let's go," he says, lovingly patting my head, but I can't even look him in the eyes. I follow him up to our apartment, and once we're closed inside, I shift back to my human form.

Ryan does a thorough sweep of my naked body with a smirk before tossing me a robe.

Still, I can barely look at him. My cheeks burn as I shrug into the robe. I threw a tantrum, plain and simple.

"Where's Lexa?" I ask, my voice like gravel.

"Being spoiled rotten by Ella and Kenna," Ryan says as he fishes in the dresser for something for me to wear. He unfurls a silk pajama set dusted with printed flowers and turns to face me, shrugging. "I'm not going to ask if you're good because I can tell that you're not."

"Thanks," I grumble, sinking onto the edge of the bed.

He leans against the dresser with the pajamas draped over his arm.

"If I'd known Ryatt was going to spring that on you this morning, I would have stopped him... especially if I'd known he was planning on doing it in front of others. I think he assumed you'd be elated."

"I was, I think," I admit, scooching back and roping my arms around my knees, tugging them to my chest. "Maybe. I'm not sure.... I just panicked."

"Why?" The question is soft and sincere.

I can feel his gaze searching my face, but I stare at a speck on the wall, honing in on it. "I'm just a girl from Endova."

"You're a hunter. A warrior. My Luna–"

"Exactly." I meet his gaze. "I'm your mate, your Luna, the mother of your child. You are the Alpha. The Alpha King." I swallow hard as a tremor of nerves rips up my spine. "How can you be so calm right now? Aren't you upset you weren't the one chosen for this?"

"Me?" He looks utterly confused. "Why would Ryatt make me a commander? You've seen me in battle. I just... roll around, hoping I run someone over."

I exhale sharply. "I'm a woman. You're an Alpha. You must feel like–like I'm upstaging you–"

"Aviva," he breathes, shaking his head. His mouth stretches into a smile. "You think I'm jealous?"

"Shouldn't you be?"

"Jealous that my wife is the most talented, vicious warrior in all the land? No, I'm not jealous. I'm turned on. It's hot as fuck."

I blush again for an entirely different reason. "But–I'm a mom now."

"Yeah, you are. That doesn't mean you're not still Aviva, the warrior." He walks toward me, sitting next to me on the bed. His hand smooths down my back. "You're exhausted. We both are, but you, especially. We have a kid now. She's... totally dependent on you. You've been giving your all to Lexa for almost four months. It's gotta be shocking to remember you had a life before this."

I exhale deeply, closing my eyes. "I don't know what's wrong with me. I'm happy, you know? I have everything I wanted–things I didn't know I wanted until I met you, and still... I don't know how to do both, Ryan. When Ryatt said that to me, I couldn't form a rational thought. I just felt scared. I can't command an army. I'm–I'm full of milk!"

"He's not going to send you out right now, Aviva. This is in the beginning stages. I talked to him after you took off, okay? He feels awful. He thought you'd be happy, and when he saw the blood drain from your face, he realized he fucked up. He feels bad about it and clarified that he wants you as commander in the Deadlands. You'd be home with us. Called into duty when necessary. We won't be separated."

"Unless there's another war." My words float through the air and suck the oxygen from the room.

Ryan rests his hand on my thigh. "Unless there's another war."

Silence hugs the room around us for several heartbeats before he says, "I think... I think we don't need to worry about this right now. I'll talk to Ryatt again. I'll handle it. If it's what you want to do, do it. If not, you're under no obligation to accept the position."

"He's the Alpha King–"

"Ah, well, I'm an Alpha King, too. And, you're part of my pack. And... he's family. He'll understand. Right now, you should rest. I'll go find Lexa and see what she's up to. I'm sure she's sick of everyone else and only wants you."

My heart swells and aches, my milk dropping and threatening to soak through my robe. "Bring her to me?"

Ryan nods then leans down, brushing his lips over mine before kissing me tenderly–a long, passionate kiss. "I love you."

"I love you," I echo as he pulls away.

I sit on the bed as he leaves the room, then the apartment, his foot-steps fading into the whisper of wind through the trees outside our bedroom windows.

I change into the pajamas he laid out for me and wait for him to return with our daughter... and a few minutes later, I'm greeted by Lexa's delirious, toothless smile, her eyes washed with relief.

* * *

I SPEND THE REST OF THE DAY IN BED, WHICH HASN'T HAPPENED SINCE Lexa was born. Ryan flutters in and out of the room, sometimes taking Lexa with him, sometimes dropping her back off to nurse and nap, but all the while, I stay tucked in the sun-warmed sheets and lose myself to the wallpaper, finding odd shapes and faces in the florals. It's near sunset when I finally leave my cave of rest and walk into the sitting room, stretching my arms above my head when the door opens.

Thinking it's Ryan, I let out a huge yawn and say, "Lexa's probably ready for bed–"

"Hey," Misty says softly, her sharp blue eyes shining in the golden light of the sunset.

Momentarily shocked out of my senses, I stare at her. I knew she was coming to Eastonia, but I had no idea when, and I definitely didn't expect to see her here, today, in my apartment.

She slips into the room dressed in jean shorts and a gray shirt with a flannel hanging off her shoulders, her hair braided away from her face.

I take one step, then another, then throw my arms around her and squeeze.

I haven't seen Misty since we had our babies. It's been months since the entire family was able to get together. I squeeze her tighter than necessary and feel tears stinging my lash line before I finally let go and hold her at arm's length.

Misty, several inches taller than me, looks down at me with a smile that hides a hint of nerves, exhaustion, and the relief we obviously share.

"Ryan said you were asleep, but I didn't think so," she says, reaching up to wipe her eyes with her knuckles. "I wanted to say hi before we tucked in for the night."

"How long have you been here?"

"Maybe half an hour." She sighs, shrugging. "Everyone's upstairs having dinner, but I felt–I needed a minute." Her eyes slide to her shoes.

I squeeze her arm. "I've been taking a break all day."

Her knowing, answering smile warms something in my heart. Her eyes meet mine again, soft and understanding. I search for the girl I met for the first time that day in Maatua, when I woke up alone, in a bed with a view of the ocean. Misty looks the same. Her skin is still a soft golden tan, and her blonde hair shines in the evening light, but the fire in her eyes is gone. That sharp edge to her voice has softened. That unwavering confidence has slipped.

"How are you feeling?" I ask.

"How are you feeling?" she echoes, and for a moment we don't do more than stare at each other.

Neither of us can answer that question. How do you even begin putting into words what the past months have felt like? What recovering from a war, and the loss of Isla and Maddox, has felt like?

Stack on having a baby, and it's damn near overwhelming to think about.

A knock on the door alerts us to company. Ryan steps inside holding Lexa in one arm, and a plate piled with little cakes, cookies, and pastries in the other, followed by Cole.

Cole gives me a brief smile and a nod of his head as he dips into the room behind my mate, and I see our nephew for the first time.

"Oh, Misty," I whisper, smiling at her before turning my attention to the baby boy in Cole's arms. I extend my hands to reach for the boy, but Lexa gives me a disapproving squawk, which sends a ripple of laughter coasting through our little group. "She gets a little jealous if I even look at another baby," I grumble, scooping my daughter out of Ryan's arms.

Cole hands Adrian to Misty, and the guys arrange some plates and pour some iced tea while I stand there beside Misty, letting our babies–cousins–look at each other.

Lexa frowns at Adrian, but he doesn't catch it. He's more interested in the ceiling fan above our heads.

"She looks like you, Aviva," Misty says a few moments later when we're sitting on the couch together. Ryan and Cole are on the balcony taking in the stars, just out of our sight.

"I think she looks more like Ryan."

"Well, she is just… huge," Misty admits, then swallows, shaking her head. "Adrian's a little thing."

"He won't stay that way." I smile, using my finger to unlatch the death grip Lexa has on my nipple. I right my shirt and finally have the opportunity to hand her off, so we trade babies for a moment.

Adrian grunts before settling into my arms. He is small… well, I'm sure he's a normal sized three-month-old, compared to my brute of a daughter who looks like she eats babies like him for breakfast every morning.

"Wow," Misty coos, smiling down at Lexa. "She is beautiful. She's going to be a real stunner. And probably a terrifyingly skilled warrior, too."

"I hope so. I want her to be able to hold her own in the world, you know? Ryan's determined to name her as Alpha of Silverhide one day, and make her his heir to his…she'll be an Alpha Queen."

"Alpha Queen," Misty smiles wistfully. "She'll be the first, I think. Everyone will know her name."

I'm not sure if that's a good thing, thinking about it now.

6

NO INTERRUPTIONS

Misty

Look, I love Shadowcrest. The suburbia nestled within the biggest city in my parents' kingdom has been my saving grace, especially after having a baby. I'm close to stores, to parks, and we've made several friends over the past few months.

Sydney has been cool, as well, which isn't normally a word I'd use to describe him. He's a great Alpha, even if he's my dumb older brother.

But Shadowcrest has nothing on Silverhide. Not by a long shot.

I breathe deeply, closing my eyes as the crisp, mountain air fills my lungs. My powers sizzle to life beneath my skin, little voices whispering in a language long lost to time in my head. Silverhide's nestled in a valley between two massive mountains and sprawls out in a sea of stone cottages and log cabins. A few small barns and farmhouses dot the horizon, nestled in rolling fields of wheat and barley. Toward the village center, the buildings become larger—some rise two, or even three stories above the ground. New homes and shops are in the process of being built while other buildings have additions being added.

It's beautiful. Simple, a bit rugged, but beautiful.

I glance up at my mate as he looks around, following behind Ryan and Aviva as we walk toward the village down a long, gravel road where the pastures fan out on either side. Cole's wide-eyed as he pats Addy's back in the carrier he's wearing on his chest–a sharply modern contrast to the fabric sling Aviva's carrying Lexa with. For the first time in many months, I feel a sense of hope and excitement fizzle to life in my chest, warming me to the bone.

Maybe Cole was right. Maybe I did, in fact, desperately need this "vacation."

We begin to pass people on the road. I have to step out of the way when a cart driven by two wolves parts our group, the back laden with baskets of grain, beans, and dried vegetables. Some people are out in the fields tending to the wheat while others watch herds of sheep and cattle graze. There's a quiet hum of energy in the air that's unlike any place I've ever been before.

Ryan's people are happy, that's clear, especially when we reach the village square and familiar faces dart forward to greet their Alpha, Luna, and their guests.

While Ryan greets his pack members, I take a moment to scan the crowd gathering around us, counting at least ten women in varying stages of pregnancy. Silverhide was always a small pack, so seeing it like this…

I could almost cry with pride knowing my brother built this pack, but I'd never give Ryan the satisfaction.

The war didn't change me *that* much.

"This isn't what I expected," Cole says over the ripple of chatter thrumming from the crowd. A trio of wolves part them before darting into the distance, howling, wearing halters lined with weapons.

I notice Aviva turning to the wolves and watching them disappear down the road, her happy expression cracking with jealousy. I gather those wolves are going hunting and follow their movements until they disappear completely, their bodies replaced by open road and rolling plains.

"I keep forgetting you've never been here before," I tease, smiling up at him.

Cole's pale gray eyes sparkle as he matches my smile. "I haven't seen you smile like that in a while."

I try to frown at him but can't get my lips to move in the way I want, but now I'm smiling so hard my cheeks hurt. "I love it here."

"I know," he replies, smoothing his hand down my back at the same moment Freya, Aviva's best-friend and the mate of Andrew, who works for Ryan, hops over to us. Her blonde hair is tightly braided away from her face as she leans down to kiss each of my cheeks, then beams at Addy, who's fast asleep against Cole's chest.

"Welcome! We're so happy you're here!"

I glance behind her to where Ryan and Aviva are moving away, swallowed by the crowd.

"Ryan wants me to show you your cabin. Come on! I figure you want some time to settle in before dinner tonight."

I'm still watching Ryan and Aviva while Freya introduces herself to Cole, however, and barely notice him giving my hand a tug to let me know we need to start walking again.

A few minutes later, we reach a tidy, two-bedroom cabin just outside of the village, tucked in a grove of apple trees.

The air is scented with sugar here, and the apples are nearly ripe. Bees dart through the branches as Freya talks our ears off all the way into the house, which is a stark contrast to what we're used to in Shadowcrest.

But, Cole and I have lived in... a lot of different places together.

There was his shitty quarters in that Goddess-forsaken fortress in the middle of the desert, then the fancy, gilded rooms in his father's castle in Oasia. We spent a week in my old dorm room, sharing Georgia's old bed because we broke mine the first night we spent together after the war.

Then, there was his apartment in Crescent Falls–our first real home together, even if we didn't stay there for very long.

After that, we shared that old cottage in Shadowcrest where I nearly gave birth to Addy before being rescued by Sydney... and now?

I step into the cabin, but I'm momentarily greeted by the foyer in our house in Shadowcrest. Spotless wood floors. Soft white walls. The furniture I picked out using Cole's credit card because I didn't have access to my inheritance yet. The staircase, and the big, muted pink rug I also bought with Cole's credit card...

"So, this is you," Freya says as my vision fades, and the cabin hurtles into view.

My vanilla scented candles are replaced by the sharp, slightly sweet smell of wood sap and spruce. The floors are still made of wood, but so are the walls and every piece of handmade furniture. A small kitchenette greets us on the right side with a wood burning oven and hearth, and on the other side, there's a small sitting area.

"Two bedrooms," Freya says, sweeping her hand toward three doors along the back wall. "And a bathroom."

"Thank you," Cole says, glancing at me before turning his attention back to Freya. He asks about the communal dinner that takes place every night in the pack house while I step toward the doors, opening the center one.

It's a bathroom. Simple, and clean. The main bedroom is also simple, clean, and rustic–with a hand woven blanket on the bed and goose down pillows.

I step into the second bedroom–a nursery–at the same moment I feel Cole approach me from behind.

I hear the front door snap closed, enveloping us in silence, at last.

"Do you think he'll sleep in the crib?" Cole asks, tilting his head toward the baby bed along the wall.

"Kenna said he'd be tired today, that he might sleep a lot... because of the herbs," I reply, shivering at the memory of the taste. Kenna had me drink an entire pot of tea before she swept us from Shadowcrest to Moonrise using her powers, then again to the outskirts of Silver-hide. The herbs were strong enough to transfer to Addy through my milk and help with the mental and physical anguish of jumping through time and space, even for babies.

Addy is out cold, tucked warm and cozy in his new bed, within seconds of Cole laying him down.

We stare at our baby, shocked by how seamless the transition was, and slowly, carefully, creep out of the room and close the door.

The second Cole's hand leaves the doorknob, he grabs me and pulls me in for a kiss.

The air leaves my lungs in a startled gasp as his lips brush over mine. He tilts his head, deepening the kiss to the point my toes curl in my sneakers.

He backs me toward the door to our room, smiling against my lips.

"What do you think you're doing?" I ask against his mouth, giggling as his hands travel down the slope of my waist, to my hips.

I get my answer when he reaches behind me and opens the door, then picks me up, clamping a hand over my mouth to stop the squeal that will no doubt wake our baby up.

With his shifts at the hospital and Addy's unpredictable sleep schedule, we don't get time together like this. We find each other in stolen moments–like when we're both getting ready for the day, and Addy's entertained by his little bouncy chair, and Cole presses me against the kitchen counter for a heated kiss, a promise of what might happen later if the stars align.

Well, the stars are aligning now, that's for sure.

We fall onto the bed together. He rises up over me, pulling my shirt over my head and unclasping my bra.

I sigh in relief when the cool, late summer air whispers over my bare skin. Cole pulls off his shirt and leans down, covering my body with his. He tugs down my shorts, his touch lingering on my thighs as he drags the fabric down.

His mouth is on mine again, hungry and desperate. I tangle my fingers in his air as he settles between my legs, one of his hands fumbling with his belt buckle.

"Please," I whimper, gasping for breath. "Cole, please hurry–"

His mouth drags along my jaw, pressing kisses down my neck, sucking marks onto my skin.

The mark he left on my body just after the battle burns with satisfaction when he shoves his pants down and–

A sharp knock on the door makes us both freeze.

We wait for Addy to wake up.

'If that's you, Ryan,' I say to my brother through the mind-link, not even daring to breathe, *'Go. Away.'*

Cole rises up on his elbows as heavy footsteps recede off the porch in the distance, then Ryan's soft chuckle rings through my head.

'Remember to get some rest,' he teases, and I feel the blood rushing to my face.

"Asshole," I grumble.

"Ryan, I'm guessing?"

Cole lowers his body against mine again, drawing teasing circles against my inner thigh with his fingers.

"We won't have any privacy here," I whisper as if the entire village can hear us, but any worry I have is quickly replaced by the insane desire beginning to course through my body at his touch.

"We don't have any privacy anyway," Cole counters, nipping at my neck.

Whatever I have to say in response is stolen from my lips when he slides his fingers inside of me with a groan, dipping his head. "Fuck, Misty."

I arch my hips into his touch, silently begging for more.

Cole and I haven't drifted apart. We've had months to find each other, actually, to fall in love all over again.

He has been nothing but strong for us. I often wonder if he's holding back how he really feels. I know he has nightmares. I know he wakes to comfort me through mine.

I decided to come to Eastonia again because of him. I thought we both needed to heal old wounds preventing us from truly moving on from the war and everything we went through–everything we had to do.

I pray that this trip is enough to actually move on. We have a life to live together, after all.

Addy starts to fuss in his crib just as we're getting down to business.

Of course.

7

WHO KILLED IT?

AVIVA

THE PACK HOUSE IS ALWAYS FULL TO THE BRIM. FOUR IMPOSSIBLY LONG tables and benches rest in the center of the wide, wood-lined space in rows where not a single seat is unaccounted for. Children dart from group to group, finding friends to play with while their parents dine.

I'm at my usual spot at the head of the left-most table, surrounded by the other young, mated, new mothers while our mates move from group to group of men, chatting over pints of home-brewed ale.

I bounce Lexa in my lap as I fork another piece of meat into my mouth, glancing down the table where Misty and Cole are seated together, unaccustomed to the noisy, damn near riotous shared evening meal.

Misty seems especially affected, which strikes me as odd, given that she spent two weeks here last year before she went back to school… but that was before everything happened.

Her eyes are empty, which worries me.

I thought I was the only one having an existential crisis, but apparently... I'm not. Freya leans over, patting her son Sam's back. "She's different, isn't she?"

"I don't think she's been feeling well," I reply under my breath as Ryan comes up behind me to give me a sloppy kiss on the cheek before scooping Lexa out of my arms. She grunts her disapproval, but she knows by now there's no use in complaining. Her cries of displeasure at being separated from me will fade into the incessant chatter of the room, and everyone loves to see their princess, regardless of her opinions on the matter.

Freya smiles as Ryan and Lexa disappear in the crowd, but then her eyes scan my profile. "Have you talked to her about it?"

"About what, exactly?"

One of the other mothers at the table leans in with a quick tilt of her head toward Misty. "She has a serious case of the *baby blues*, Luna."

I nod because it's all I can do. I already know it's more than that. Misty's vibrancy is gone—staunched like water to flame. Her razor sharp edges are chipped. I can see it in her eyes.

I can see it in Cole's eyes, too, as he tries to engage her in conversation. His worry is palpable, which gives me an idea about where I need to begin to fix this.

I set my fork down before leaning over to tickle Sam under his fat chin. "I'll see you guys tomorrow."

"Where are you going so soon?" Freya complains with a scoff. "You barely touched your food!"

"I'm going hunting tonight, *Mother*," I tease, rolling my eyes as Freya scowls. "I don't want a full stomach slowing me down."

"But you'll still come by my loom class in the morning?"

"Absolutely not." I give Freya a dazzling smile that only makes her scowl grow, but I'm beyond caring. Freya knows me better than to expect me being mated and a mother to have changed me on a biological level. My fingers don't long for the loom. My body can't sit still for that long, either.

I'm better suited to what I've always done best—killing things. For food... and fun, of course.

"Be careful out there!" Freya calls out. "There was a report of a hellhound nearby!"

"The hellhound should be more worried about me!" I call back, but my voice is absorbed by the cascade of conversation pinging from one side of the room to the other.

I head for the door, hooking my arm around Ryan's, pulling him away from a conversation regarding some water wheel apparatus some of the guys are constructing near the lake.

"Did you even eat?" he asks, switching Lexa to his other arm to prevent her from tangling her fists in my hair in an attempt to get to me instead.

"Doesn't matter," I rush out, pulling him to a stop just outside the pack house. "Your sister is really going through it, Ryan. You need to talk to Cole."

Ryan's cocky smile fades immediately. "What do you mean?"

"Somethings wrong with her. She's so sad."

"I picked up on that," he says under his breath. "Cole and I talked–"

"So you have talked to him about it?"

"The last time I was in Crescent Falls, when he and Sydney pitched the idea of sending Cole to Eastonia to train with a healer. I was the one who suggested they come here, and he told me he was starting to worry about Misty."

"Worry how?" I press.

Ryan, being of the male variety, shrugs, "She's just not herself."

"Okay, elaborate!" Men. I swear.

"We didn't really get into it."

I point to the door to the pack house. "Misty's going hunting with me tonight, and you're going to talk to Cole about her and gather some information. I want details from his point of view."

Ryan huffs, giving me an exasperated look. "What do you want me to say to the guy?"

"What would you want to know about me if I wasn't feeling well? If I wasn't myself?" I give him a little shove toward the door. "I'll reward you for it later."

"Reward?" he tosses me a wry smile. "Elaborate–"

"Get in there and send her out. I want to get going."

Lexa gives me the most furious look as Ryan carries her back inside, and I wait, and wait, and wait for Misty to come out… but she doesn't.

It's Mercy slipping through the door instead, her dark green eyes shining in the moonlight as she shakes her head. "She's not coming tonight. She wants to sleep. Be careful, okay?"

I nod, resigned, and turn from the pack house, grabbing my halter and bow where I'd left them hanging over a lantern post.

I know why I'm tangled up about Misty. It has more to do with caring about her, if that makes sense. I love her. She's a sister to me, metaphorically and literally because I'm married to her brother, but we went to war together. I fought by her side. I watched her get sucked through a portal to a place she hasn't spoken about yet. I stayed upright long enough to bring her back. I was with her in the days that followed, but even then, she hadn't been like this.

It's a good distraction from my own anxiety, I guess.

I break into a sprint and shift, tearing toward the mountains. I pass the lake and hot springs in a blur of dark woods and moonlight with no direction in mind, only the knowledge that a hunting party came home this morning with a report of seeing a hellhound thirty miles north of Silverhide, and there is no way I am letting an opportunity like this pass me by.

I descend into the valleys behind Silverhide, racing deeper into the forest, following the scent the hunters' left behind on their return.

It's fully night when I reach their old camp. I pick up Jacob's scent first, likely when he'd gone out on patrol and spotted the hellhound, but he didn't go that far from camp to begin with, it seems. They got an elk. The remnant of blood and silver skin from the butchering are still evident as I pick through the forest.

The smell of blood lessens the further I travel from camp, mingling with a new scent–something even more metallic–magic.

The hunters weren't lying about seeing a hellhound.

Because there was a hellhound.

Only, it's dead now.

I shift back into my usual form and adjust my dress in a rush, my mind spinning over the figure lying still in front of me. Warmth radiates from its mutated form. This hellhound is more wolf-like than the others I've seen. Almost a cross between a rogue and a regular shifter; its body is lean and strong, but its facial features are all wrong. Its eyes are huge and extremely far apart. Its mouth is wide open, three rows of razor sharp teeth glinting in the moonlight.

Its magic pours from its broken body, but I can't figure out where it was injured. In fact, it's in one piece. No blood seeps from its skin, and normally hellhounds—which can easily be hundreds of years old—dissolve into ash when they die, but this one... something's odd about this one.

A flicker of panic skitters through my mind as I instinctively look for green-hued magic but don't see anything that color.

But there's still a smell I don't recognize. Some kind of herb... something spicy and extremely pungent to be sticking around despite the warm breeze whispering through the trees.

I edge toward the hellhound, wondering if it might still be alive, a second too late. Its body begins to cave in on itself, its skin falling away, bones turning to dust.

I lean on my bow and watch the breeze carry the last remnants of the hellhound away but notice something odd about the area where it was just lying.

The ground here is... wrong. I'm standing in a clearing where new-growth trees fan out in all directions, creating a circle of spindly aspen and alder. Beyond that, the trees are absolutely ancient, towering dozens of feet above my head.

This place—this circle—is new. Something used to rest here—a building. A temple, perhaps.

Excitement blurs my senses as I begin to search for ruins, ignoring the prickle of unease making the hair on the back of my neck stand on end.

A twig snaps nearby, followed by the scurrying of something larger than a rabbit but smaller than a wolf, and I jerk back to reality.

I just found a hellhound, dead. It wasn't injured. Something killed it, but how? They don't just die of old age. They're immortal souls trapped in bodies mutated by magic–bodies that never belonged to them in the first place.

Nothing about this place feels right, and I decide I'm not sticking around to find out why.

I wish Misty had come with me and been able to use her powers to show me exactly what happened here. I'll convince her to come back with me, one way or another.

On my way back to Silverhide I grab a few rabbits just to bring something home, but by the time I reach our house on the outskirts of the village, the moon is dipping back toward the horizon, and another day is about to begin.

I leave the rabbits hanging on the deck and creep into the house to find Ryan awake and sipping coffee on the couch. I pause in the doorway, furrowing my brow. "Did you… wait up for me?"

"You know I don't sleep much when you're away," he says, taking another sip. "Lexa's still asleep by some miracle. I think she accepted the fact you weren't going to be up with her every hour tonight."

"She'll be strapped to my back all day today," I say, feeling slightly guilty but unsure how to tell him about what I found. "Uhm, did Jacob say they saw a live hellhound or a dead one?"

"Live," Ryan replies, narrowing his eyes at me. "Why?

"Because I found it, and it wasn't alive anymore." I pour myself a cup of coffee. "It was very dead."

Silence swells between us for the space of several breaths before Ryan rises with a groan and saunters over to me. Dressed in nothing but a pair of navy blue boxers and a fitted gray shirt, his massive frame flexes as he sidles up to the table and leans his thigh against it, reaching out to brush a lock of hair away from my face before cupping my cheek.

I can see the words unsaid in his eyes. He doesn't want to deal with any more threats. He's trying his hardest not to care that a fucking hellhound, of all things, died mysteriously only thirty miles north of our pack.

An easy year.

That's all we wanted.

"Take a shower with me," he orders, his eyes darkening a shade. "You have sticks in your hair."

8

IT'S A FEVER

AVIVA

HOT WATER ROLLS OVER MY SKIN AS I PRESS MY FOREHEAD AGAINST THE tile. The shower is a new addition to our house, built along with the second story and unused bedrooms in the upper level. For me, the shower is absolutely massive–unreasonably so. For Ryan, it was a much needed upgrade from our copper tub downstairs.

He stretches his arms over his head and groans as the scent of lavender soap fills the air, mingling with the steam. The window cut into the tile fogs up, blocking our view of the woods, but the first inklings of morning sunlight are trying to stretch toward Silverhide.

"So," he says behind me, gently tugging twigs from my curls and tossing them out of the shower. "This hellhound you found... what did it look like?"

"A wolf," I say, closing my eyes as his large hands drift to my shoulders, working out the knots from being in my wolf form practically the entire night. My breasts begin to ache with fullness but it's a sensation I'm eager to ignore, especially as his touch burrows into my body, making me feel… other things I'd rather focus on. "Like a cross between a rogue and a shifter, but mutated, of course. Big and ugly."

"That aligns with what Jacob and the hunters saw. He found it strange that it didn't approach them."

"It was guarding something," I whisper before I can stop the line of thought from leaving my lips.

"Guarding what?"

I shrug, and his hands move down my sides. "I found it in a clearing a few miles away from their camp. The clearing was strange— like, something had been there at one point, but I couldn't find any ruins. It gave me a weird feeling and the way the hellhound died was almost like a natural death… due to age. It's like it laid down and took its last breath there."

Ryan turns me around to face him, concern lighting behind his eyes. He looks handsome with his dark, curly hair wet and sticking to his face. He grew his beard out again over the winter after the war but has been shaving it clean every couple of days. He's clean shaven now. I reach up to run my knuckles over the sharp line of his jaw then graze my fingertips down the column of his throat.

"I like to think dying of old age is a possibility for those creatures," he says quietly over the rush of the water.

"We both know that's not possible," I reply, meeting his eyes. Hellhounds live forever, trapped in their immortal, devastated bodies.

"Maybe things are changing," he says, leaning down to press his forehead against mine.

His proximity is also intoxicating but more so when he's completely, utterly naked. I have a hard time focusing as my hands slide down his slick chest, over the firm muscles of his abdomen, and lower….

Ryan groans, moving his hands from my waist to cup then squeeze my ass, as I press the heel of my hand down his length. His cock stands immediately, harder than steel, and I only have a heartbeat to inhale a breath before his mouth is on mine, ravenous.

He built a ledge into the shower for our soaps and shampoos, but I found out rather quickly that he had something else in mind when he designed it. Our height difference makes this rather tricky, unfortunately, unless we're in a bed, or on a couch, or if he has me sprawled over a table. In one swift motion, he hauls me onto the ledge, ignoring the bottles of soap that fall around his feet, and spreads my legs wide.

I wrap my arms around his neck and pull him in for a kiss while his hands slide up my soapy thighs. He growls in satisfaction when his fingers find my entrance—wet and hot for him. Ready for him.

"One day, I'll have time to lay you down and fuck you like I want to," he rasps against my lips. "With candles and shit."

I choke out a laugh that quickly turns to a moan when he drags the head of his cock through my folds. We both tremble. "You know that doesn't matter to me," I whisper, my breath hitching as he enters me, inch by inch, stretching me wide to the point of fullness.

I doubt I'll ever get used to his size, even after giving birth to his giant baby, but still, no one can make me feel the way Ryan can. My body was made for his—and vice versa.

"Goddess," he curses, groaning as my muscles flex around his cock. "Aviva, I want to do this all day, all night. I want to make you come until you're spent—"

I gasp as he pulls out and thrusts deep, hitting the spot that makes my toes curl. I wrap my legs around his waist on impulse, leaning back to take him deeper, to give him better access to everything he desires.

Any stress and anxiety I felt on my return to Silverhide vanishes, replaced by that tight, coiling tension in my muscles and a deep ache that edges on desperation as Ryan thrusts deeper, his pleasure loud and untethered. He nibbles my earlobe, whispering filthy things against my skin as my body begins to unravel, pleasure washing through me in waves.

He groans deep in his throat and slams his hand against the tiled wall as my inner muscles spasm and clench. I bite down on my lip to stop from screaming, my legs locked around his waist, my head rolling back and my eyes squeezed shut in ecstasy.

"Good girl," he rasps, jerking into me once, then twice, then pulls out and spills himself on my belly.

I can barely catch my breath. He leans in to kiss me again–full and tender, brushing the words, "I love you," over my cheek, into my hair.

I can't choose just one reason I love Ryan so much, but his gentle, loving care is at the top of my list. He washes my entire body. He lathers shampoo through my curls and untangles them, brushing them out as the water pours over us, washing my late night journey down the drain.

Afterward, dressed in a robe with my hair wrapped tight in a towel, I creep into our bedroom, where Lexa is still fast asleep, sprawled in the center of the bed.

I curl up beside her, waking her gently to nurse, and notice she's running a little hot as she nurses, not even bothering to open her eyes.

Ryan creeps into the room to grab some clothes. I turn to him, concern ripping through my body as I press a hand over Lexa's forehead. "Is she sick? She's hot."

"She seemed fine last night," he says, his eyes narrowing as he pulls a shirt over his head then pulls a belt through his jeans. He walks over, cupping Lexa's head. "She is warm."

"What–what do we do?"

"Shifters rarely get sick," he mutters under his breath.

"But she's–" I look down at Lexa, confused. She's more peaceful than usual. "Was she like this last night?"

"She was calm and slept through the night. I thought she was just getting over her separation anxiety," he explains. Lexa unlatches, sighing deeply before slumping back into sleep.

This is abnormal behavior on her part, and we both know it.

Ryan bursts into action, scooping her up and wrapping her in a blanket. I roll out of bed and quickly dress, ignoring my wet hair and rushing out the door following my mate, struggling to keep up with his long stride.

The village is just waking for the day. Sunlight hasn't reached the valley yet as we move under the cloak of amber light falling from lanterns, but he doesn't turn toward the new healer's cottage that was built this spring.

His pace is just under a brisk jog as he bee-lines toward the cabin where Misty and Cole are staying.

He knocks once, raising his fist to knock again, but the door swings open, revealing Cole, mussed from sleep but wide-eyed as he looks at Ryan, then down at Lexa.

"She's running a fever," Ryan rushes out.

Cole nods, motioning us inside. Misty peeks out of their bedroom holding Adrian, looking skeptical with hooded eyes like she just woke up, but her expression shifts when she notices it's us.

Ryan hands Lexa to Cole, and I have a visceral reaction to seeing Lexa in his arms.

Memories of the war and what happened prior sprint through my head. I remember the day we gathered in the kitchen in Crescent Falls after finding out Cole planned to use Misty as a breeder. I remember seeing her for the first time after her abduction, screaming in that pink gown while Ryatt and Isaac tried to calm her down... and she shifted for the first time.

Cole isn't the monster he was forced to be, but I don't know him that well yet. He's a physician. A doctor. He's here to learn the more traditional shifter medicine Eastonia is known for... but I still imagine him in the black cloak Misty described–with a dead look in his eyes.

Right now, he's wearing a white T-shirt and sweatpants, his curly blond hair sticking out at all angles as he lays Lexa on their kitchen table, unwrapping her blanket.

"Misty, can you please grab my kit?" he asks, looking up at his mate, who nods and hands Adrian to me before disappearing back into their bedroom.

I rest Adrian against my shoulder and absently pat his back while Cole examines Lexa, who has barely even started to wake up from the longest sleep of her life so far.

"She is running a fever," he confirms, glancing at me and Ryan. "It's nothing to be worried about."

"She shouldn't be," Ryan says as Misty reappears with a large metal box balanced in her arms. She sets it down, opens it for Cole, and steps to the side while he pulls out a variety of instruments I can't begin to name.

But then Lexa sputters a cough.

Panic echoes through my body. I grab Ryan's hand. He squeezes.

Cole listens to Lexa's chest. I feel Misty gently taking Adrian back, cradling him as we all watch Cole work. Finally, he wraps Lexa up tight, turning to me with a resigned look in his eyes. "Is she nursing like normal?"

"She did, just recently," I say, but my voice cracks. "I was gone last night–"

"She took a bottle around ten in the evening and fell asleep right afterward and slept through the night for the first time ever," Ryan cuts in, sensing my rising guilt.

"I was gone," I sputter. "I shifted and went hunting–"

"She's okay," Cole assures us. "It's probably a little respiratory virus."

I turn to Misty. "Your powers–"

"On someone this young, it's not a good idea," Cole says before Misty can answer. "It's better that we let her ride this out, but I'll check on her again today. If she stops nursing, we have a problem, otherwise... the fever will burn out."

But Cole has an odd look in his eyes as he turns to Ryan and asks, "Has anyone else been sick lately? With a cough and fever?"

"It happens from time to time, but rarely in children," Ryan says. It's true. It's incredibly difficult for shifters to get sick, and when we do, it's usually not that serious.

"I'm just asking in the event this is contagious."

I close my eyes. Several years ago, a sickness swept through Endova at the tail end of our harvest season. It was a mess. Everyone got it and was in bed for a week, at least, meaning half of our harvest went to waste, and we barely made it through the winter.

After last winter and the war, our supplies are minimal at best. We've had to work insanely hard to restock for this coming winter and to trade at the harvest festival.

As a pack, we can't afford to miss that much work.

As parents, we can't sit here and let our baby suffer.

"I could… I could nurse her," Misty says quietly, glancing at Cole before turning to me. "My healing powers might transfer through my milk. It wouldn't overwhelm her little body like my full powers might."

Cole nods his agreement. "That's a great idea. If you're all right with it." He turns to look at us, and I… I can't decide.

Ryan looks down at me.

"Okay," I whisper, and Lexa's feverish body is handed to Misty, who hands Adrian to Cole, and I sit on the couch and watch–and wait.

At some point I fall asleep and wake up to Lexa tucked snug in my arms and the room empty and quiet.

Misty steps out of their bedroom with Adrian, the two of them now dressed for the day. I run my hand over Lexa's head, noticing that she's still warm to the touch. My heart sinks.

"Where'd the guys go?" I ask. The sun is high in the sky now, so it's likely just past noon.

"A few others are sick. Cole confirmed it, and Ryan is doing whatever Alphas do in this situation."

I lean my head back against the couch and close my eyes, the memory of the hellhound and the strange clearing slipping away, replaced by worry for my pack.

Misty sits down beside me, groaning softly.

And we sit, and wait, for news.

9

WHAT A WITCH!

Misty

IT'S EARLY AFTERNOON WHEN I FINALLY LEAVE OUR CABIN IN SEARCH OF Cole. Aviva–who stayed up all night hunting, and then the entire morning caring for Lexa–is asleep on the couch with both babies at the moment.

The tension in the village is palpable as I walk through the village square, which is quiet… borderline empty. A few people mill around going about their chores, but the square isn't filled with conversation, children playing, or food being cooked and shared.

It's a bright, sunny day, which is being wasted. I sigh heavily and hike the bag I packed with a few sandwiches and treats for Cole over my shoulder and lower my head as I pass a group of men then turn toward the healer's cottage.

In the few days we've been in Silverhide, I haven't had a chance to meet the pack's healer–some witch sent down from Moonrise a few weeks ago to serve in his pack. That's the norm across Eastonia. Witches trained in Moonrise spread out, taking up residence in packs from Veiled Valley, through the Roguelands, and even as far as Tarsian.

But there haven't been witches in the Deadlands for a long time, and according to Ryan, this is a huge deal... a shining declaration that the Deadlands stand with Ryatt, Ella, and their leadership.

In my head, the healer's an old, gnarled woman who smells like herbs and whose age-bent frame is swallowed by her thick, intricate witch's robes.

But I'm sure as hell not expecting the lithe, tall, drop-dead gorgeous witch whose giggles slice through the air and cut out the second I slide through the door, her dark brown eyes narrowing on mine as she steps away from my mate.

Cole's bent over a counter full of jars and herbs, writing notes, like usual. Using the new pens I bought him, the new notebook...while she, the so far unnamed witch, leans against the counter just a few inches too close for comfort.

I'm immediately put out by the surprised, and disappointed, look on her face.

Cole, however, beams at me. "Misty," he breathes, giving me a real, genuine smile.

My heart shudders. This is the four-hundredth time I've seen that smile. Yes, I count them. No, I can't stop and doubt I'll ever stop counting those smiles because I worked so hard to get us here— to happiness, to safety. To a life we desperately wanted and deserved.

I did not go to war, watch my grandparents die, and settle into a mundane suburban life to have a witch I don't know wrinkle her nose at me because I interrupted a moment she thought she was having with *my* mate.

I'll scratch her eyes out.

I narrow my eyes at her before quickly fixing my expression and meeting Cole's gaze, shaking my bag of goodies. "I thought you'd be hungry."

"Thanks, sweetheart." He steps toward me smelling of chamomile and pepper corns—an odd mix of scents compared to the astringent, sharp scent of the sterile scrubs I'm used to him wearing. "How are Misty and Lexa?"

"They're fine. They're both asleep. I left Addy with them." I cut myself off and sigh, feeling a little unsure if that was the best decision. "If he gets sick… I'm sure he'll be fine, right?"

The witch, who I'd been purposefully ignoring, clears her throat. "He won't get sick. He's not from a tribal pack. He's stronger."

I blink and lean to look at her over Cole's arm.

"Misty," Cole says with a hint of a bite in his voice that immediately makes me feel a little better about my quick judgment of the woman, "this is Kyra."

Kyra smiles at me. I don't smile back. "You must be his wife."

"I am," I reply, straightening up as Cole takes the bag of food and sets it on the counter. I love Cole dearly, and he's as sharp and intelligent as they come… but he's still a man. I'm sure when it comes to other men, he's a great judge of character, but he's useless when it comes to women.

I noticed that about him when we integrated ourselves to the culture at the hospital in Crescent Falls, which serves all the packs. His colleagues are from different packs, bending the knee to different Alphas. Being the wife and mate of a physician, I've gone to the garden parties and fundraisers for the hospital, of course. I've met the other mates, the other wives, the girlfriends.

There's a few I love…and more I can't stand, and Cole doesn't get why.

It's because women just know, okay? I'm not sure how else to explain it, other than one look at Kyra has my hackles raising and my powers simmering closer to the surface than they have in months.

"You shouldn't be worried about your son getting sick. He won't."

"If it's contagious, then he likely will," I counter, glancing at Cole as he turns to face us, leaning his leg against the counter as he bites into a sandwich.

"It is something to consider," Cole tells Kyra.

"I don't need to consider it at all," she says brightly, shrugging. "Cole and I canvassed the village this morning. Those who are sick are from Endova and/or refugees from Navvan, not anyone from Ryan's pack–"

"Everyone here is part of Silverhide," I interrupt, my voice clipped.

She purses her lips, tucking a strand of raven black hair behind her ear. "I meant that those who are sick came here from other places originally. The Navvan refugees who assimilated... they're sick. Everyone else is fine and will be fine."

"That doesn't make any sense," I say, but I can feel Cole watching me with marked curiosity as I take a ginger step toward Kyra. I hate that I have to look up into her eyes, and she gets to look down at me in return, but so be it. She hasn't given me a reason to like her yet, and talking shit about Ryan's pack members isn't helping her case. I think Cole is catching on.

He raises a hand to begin to diffuse the situation, but I barrel forward. "Do you have a problem with people from the Deadlands? Those born here, in the tribes?"

"Of course not," she scoffs. "But you have to understand they're not like us."

I raise my brows. "Us? You're a witch, if you've forgotten. If anyone is *not like us*, it's *you*."

"Misty," Cole says under his breath, but I ignore him.

"You're a scholar aren't you, Princess?" Kyra says hotly, crossing her arms beneath her... unfortunately ample breasts. "You should know that the people of the Deadlands are an entirely different kind of wolf than you, therefore, genetically predisposed to sickness like this–"

"There's absolutely no correlation–"

"All right," Cole breathes, grabbing my shoulder and swiftly whirling me toward the door. "Let's take a walk. I haven't seen you all day."

A growl works its way up my throat as I snatch the bag of food off the counter before Kyra can get her hands on it and allow Cole to lead me out of the cottage, but I'm worked up, itching to shift or use my powers.

He can definitely tell.

"What was that about?" he asks, his hand dropping from my shoulder to my arm while I stomp back across the village square with him at my side.

"Did you not hear her?"

"Of course, I did," he says under his breath. "I don't agree with how she said it, but she's right."

I grind to a stop. "She's right?"

He sighs and turns to me, sunlight catching in his hair. "This is part of the reason I needed to come here, Misty. You know that. You know that people like Aviva are different–a different kind of wolf. Her people have been secluded and separated from the rest of us for centuries, and now we're commingling in droves. If this... virus is only affecting those from the Deadlands, it's something we're immune to, which means Addy will be fine."

"She said he was stronger," I growl.

"There are better ways to word it, I know. I didn't like that, either."

"Well I don't like her."

He purses his lips. "She's not that bad. She's strange, definitely, but talented in apothecary style healing."

I want to say I don't care. I don't care about herbs, potions, or tonics. I care about the way her eyes were bright and shining as she stared at my mate, leaning close to him, and then went dark as night and deadly the second she saw me walk through the door.

I've never considered myself a jealous person, but I am territorial, if what I went through to save Cole's life is any indication of that.

But, maybe I am being a little uptight.

"I'm tired," I admit, and it's true.

"You didn't sleep well," he confirms with a sigh. "I know. That's what you should do today, while you have help with Addy. There's so much help with kids here, it's amazing, honestly, the community–"

I'm barely following his words. My heart is beating fast, my powers still trying to claw to the surface, and for whatever reason, memories I'd tried to bury work in tandem with those powers, fighting for dominance.

Something doesn't feel right, and I hate it. Something feels a whole lot like it did when I was cloistered away in that Goddess forsaken fortress in the middle of the desert, trying to figure out if Cole was mine… or if he still belonged to that fuckhead Richard.

When we reach our cabin again, Cole has effectively calmed me down enough I can pretend I'm fine, which I do, shoving the bag of food in his hands and resisting the urge to tell him never to go near that witch again.

But it's not my place. He's here to learn, and she's the pack's healer.

But I will be telling Ryan and Aviva about what she said, just for good measure.

Aviva's still asleep with Lexa when Cole leaves. Addy's just waking up, which is great timing, so I scoop him into my arms and check Lexa's temperature by laying my hand over her forehead. Still hot, but not as bad as this morning. Cole was sure she'd be able to burn this off on her own, and I'm praying that's the case.

But Aviva's looking pale now.

I nurse Addy for a few minutes then settle him in his chest carrier and stalk back into the village, looking for my brother.

Ryan's at the forge with Andrew, who gives me a tight nod in hello and goes back to work as Ryan turns me toward the door. "You shouldn't bring Addy in here, it's too hot–"

"Aviva's running a fever now, but she's asleep. I think you should take them home and take care of them."

He chews his lower lip. "Shit."

"Right," I grumble, following his gaze across the sleepy village to the pastures and the hills beyond.

"Everyone's ill," he says under his breath. "Most of the guys are okay, but the women–"

"Your bitch of a healer said only the tribal people are getting sick because wolves like us–from Crescent Falls–are stronger."

Ryan looks down at me. "What?"

I shake my head, feeling overwhelmed by my simmering powers and uncertainty. "Look, just–just take care of Aviva, please? She's so pale, and I need to–I want to use my healing powers on her, but I'll need help with both babies, okay? Can you step away from your Alpha duties for the afternoon?"

"I'm sure the healer has this handled–"

"I don't trust her, Ryan. Something's off." I barely recognize my own voice. It's been months since I've let myself lean into this intuition I know I inherited from Grandma–that little voice in my mind screaming to keep my head on a swivel.

I wonder if she'll send me visions tonight. I haven't had a vision in ages.

I hope she does.

Ryan searches my face. "Misty, what's wrong?"

"I don't know," I growl under my breath. "But I need to do something. My powers are begging me to do something. *Please.*"

10

____

WHERE BUT NOT WHY

Misty

NIGHT FALLS ON SILVERHIDE AGAINST A CHORUS OF COUGHING AND sneezing. I'm not sure how else to describe it, but I've also never been sick before, so seeing half of Ryan's pack under the weather is absolutely alarming.

Everyone seems to be doing okay, however. Aviva snapped out of what ended up being a very short-lived fever, and Lexa is back to her usual self, but they're both exhausted. Freya, Andrew, and their son, Sam, were somehow spared by the worst of the illness and have taken over care of Aviva and Lexa tonight so Ryan can take me on a run.

I stare at the sleeping forms of Cole and Addy before closing the bedroom door and slipping out of the cabin to meet my brother on the road leading out of Silverhide. The dress I borrowed from Aviva feels strange against my skin as the warm night air wafts over me, lifting my hair from my shoulders in a soft breeze. It's one of those Endovian dresses designed for shifting, of course, which means I'm practically exposed, but when I catch up to Ryan, I notice him in a pair of Endovian pants and not much else.

He looks equally as uncomfortable as he glances away from me to scan the quiet stretch of road and the pastures rising on either side.

We shift, and that's that. No more talking, no more fussing. I spent the entire afternoon reeling from meeting Kyra for the first time, and my reaction to her presence in general, which was completely unnerving. Sure, she'd said some things I hadn't liked… but I'm starting to wonder if I overreacted.

Shifting is exactly what I needed, but as an hour passes, then another, I start to wonder what exactly I got myself into, especially when Ryan dips into another valley where the forest is so thick I can't make heads or tails of what direction we're traveling in.

But then, I pick up Aviva's scent—faint, but it's still there.

'*Where are we going?*' I ask through the mind-link, following several paces behind Ryan's massive, dark brown wolf.

He lumbers ahead, not bothering to stay stealthy and quiet on his paws as he crashes through the woods, scaring the absolute wits out of the birds and whatever tiny creatures were trying to get some sleep on the forest floor.

'*I needed to come out here and check something, and you gave me the perfect opportunity to make time for it because of your tantrum earlier.*'

'*I wasn't throwing a tantrum,*' I growl, but he shakes his massive head, moonlight rippling through his thick fur.

'*Misty, do you trust Cole?*'

'*Of course, I do. What kind of question is that?*'

'*You freaked out because he was in the company of another woman.*'

I nearly skid to a stop, livid. '*No… that's not why I don't like Kyra. But she was—she was looking rather cozy with him when I came into the cottage and looked furious that I'd interrupted—*'

'*Interrupted what, exactly?*'

Nothing. Absolute nothing. At least, Cole thought nothing was off or strange about her proximity. I realize at that moment that I'm the problem.

'*Cole shouldn't be as trusting as he is,*' I reply, feeling a burden lifting from my shoulders at the admission.

'*Why do you say that?*'

'Because, when the war ended, and we went home and started our life together he just... moved on. It hasn't affected him.'

'Has he said so? Have you asked him if he's been affected by the war and what he went through?'

I want to say yes, of course, but...

'He doesn't like to talk about it.' We've never brought it up–at least, not how he's faring after everything that happened. There were a few times, especially toward the end of my pregnancy, when we'd visit his mom and sister on their cozy island up north, and he'd talk somewhat openly about his father, but not about his time in Tarsian during the war, or Richard, or the curse.

But Cole's so different than he was when we met last year. He's happy. He smiles, and laughs, and he loves me so much and isn't afraid to show it.

He's my dream, and I don't want to hurt him by bringing up the past, even if he's the only one that's been able to move on.

'He had it the worst, you know,' I tell my brother as he leads us through the trees. *'What he went through–what he had to do–'*

'You're worried about someone else using him like Richard used him, aren't you?'

That comment stops me in my tracks.

Ryan senses that I've stopped following him and turns, his dark blue eyes shining in the moonlight. *'Kyra's just a witch. I didn't get to choose who was sent here, and trust me, I would have chosen someone older and more experienced, but I brought a healer from Moonrise to Silverhide because we needed one–someone able to take care of the pack outside of delivering babies and tending wounds. She can make potions and herb blends that could help us thrive through another hard winter. Her opinions about the tribal packs... admittedly, I didn't know, and I'll talk to her about it.'* He steps toward me, lowering his head. *'Everyone in Silverhide is equal, regardless of where they're from. I won't tolerate those kinds of comments, period. You have my word.'*

I nod. That's all I can do.

But Ryan continues, *'You went through so much last year. I don't think any of us can relate.'*

'We all went to war. We all nearly died–'

'You and Cole did most of the fighting. You went through a fucking portal, Misty. It's okay to be fucked up, but you're holding it in. Mom said you've been closing yourself in the library for months cataloging every shred of information about the war, putting together some big book about it.'

'So?' I ask hotly, shivering suddenly as we step into a clearing drenched in moonlight.

Ryan lifts his snout, sniffing the air before taking a timid step into the moonlight. *'So, don't forget to write your own story, too. Cole's story. Addy's story. How he came to be, and how his mother found his father.'*

'I'm not sure I ever want him to know.'

'And that's why you can't think straight. That's why you're hurting. You haven't let it go.' He looks at me in the eyes, holding my gaze, showing me a glimpse of what I can only describe as hurt that he's kept long buried, too. *'I killed my first mate, remember? I spent two years feeling like you do now–absolutely fucking wrecked. In pieces. Ready to just let go–and die. Aviva pulled me from the edge, Misty. Cole's been pulling you away from the edge since the end of the war–'*

'He hasn't–'

'He has. Cut the guy some slack. He's not going to cheat on you with a fucking witch from Moonrise after everything you put him through, trust me.'

For a moment I honestly believed I was having a heart to heart with my favorite older brother, but as he shifts back into his human form, still dressed in those weird pants, his mouth plays into that fucking smirk again, and I growl.

'It's time to wake up, Misty. I need your powers.'

I shift to my human form with a huff, shoving my hair out of my face. "What do you need my powers for? And what's that smell? It smells awful!"

Ryan grinds his teeth and steps further into the clearing. "I need you to show me what happened here."

"Something died, obviously. Recently." I cover my nose with my mouth, but the heavy scent of fresh death isn't the only thing hanging low in the air around us–metal coats my tongue. The sharp, thick taste of magic… and it's not mine.

"Jacob and some of our hunters came here two nights ago tracking a herd of elk. They set up camp ten miles south, and that night Jacob's scouts came back saying they'd had a run-in with a hellhound."

"A fucking hellhound–"

"Which is odd," Ryan cuts in sharply, raising his fingers to motion for me to keep my mouth shut for a moment, "because generally, running into a hellhound either means you're with the witch controlling it, or it's without a master... and those without masters are the deadliest, yet this hellhound didn't even know they were there."

That doesn't make any sense.

Ryan seems to agree, nodding to himself as he scans the clearing. "Aviva came here last night. This is where she was when Lexa got sick. She found the hellhound, saw it take its dying breaths."

"She killed it?"

"No, it was... it was dying." He rushes out a breath, his chest contracting with the movement. "She didn't see any injuries. It wasn't wounded, and hellhounds don't just die of old age or illness. But it died and turned to ash. That's what you smell, I think. That spice in the air."

I feel a little sick to my stomach as a chill creeps through my body, making my skin pebble with unease.

"I need to know what killed it. Can you show me?"

I nod. It'll be easy. My powers are simmering here just like they were when I met Kyra, so I raise my hands and let my powers flow, painting Ryan a picture of mist and light.

I watch the hellhound staggering into the clearing. It's unsteady on its feet and topples over. But even while my powers show us the hellhound's death, I can... feel it–the ungodly creature–it's an overwhelming sense of peace that this is finally the end of what was an incredibly long life spent in the hell of a witch's making.

The hellhound–a male, I believe, based on the flicker of voices in my head–lays his head down and closes his eyes at the very moment Aviva's wolf bursts into the clearing and freezes.

We watch the hellhound drift into death, and the breeze carries its ashes away.

Ryan huffs beside me. "No, I need to see how it died."

"It didn't happen here," I tell him, but then my powers surge to an unholy degree. I nearly scream, choking on the pain from the pressure of my powers leaving my body through my fingertips, the mist building something right before our eyes–a castle. A castle that rivals the size of the one in Moonrise.

Ryan grips my arm tightly and yanks me back as my powers shudder, failing to complete whatever picture they were painting.

The clearing falls dark and silent once again, but my heart is beating out of rhythm, and those voices in my head are loud.

"There used to be something here, didn't there?" Ryan says, meeting my shocked, wide-eyed gaze. "Aviva mentioned she thought so but couldn't find any ruins."

"Obviously. This is a Firestone sight." I swallow back my surprise and wring my aching hands. "I need to do some research, I think, on hellhounds and whether the Firestone's used them. What if the hellhound did just in fact... die? And he came back here, to where his home was once, to take his last breath?"

"You're giving those creatures too much credit–"

"I'm serious, Ryan. When you moved to Silverhide, you told me all about the hellhounds and the rogues that were here, as well. That the hellhounds here were unburdened by witches and simply roamed, but what if it's more complicated than that? What if they were guarding things–bound to specific places? I look at the ground, feeling my powers flickering back to life, reaching toward something beneath my feet....

Ryan grabs my arm again, tugging me toward the woods. "We need to go back. I'm getting called through the mind-link. We have visitors."

"It's the middle of the night. Who?"

"Someone I've been wanting to meet for a few weeks now. We'll decide what to do about this place later."

11

SWALLOWED GLASS

A VIVA

I WAKE FROM A DEAD SLEEP THAT LEAVES ME IN AN ABSOLUTE PANIC. I roll off the bed with a crash, and then Ryan's voice cuts through the air in alarm over the sound of him ripping the sheets from the mattress in his haste to follow me out of bed.

"Aviva–Goddess–" he grumbles, scooping me up right by my armpits and tossing me back in bed just as a wail echoes through the house.

"Where's Lexa?" I croak, my throat throbbing painfully like I've swallowed glass. I clutch my neck in alarm, swallowing hard past a massive lump nearly blocking my airway.

I've never felt so terrible in my life.

Ryan disappears and returns a few moments later with an incredibly fussy Lexa and a giant glass of water for me. Then, he fusses over us, propping me up against the headboard with several pillows and whisking Lexa away when she's done nursing, all while I sit there in a haze, my head pounding and my joints aching so badly it nearly brings me to tears.

It's early morning. I don't even remember going to bed last night. I just remember Freya being here to help with Lexa. She told me to go lie down, and now?

I turn my aching head toward the bedroom door as the house goes ghostly quiet.

I've never been sick like this. Sniffles, sure. But never a dull, whole body ache. I rub my temples and nestle into the pillows, whimpering pathetically. Some commander, huh? I can't even function through a fever… a fever that apparently returned overnight.

Several sets of footsteps reach the house, moving through the living area and toward our bedroom. Ryan opens the door, holding Lexa in his arms. She's bright and alert–no longer plagued by the same fever threatening to drag me under. Cole steps into view carrying his medical kit. He gives me a flat but sympathetic smile as he edges into the room, asking, "How're you feeling?"

"Absolutely fucking miserable," I croak like someone stuffed rocks down my throat.

"Is that an improvement from yesterday?" A hint of sarcasm laces through the words as he sits on the edge of the bed to listen to my chest. He glances at Ryan, who's darkening the doorway with an exhausted expression.

I want to ask how his night went. I know he went on a run with Misty, which I think she really needed, but I didn't hear him come in. He looks like he didn't sleep well, if at all.

Cole pulls a long, white stick with a fluffy end out of his medical kit, carefully removing it from a length of plastic.

"What is that?" I wince.

"I need to take a sample from your throat. It'll feel weird, but it won't hurt."

"Why?"

He glances at Ryan again.

I realize that Ryan has had a very long night when he says, "Several of the adults are very ill now, Aviva."

Cole adds, "The children, especially the ones still nursing from their mothers, are fine. But yes, whatever this is, it's more serious than we thought."

"What are you going to do with that?"

"I'm sending this sample to Crescent Falls and Moonrise to see if it's something we can treat with medicine that's not available here."

"Misty," I croak, but Ryan shakes his head.

"She tried. Her healing powers aren't working well on this for some reason."

I notice Cole's eyes going a shade darker than normal and feel unease creeping in. "Are we sick? Or is this something else?" I ask my mate.

"Our food and water supply is being tested as well," Ryan practically growls.

I sit up a little straighter. "Were we poisoned?" My throat burns as I look from Cole to my mate. Ryan must have considered this given our somewhat sour relations with the new packs that moved in just north of us.

"You'd likely be dead if that were the case," Cole says point blank, and I grimace, falling back against the pillows.

He then proceeds to stick his torture device down the back of my throat. I nearly bite it in half on instinct but try to be good, at least for a moment.

"Kyra has herbs that've been helping some of the others with their symptoms. I'll have her drop some off this morning, to be brewed into a tea," he tells Ryan before taking his leave.

Ryan lingers in the doorway for a few moments before walking toward me, setting Lexa in my waiting arms. I'm immediately relaxed by her presence, but still, I feel like walking death.

"If I was poisoned," I grind out, "I'll kill–"

"I know, babe," he says with a sad kind of smile.

"What happened last night? This is insane!"

"Well," he says with a deep breath, exhaling slowly. "Misty and I went out and... to begin, you were right about something being in that clearing–something old. She thinks a Firestone castle used to be there. We didn't have much time to debate it, though, because

Andrew blew up the mind-link saying Teshkan warriors had just arrived with the boy."

"The boy?" My foggy, fevered memory whirls. Then, I remember. "Oh, the boy from… Emberfyll? From the sea?"

"Yeah, he's here in Silverhide and fucking terrified, I'll say that much. He's holed up with a household who didn't get sick, but he's not talking. The Teshkans seemed ready to get rid of him, though, saying he was a bad omen or something. I can't really understand much of what they say because of their accent."

I close my eyes, shaking my head. "What the hell is happening, Ryan?"

"I don't know," he says on exhale, slumping his shoulders and running his fingers through his hair. "But I have the harvest to worry about. Mercy's sick."

"Oh, no," I whimper.

"She's going to be okay. Reuben's just fine, like Lexa and Sam. Addy's still healthy. The babies are okay, but anyone originally from the tribes is hurting right now, so I have to deal with that. Jacob doesn't want to leave Mercy's side for obvious reasons, same with Andrew when it comes to Freya, so I have to put a hunt together so the guys can nab a few elk–"

He goes on to explain his plan to save our harvest season in detail like he just needs to say it out loud, but my brain is having a hard time keeping up with the onslaught of information.

"I'm in contact with Kenna. She's going to come get the tests Cole's taking on everyone who's sick and take them back to Moonrise to determine what this is, exactly."

Because shifters don't get sick. Not like this.

Especially not me.

"You need to stay in bed today," he says, lifting Lexa off my lap. She squawks, her face twisted in fury, but I'm not sure I have the strength to even hold her right now.

Ryan says something about making me some tea, but my eyes are already closing, and when they open again, hours have passed somehow.

I'm too weak to even reach toward the curtains to see the last stretches of sunset playing across the sky. An entire day wasted. I could have been hunting. I could have been helping with the crops. I could have been weaving. I could have been holding my daughter.

I turn to the corner of the room where a figure appears out of nowhere, sitting in a chair they obviously dragged from the living room. It's Misty, scribbling in a notebook. She notices me turning my head and looks up, sighing with relief. "I thought you were going to sleep all day. How're you feeling?"

I swallow, feeling more of a dull ache than shattered glass. "Better, I think."

"I knew it," she says, smiling as she tucks her pen behind her ear and rises. "I dosed your tea with my tears. I wasn't sure it was going to work. It hasn't on most people, but it broke your fever."

"Cole said the healer was dropping off herbs–"

Misty clicks her tongue. "Yeah, she did, and they didn't smell right, so I threw them out and made my own concoction."

"What do you mean?"

"You need to rest. We don't need to talk about this now–"

"No, what do you mean? What didn't smell right?"

"I just got a bad feeling when I got here a few hours ago and found Ryan brewing whatever herbs she brought up. I don't know how to explain it, but my powers go haywire when Kyra's around. Do you... know her well?"

"No, not really." She keeps to herself. She doesn't join the pack for meals or confer with the women during the day. She showed up one day, and that was that–Silverhide had a healer... who stayed in her cottage and didn't speak to anyone unless she needed to.

"Well, you're drinking mint tea and my tears from now on, and I think it's working."

"Where are Ryan and Lexa?"

"Down at the pack house having dinner. I've been nursing Lexa today, I hope that's all right."

"It is." I sit up, groaning but feeling... much better. My head feels fuzzy, for sure, but my joints don't feel like they're about to disintegrate.

Misty moves toward the bed, sitting down, her fingers picking at the spine of her notebook. "Aviva... what do your people say about the Firestone witches?"

"Why?"

"Because of that clearing. Something happened there, and it wasn't just the hellhound dying. It smelled... strange."

"Like heat and sulfur... like death."

"Yes," she confirms, her voice low. "Why?"

I shrug. "I don't know, but when I'm well, I want to go back and explore it a little closer. I feel the same." I sense a growing excitement between us that I know for a fact neither of us are ready to admit we feel.

"I want to go with you," she says.

I nod. I wouldn't go without her, honestly. I don't have powers, but she does. If that place is calling to her like it's calling to me, I'm going to need backup.

Two cups of tea with tears and an hour later, Ryan and Lexa return. Misty leaves to join her family, and I lie in bed with mine while Lexa falls asleep in my arms.

But I can't sleep. I've been in bed all day, and with a copious amount of Misty's powers working through my body, I decide enough is enough.

I sneak out of bed, snuggling Lexa close to Ryan, who is so exhausted he doesn't even stir.

Then, I walk out onto the deck to look out over the especially quiet village.

A small, hooded figure emerges from one of the houses in the center of town. I watch the shadow scale the side of the house, jumping to the ground from a second story window, and walk stealthy into the night.

Obviously, I'm going to investigate.

Wearing a nightgown and slippers, I move with practiced grace, dipping into shadows cast by lanterns to stay hidden while the figure–a child–creeps through the village toward the road.

He has no idea I'm behind him, so when he finally looks over his shoulder, he freezes–pale green eyes holding mine.

"You're a long way from your homeland," I tell him in the old tongue.

His eyes go wide, but he doesn't say anything. I edge a step closer to him, holding my arms out in surrender.

"It's a very long way back to the coast."

"I want to go home," he says, heartbreak evident in every word.

"I know," I reply, holding back my grief as his eyes shine with tears. He's definitely young, but not really a child. A young teenager, perhaps, maybe only twelve.

Far too young to be without his parents.

"Are you tired? Hungry?"

He shakes his head, trying his hardest not to cry.

I take another step toward him like I'm approaching a skittish wild animal, but he doesn't move away.

"Do you want to see something..." I try to find the world *cool* in Firestone, but I don't think they used it. "Something incredible?"

He hesitates then nods.

12

LOGAN

Aviva

"What's your name?" I ask in the old tongue as I lead the boy through one of the pastures, shoving chest-height strands of wheat to the side to give us a path.

He doesn't speak for a while. I don't press him for information, either. The fact that he's following me is enough.

"Logan," he says after a moment, his voice calm and cool like the breeze coming off the rolling hills in the distance.

"How old are you?"

"Twelve."

"I thought so." I look at him over my shoulder, smiling, but he doesn't return the gesture. Dark circles line his eyes, and he's incredibly thin, even for a boy his age, who all seem to be gangly and lanky. His dark, nearly black hair is pin straight and sticks up at all angles, rustling in the breeze, and he's pale with freckles across the bridge of his nose.

A scar wraps from his left temple, over his nose, and across his right cheek. It's... horrific, honestly. Wide and gnarled.

"How'd you get your scar?"

"I don't remember. I've always had it."

I nod, turning back to the field, squinting into the darkness as the first hill begins to rise before us. He dutifully follows as I trudge forward up the incline, my legs burning from lack of use after spending the entire day bedridden.

When we reach the top of the hill, I turn back to the village, plopping down on my ass with a dramatic sigh.

"This is what I wanted you to see."

He stands beside me for several moments before sitting down a few feet away, his eyes reflecting in the moonlight. Silverhide sprawls out in a wash of soft, flickering amber light and raised stone buildings nestled in fields of wheat and barley that shimmer in the light of the moon. The mountains rise around the village, the highest peaks still topped with snow, and above them?

Stars fan out across the night sky in shades of the purest white to the richest blue. Violet waves of light dance against the backdrop of stars like ribbons of silk.

Logan takes a shallow breath beside me that edges on a sob.

Poor kid.

"I came here last year after leaving my homeland," I tell him, slipping into the old tongue to the best of my ability. I'm sure the accent is off, and I'm messing up words, but so far, he seems to understand me.

"Why?"

"Because I got married," I answer, wrapping my arms around my knees. "I left everything and everyone I knew behind. I didn't have a choice. I was terrified. I was lonely. I wasn't sure what my future held."

"Did you try to leave?"

"No," I whisper, meeting his gaze. "I had someone here keeping me tethered to this place. But he was a stranger back then. Now, he's my family, and these are our people. I'm the Luna."

He goes pale and glances away from me.

"You don't have to be scared of me. I'm Aviva, but you've probably heard my name already. I'm Alpha Ryan's mate."

"He's the big one."

"Yes," I laugh, resting my chin on my knee. "That's him. He's a kind man. A good man, and you're safe here… but I wanted you to see the valley, to see the mountains and road leading back into the Deadlands before you make your decision."

"You'd let me leave?"

I roll my head to look at him. I can already tell he's a smart kid. He has a certain kind of sharpness behind those big eyes of his–something honed and deadly, perhaps, that will develop more as he gets older.

Something that tells me he's already fully aware of the severity of his situation.

"You can't cross the sea and go home," I tell him. "No one has… you're the first person to ever show up on our shores. You are in a new place, but you don't need to be here alone. Silverhide is a friendly pack. You can stay here. If you don't want to live with a family, we can set you up with your own house, if that would make you more comfortable."

He picks at the grass between his legs.

"You could go to school," I continue. "There're boys your age in the village. They're always causing mischief. Once their chores are done, they run wild and free through the valley. You could join them."

He licks his lips. "I don't know how."

"How to what?"

"Play."

It feels like I have a rock stuck in my throat, and it's not because of the illness I'm trying to fight off. I should ask him the questions I have… things everyone is dying to know. Things like, "Is Emberfyll a threat to us? Are you a threat?"

But he's just a kid.

"What do you like to do, Logan?"

"Draw," he says quietly.

"Okay... I have paper and pencils at my house..." I roll my lip between my teeth. "What if you stayed with me?"

"And the Alpha?"

"Are you afraid of him?"

"No," he says in a near whisper, refusing to meet my eyes. "But–the other one. Who has–" He motions toward his face and then looks at his hands.

"Alpha King Ryatt," I say under my breath, nodding, his facial scars and numerous tattoos coming to mind. "You met him?"

"He came to...to..."

"Teshka," I say, and he nods.

"I couldn't understand what he was saying."

"He was just concerned about you. We all are–"

"Because you think I'm dangerous," he says, point black. He finally meets my gaze, holding my eyes without so much as blinking.

"No. I think you're just a kid who lost his parents and went through an incredible tragedy. A kid who ended up here, with strangers, in a land far away from his home. I think you're just a kid, Logan. A kid who wouldn't survive very long out there by himself, but one day, when you're older, you can go find your people again."

I rise, looking down at him. He curls into himself, tucking his head between his knees. He's likely crying and doesn't want me to see. There's not much else I can do or say to the boy. My heart breaks for him, though.

So, I start walking home, deciding he's old enough to spend the night outside if he really wants to. Hell, I was out hunting at his age, spending my nights under the cover of stars. But when I reach the village, I'm not alone. He follows several paces behind me, sniffling and rubbing at his eyes. Wordlessly, he follows me up to my house where I let him inside, and quietly, almost silently, take him upstairs to the so-far unused bedrooms Ryan built this spring.

We already have a bed ready for him. He'll have a dresser he can fill with the clothes I'm sure Freya will knit and weave for him. He stares out the window at the village below as I leave to gather some extra blankets and the paper and pencils I promised, setting them on his dresser before going down to the kitchen to rummage through the cabinets, coming up with a snack of bread, dried meat, and fruit for him.

But when I return to his room, he's curled up in the bed, already fast asleep, tear stains on his pillow.

I back out of his room and carefully close the door, leaving it open a crack, turning the hallway light on in the event he's scared of the dark.

But the moment my feet reach the bottom step, Ryan turns to me, stepping out of our bedroom. "Is everything okay?" he asks, running a hand down his face. "Are you okay?"

"I'm fine," I whisper, trying to smile, but my lips only twitch. "Uhm, Logan... the boy? He's asleep upstairs."

Ryan raises his brows and blows out his breath. "It's the middle of the night."

"I know." I walk to the couch and sit down, pinching the bridge of my nose. "I woke up and couldn't fall back asleep, so I went out on the deck to get some fresh air and saw him scaling the side of a house and trying to run away."

Ryan sits beside me, stretching out with his arm roped over my shoulder. I lean against his chest, breathing in his scent, and explain the conversation I had with the boy.

He quietly listens as he draws little circles across my shoulder.

"He followed me home, so I set him up with a bed. I think he trusts me, especially since I can understand him."

"He can stay here, of course," Ryan says. "Poor guy. You said his name is Logan?"

I nod. "Yeah, that's what he said. But... he could be lying about that. He's got this scar on his face.... It's horrible, but he told me he's always had it."

"Yeah, the Patriarch of Teshka was weary of that." Ryan chews his lower lip in thought. "They tried to tell me he was a sea creature, some type of water shifter, a demon, and we should take him back out to sea, but I... obviously don't believe that."

"He's a shifter, a wolf, I can smell it."

"Me, too."

Silence falls for several heartbeats. Then, Ryan asks, "Ryatt's concern is that if the original story is true–that he was on a boat leaving Emberfyll, wherever that is, whatever it is, and his parents died fleeing some conflict there–there could be more people coming."

I sit up a little straight at his tone. "What's happening?"

"Evander is sending some of his forces to the coast, just for surveillance. He'll be in the Deadlands for a while, it sounds like, which is great, honestly, seeing as I could use some extra help around Silverhide."

"But he'd be at the coast, near Teshka."

"Evander is a commander, not a grunt soldier. He'll be here. I'm sure he'll bring the whole family after the conversation I had with Kenna. We'll figure out what to do with Logan–even if that means he joins our pack."

"And he stays with us?"

We look at each other, and I think we're both asking ourselves what we know about teenage boys–nothing, honestly, from a parenting perspective. We have an infant daughter who continuously kicks our asses, metaphorically, of course, but still.

Can we be what he needs?

"He'll stay with us as long as he's comfortable with it. It'll actually be a good thing for him, I think, when it comes to integrating into our pack. He'll have me, and you, the Alpha and Luna as backup if the other boys give him any trouble... which they will."

"What do you mean?"

"Just like wolves, Logan's going to have to find his place in our pack, even if it's just temporary. That might mean getting roughed up and roughing up in return."

"You're not serious," I laugh, but he's dead serious, it seems.

"I was twelve once, remember?"

"I don't. I didn't know you then."

"Well, you likely wouldn't have recognized me, given that I was always covered in bruises from scrapping any chance I got."

"You haven't changed much," I tease, leaning closer and resting my head on his chest.

"You're feeling better, aren't you?"

"I am."

"Thank the Goddess," he groans, sighing deeply.

"Thank Misty," I correct. "Her tears actually started to work."

13

WHAT IS THIS PLACE?

Misty

LOGAN IS QUITE GAUNT. THAT'S THE FIRST THING I NOTICE AS I LINGER in the doorway of the healer's cottage, watching Cole check Logan's ears. Cole is amazing with kids, and it shows, because Logan cracks a smile at something Cole says and Aviva interprets.

But Cole's eyes are heavy with concern when he turns away from the boy, his eyes scanning his notes before closing his notebook and setting it on the counter. Aviva, wearing Lexa on her back, takes Logan's hand and leads him out of the healer's cottage, closing the door behind her.

I watch through the window as they walk away, into the rolling, morning fog. It's a chilly late summer morning–the first truly cold morning since we arrived last week.

It's been four days since almost everyone fell ill, but thankfully that's over.

And, Kyra isn't here right now. She's off doing something in Endova, according to Cole and Ryan.

I feel immediately more relaxed in her absence.

"So? Is he going to live?" I try to tease to break the tension in the cozy, herb filled room.

"He will. I think he'll be fine with a better diet and some exercise. He's stressed, that's obvious. I'm mostly worried about his bones and teeth right now. He looks like someone who went months without adequate food–minerals and vitamins, especially."

"Which aligns with his story that he was on a boat," I add, and Cole nods.

"I wish we were in Crescent Falls with him right now. I could run a full panel on him to find out for sure what he needs, what he's lacking but... for now, I think Aviva and her friends are going to keep him fed and happy. That's what matters most."

"How do you think he got the scar?"

Cole stills, leaning over his notebook with a sigh. "I have no idea, but whatever did that, it would have been a horrific injury. It's an old scar, definitely, and looks like it wasn't stitched up or mended every well, but anything could have caused that."

Addy coos faintly in my arms, tangling his little fists in my hair. The thought of Addy being injured like that makes my stomach ache, but I ignore the feeling, saying, "Logan loves Aviva, at least. He's been following her around like a little duck."

"And she's the mother duck," Cole smiles, nodding his agreement. "I talked to Ryan about that last night, actually, during dinner. They like having him around, but he's weary of Ryan and most of the men in general. Ryan's hoping Aviva convinces him to open up soon. Anyway," he breathes, stretching out his arms before reaching for Addy, "are you leaving soon?"

"Yeah, we are. I need to go now if we're going to be home at a decent hour tonight." I kiss Addy on the forehead then rise on my toes to kiss my mate–just a little peck–but Cole wraps his hand around the back of my neck and kisses me deeply, so deeply in fact, I feel my toes curling, and a warm ache beginning to spread in my lower belly.

Unfortunately, I have to pull away. "I'll be home tonight, I promise."

"I know," he smiles. "Have fun, okay?"

I kiss him once more for good measure and take off in search of Aviva, who I find tucked up in her house, laying out her weapons and some shifting clothes for me.

I glance at Logan, who's kneeling on the ground next to the couch, scribbling frantically with a set of colored pencils.

I smile at the sight, especially since Lexa's lying on a blanket beside him, totally enraptured by the movement of his hand.

"Ready?" Aviva asks, her dark, amber-hued eyes meeting mine. "It's going to be a long night, I think. I'm packing snacks."

"How long?"

"Well, that depends on what we find."

I swallow hard. Maybe I shouldn't have told Cole I'd be back soon, judging by the shovels resting against the wall near her front door. How we're going to carry those over thirty miles away, I have no idea, but apparently, Aviva has a plan.

Ryan arrives at the house a few minutes later, just as the light is pulled from the sky and dark rain clouds move in. I feel the temperature drop several degrees and glance out the windows, sighing.

I know this is important... finding out why that clearing is so special and what lies beneath... what's calling to my powers, and to Aviva, who is powerless.

I reach along my side to my leather satchel, drumming my fingers against its side... and the book that lies within.

A book I haven't touched since Cole got it for me for Solstice. The copy of the *Book of Whispers.*

"It's about to rain, hard, I think," Ryan says apologetically, scanning the weapons and halters on the table.

"We'll be fine. It's just a bit of water," Aviva murmurs under her breath. "I want to get some hunting done on our way back."

I can feel tension in the room. It simmers between Ryan and Aviva... but not in a sexual way, thank the Goddess. Ryan's worried about her, that's clear. While Aviva has had four days of rest and recovery after the strange illness that swept through the pack, she's still on the pale side.

Regardless, we spend the next twenty minutes gearing up in

those strange outfits and harnesses and follow Ryan outside. Aviva and I shift, and he takes a few minutes to secure the shovels–smaller than the average, another thing I'm grateful for–to our backs.

I'm weighed down by the weapons and gear, but Aviva moves with grace as she throws him a wolfish look over her shoulder, likely saying goodbye to him through the mind-link.

We trot out of the village. I can feel the stares of the pack as we weave through the village center, then out onto the road, where everyone has gone back to their usual chores with vigor. The clock is ticking on the harvest, and there's no time to waste.

We pass the smoke shed, which is only half full. No wonder Aviva mentioned hunting on our way home tonight.

But my heart lurches when I see Cole and Addy waving from the door of our cabin. Cole's smiling, but his eyes are dark, full of concern.

Into my mind, he says, *'Be careful.'*

'I love you,' I reply, my chest squeezing painfully as my intuition flares to life, sensing I'm about to walk into something bigger than I can chew.

'I love you,' he replies, and I reluctantly turn toward the road.

* * *

It takes us several hours to reach the clearing. Rain pours over us, soaking our fur and making it nearly impossible to see past the sparse ring of alders lining the clearing. Any scent that'd been lingering is now washed away, replaced by ozone and damp earth.

Aviva rolls into her usual form and slides to a stop, panting, her face twisted in disappointment. This isn't ideal weather. Not in the slightest.

I shift with her, shivering against the cold rain and squint into the ever growing darkness, deciding not to waste a second of time. My powers of mist rumble to life, filling the clearing with light, showing her the same vision I'd painted for Ryan. A massive castle grows around us, reaching toward the sky with twisting spires and walls stretching twenty stories high, maybe further.

Bigger than the castle in Moonrise, by far.

"What was this place?" Aviva asks over the downpour.

"The Firestones had castles all over the place," I shout back as my powers curve and fade, the castle falling in a cascade of mist. I'm not sure if it's my powers flickering out or if they're giving us a glimpse of how this place actually fell to oblivion. The ground beneath us fills with silver mist, rising around us in a bubble–a cavern... a cave.

Aviva whirls, wiping water from her face with the back of her hand as my powers create a shield from the rain. "What is this?"

"I don't know," I whisper in awe, looking upward at the vision of crystals and stalactites hanging from a domed, rock ceiling. A great... something rises before us–between us–spreading out in a wide circle of stone.

Aviva jumps back as a roaring sound splits the air around us, and voices explode, their words unfamiliar and pitched in what sounds like a song.

I have no idea what my powers are trying to show me, but Aviva looks ghostly pale as she listens, and looks, at the silver-white flames breaching the stone circle–the well.

Her eyes meet mine, the fire dancing in her irises. "I know where we are. I know what's beneath us."

She waves a hand through the mist, my powers snaking between her fingers and around her wrist.

"There's a forge here, isn't there?" I shout.

She's staring at my magic playing over her skin, but then her eyes meet mine, and she nods gravely.

I let my powers shut down completely, the mist dissipating so rapidly we blink, and the vision's gone, replaced by rain and darkness.

Aviva looks at the ground beneath us, heaving a breath. "We need to make camp."

"We didn't tell the guys we'd be gone all night."

"Misty," she says sternly, holding my gaze with a predator's intent. It makes me start and straighten. I've only seen this look on her face in battle. "The Firestone forges haven't been active in thousands of years. This one is, isn't it? You feel it too. I know you do."

"What are you suggesting?"

"We're going to dig and find the entrance to where it's being kept."

"No," I say, barking a laugh. "Are you insane? We don't know enough about the forges to–"

"They're supposed to be dormant. Something's wrong. The hellhound that came here… he must have sensed it. He was guarding this place for a reason."

I take a step in her direction. "And you want to… what? Dig a hole? Hope we find an entrance? Then what? We don't know what this thing can do."

"We need to put it out," she says under her breath. "Before someone with malicious intent finds it."

"We need to tell Ella," I rasp, shaking my head. "First and foremost. The only active forge is in Moonrise, and the Mystics will know what to do."

A shuddering howl breaks through the forest, echoing over the rain. I shiver, whirling toward the ungodly screech that follows.

I hear the swift metal song of Aviva drawing her golden bow. "That was a rogue. We need to make camp now. We're not the only ones who can feel this thing bubbling back to life." She lifts her chin, sniffing deeply, her eyes going as dark as polished onyx. "More than one, I think. Come on, our hunters made camp a few miles away. It's likely dry there."

"We need to tell Cole and Ryan–" Another snarling howl rips through the clearing, closer this time. Close enough to cause my heart to skip a beat and freeze.

"Misty," Aviva breathes, her entire body locking up as she lifts her bow. "*Run.*"

14

HOLE LOTTA TROUBLE

Misty

"Aviva, stop!" I shout as she begins to turn toward the woods, her bow raised and arrow primed and ready. My powers ignite, stronger than they've ever been, and explode through the clearing in bright, blue light that sizzles into the ground.

I swear, somewhere deep in the swirling, blue ether, I hear what sounds like a lock clicking–like I've just jammed a key into a padlock and wrenched on it until it turned–and then the ground shakes violently, a crushing, grinding sound beginning to echo through the clearing.

Red eyes appear near the tree line–three sets–barreling toward us. Aviva roars as she pulls back on her arrow again, but then she... disappears with a surprised scream.

"Aviva?!" I shout, then choke on her name as the ground beneath me falls away.

My powers burn out. I'm falling through the darkness, reaching blindly for anything to grab onto. Something beneath me hits the ground with a crunch, and then I'm landing on top of the object, which turns out to be Aviva.

We both choke and yelp, rolling to opposite sides. My healing powers tremble to life, attacking the pain in my hips and back from the fall, while Aviva snarls and tries to untangle us.

"What did you do?" Aviva pants, desperate to catch her breath as she stands on unsteady legs.

I don't have a chance to answer. Red eyes float in the rainy darkness above our heads.

The snarling, gnarled growls of the three rogues echo down to us. Aviva grits her teeth and picks up her bow, letting go of an arrow that pierces the first one right between the eyes.

The other two circle the opening we've fallen into, snapping their massive jaws, their naked, molted skin dripping with rainwater as their talons grip the freshly overturned earth.

Aviva shoots another arrow, but she's squinting against the rain, and the arrow pierces the shoulder of the rogue, which causes it to pitch forward and fall.

"MOVE!" Aviva shouts.

I jump out of the way, flattening my back against… solid stone.

The rogue's scream of pain pierces the air, making my ears ring. I narrow my eyes against the rain in time to see Aviva going absolutely ballistic on the rogue, slicing its head clean off its neck with one of her long blades.

Blood sprays. I find it hard to breathe as Aviva picks up the rogue's head and stares into its dead eyes before chucking the head so hard it flies straight out of the hole and smashes against the one rogue still standing, who yelps and scurries away.

Holy shit.

Aviva, coated in blood, turns to me with a vicious look in her eyes. She scans the stone wall behind me, her chest heaving as she catches her breath. "Where are we, Misty?"

I choke back my shock and whirl toward the wall, laying my hands against the cool stone.

The rest of the hole is packed dirt. I follow the stone until the dirt begins, and back again, my fingers slipping over symbols and swirls that make little sense to me.

Aviva comes up behind me smelling sharply of blood and mud, extending her hand to swipe her fingertips over the symbols, then retreats, clearing her throat.

"It's a temple," she says under her breath. "The symbols are Firestone."

I start pushing on the stone like a trap door will miraculously open for us, but nothing happens. Instead, rain continues to thunder overhead, soaking us to the bone. Water begins to pool around our feet, turning the dirt beneath us to sticky, soupy mud.

Shivering, I turn my eyes to Aviva, whose eyes–once full of blood-lust–now shine with concern as she squints up at the sky.

We're twenty feet below the surface. There's no way up.

"Fuck," she hisses under her breath and turns to start picking up her weapons. She examines her blades before sticking them in the muddy wall of the hole.

"What are you doing?" I ask, watching as she tries to jump with her blades in each hand, slamming into the dirt wall, sinking her blades deep… but not deep enough to climb, like I'm thinking she's trying to do.

The blades slide down, dragging more dirt and soggy earth with them. Dirt tumbles into the hole, scattering around our feet and soaking into the water still gathering, nearly to our ankles.

"We're stuck," Aviva says under her breath, running a hand over her face.

"I'm sorry–"

"It wasn't your fault. I shouldn't have come back here."

"Well, you were right about things being drawn to this place. The rogues…"

"Maybe," she says, sinking into a crouch. "I mind-linked with Ryan. He's on his way with help, but it's going to be a while."

I'm sure Cole sensed whatever was going on and is racing here, as well. I lean against the stone and close my eyes. I'm freezing, but my powers are exhausted, and trying to shift right now sounds more miserable than shivering in the rain.

Aviva cleans her blades in the water and slides them into her halter, but her eyes are wide and distant as she asks, "Have you been studying *The Book of Whispers?*"

I chew my lower lip, eventually shaking my head. "No. Not yet. It's in… in an early form of Firestone, I believe. I've been trying to learn how to read it, but it's proving to be impossible and I… I'm not sure I want to know what's in there."

"I want to know," Aviva whispers over the rain.

"You can read it. I don't care."

"Maybe you should care, Misty. That's our history, as sordid as it is. We need to know what to expect–"

"You think the book can give us a glimpse of the future?" I laugh sardonically, shaking my head.

"I think it'll tell us what we should be weary of so history doesn't repeat itself." She rises, coming to my side, and leans against the wall as water begins to rise over our ankles. "What did you see when you went through that portal?"

I grind my teeth. I haven't told anyone the truth. When asked by my parents, and my aunt and uncle, I told them it'd been dark. Black, empty nothingness… which is a half-truth.

I think of the women. Emory, and Faye. Whoever they were, wherever they lived…

"We're connected to another world somehow," I say, closing my eyes at the memory of Faye's fangs. "It's quiet there. Foggy and slightly cold. I didn't see much before you rescued me, but I met–"

A distinctive howl cuts through the rain, followed by others–an army of rescuers.

Aviva doesn't make any moves, however. She's looking right at me, her gaze burning into my profile.

"Who did you meet?"

I turn to face her, both of us soaked to the bone. Aviva's hair sticks to her filthy, blood covered face.

"I met someone who wasn't like us. Someone that wasn't a shifter, or a witch... and she was kind. There was a child with her. She looked important," I admit. I meet Aviva's eyes. "We're connected—our world, and theirs. I don't know why, but I feel responsible for them now, and I think that's why I can't make myself learn the secrets of *The Book of Whispers*... yet. If anyone were to find out... Aviva–"

"I understand," she says, lacing her fingers in mine and squeezing. "I won't tell anyone."

"Thank you."

Our names are shouted into the gloom from above, and then several lanterns appear, shining golden light down into our muddy prison.

Cole appears first, looking borderline manic, his eyes wide with concern that softens to frustration when he sees me in one piece but stuck twenty feet below. Ryan crouches at the edge of the hole, raising his brows at his mate.

"Well, well, well–"

"Shut up, Ryan," Aviva says dismissively, glaring playfully up at him. "Just get us out of here."

* * *

I LIFT MY HEAD FROM A PILLOW FASHIONED FROM A ROLLED UP LENGTH of wool as Cole's shadowed frame enters our tent. Rain pounds against the tarp roof while I sit up, scooching over to give him room to sit beside me.

He pushes out of his muddy boots and shrugs out of his jacket before reaching for the piles of blankets I've been buried under for the better part of three hours. It has to be nearly morning by now, but the sky is so dark from the storm raging overhead that it's impossible to tell the time.

Dressed in nothing but one of Cole's shirts, I shiver as the cool night air touches my skin, but Cole turns to me as he pulls off his shirt. "I didn't think you were still awake."

"I couldn't sleep," I tell him, giving him a small smile as he rises over me, having to bend down at an odd angle to slip out of his wet pants.

He curls up beside me on the sleeping mat separating us from the cold, dirt floor and piles the blankets on top of us. "You're freezing."

"I think I'll continue to be cold until I can take a shower," I reply a little dreamily, sighing as his body heat fans around me. He pulls me against his chest, wrapping his arms around my waist. His warm breath tickles my neck, sending flickers of heat down my spine.

"Ryan wouldn't let Aviva into their tent until she was clean. He dunked her in a nearby creek repeatedly."

"Really?"

"That's where I was... well, I was treating Ryan's wounds after Aviva got her hands on him after the fact."

"Did she find that third rogue?"

"Yes," he says with a sigh. "A few warriors got hurt in the fight that ensued, but it was good experience for me, honestly, doing some field medicine." He snuggles closer, his voice edged with exhaustion. "I'm glad you're okay."

"Are you mad?"

"For what?"

"Using my powers to open a hole to the underworld?"

I can feel his smile against my jaw. "No. I wouldn't expect anything less from you. It's not the first time, and I doubt it'll be the last time. Plus, we got a night alone out of it."

I chuckle, nestling deeper into his touch. It has been a while since we've been alone like this. The rain drowns out any other sounds from the tents scattered nearby, closing us into a vacuum of silence where the only noise is our heartbeats.

Addy's staying with Freya, the village babysitter, it seems, who's also caring for Lexa in our group's absence.

Cole already knows what we found, of course. It would have been hard to miss the strange exterior wall we'd uncovered during our fall, but neither of us are keen to talk about it right now.

His hand slides over my belly, pressing me closer to him as he kisses across my jaw. I turn toward him, catching his lips with mine in a heated kiss that warms me through and through.

I missed him. I missed us, when it was just us, and we were learning each other outside of the war that brought us together. Those first few weeks spent in freedom, building a life together... it was bliss. Bringing Addy into the fold felt natural, but our life suddenly felt so busy, so loud.

I missed quiet nights like this, when it was just me, and him. Is that selfish?

"What are you thinking about?" he asks against my lips, sliding on top of me.

"Just you," I whisper, sighing as he nudges my knees apart. "Just that I missed you. I missed this."

He steals the words with a kiss that banishes any thoughts in my head.

15

FIND THE ENTRANCE

Misty

COLE GROANS AGAINST MY NECK AS I REACH BETWEEN, RUNNING MY hand down his chest to the deep V of the muscles of his waist. He kisses me again, hungrily this time, his tongue sweeping over mine in a slow dance that has sparkles of pleasure rippling over my skin. I sigh against his mouth as he grinds his hips against mine, rocking us back and forth, his hands drifting down my sides and settling on my ass with a squeeze.

He slides his hand beneath my shirt, revealing how naked I already am.

"I didn't bring any pajamas," I admit, my voice pitched with excitement as he smiles against my lips. There's no panties in his way tonight.

A dull, throbbing ache radiates through my lower belly. My inner folds are already slick as he drags his fingers through them, lowering his head against my shoulder and trembling with anticipation. "Fuck, Misty, you're soaking wet."

I close my eyes and arch when he presses two fingers inside of me, his thumb stroking slow, teasing circles over my clit. I rock into his touch, rolling my head back and forth as the sensation edges on too intense, and all the while, he presses kisses to my neck, my jaw, his teeth nibbling that sensitive spot just behind my ear.

Cole's touch has a way of unraveling the tangled thoughts in my mind. They flow away, replaced by pure pleasure. He removes his fingers, grunting under his breath as he slips his boxers down and slides his cock between my legs, entering me without ceremony.

He groans–loud and deep–as he buries himself inside me but claps his hand over my mouth when I let out a pitched cry of ecstasy I'm sure the entire camp can hear, despite the rain.

"Hush," he breathes, giving me a cocky smile as he pulls out slow, teasing me. "I don't want anyone to hear you. The sounds you make while I'm fucking you are for me only."

Goddess, I'm going to come right now.

I've forgotten how possessive Cole can be. It has been almost a year, I guess, since we first met, and he used that tone with me. That dark, rasping voice that demands submission–my submission.

I think about our first kiss. It's one of the only memories I allow myself to dwell on, to pull back from the recesses of my mind.

That initial kiss had been mind blowing, nearly intense enough to knock me off my feet. Sometimes, I wish I'd been older when it happened–old enough to know in that moment that he was mine–my mate.

Now, my wolf side cries out for him and his for me, and it's bliss.

I drag my nails down his back as his movements become more erratic, his voice hoarse and strained as he whispers filthy things in my ear, praising me and my body.

But he slows down, panting, switching from hard thrusts to deliberate strokes at the very moment I'm about to fall over the edge.

I whine, trying to pull him back to me, but he rises over me instead, lifting my right leg and resting it on his shoulder.

"I mean to take my time," he says, his eyes dark and locked on mine. His hair is wild–curling tightly from being wet. He's lost some of that sharp edge over the past year, sure, but right now, the old Cole is between my legs. The stern one. The bossy one. The one I miss more than anything during our most mundane days of work and parenthood.

I shouldn't be longing for that side of him, though, should I? He was only like that because we were going through hell together, and he needed to be hard and scary to protect me.

But this... this is really him. He's obsessed, and that's evident in the way he presses a kiss to my calf and grinds into me with renewed fervor.

I can barely breathe as my muscles contract, trembling with tension. I bite back a scream of pure pleasure while he begins to stroke my clit and lifts me back into an orgasm I know is about to rock me to my core.

"Come for me," he commands, his mouth lifted in a dark, wry kind of smile.

My arms fall to my sides. I grip the blankets all around us, arching into his touch when he thrusts so deep I see stars and come completely, utterly undone. My inner walls spasm around his cock. He chokes out a breath, leaning deeper into this position and riding out my orgasm with enthusiasm.

I try to be quiet. I hope the thundering rain is enough to shield my moans and whimpering from the rest of the camp, from the wolves lingering on the outskirts of the clearing doing their rounds.

Cole pumps into me hard, squeezing my thighs as he spills himself inside of me, filling me with warmth. My chest heaves as he gently lowers my leg and pulls out. He scoops me into his arms, kissing me soundly. We're both slick with sweat when he lowers us against the blankets and holds me to his chest, his breathing slightly uneven and his heart beating rapidly.

"I love you," he breathes into my hair, his fingers drawing lazy circles over my naked hip.

"I love you," I echo, stifling a yawn. Pure exhaustion settles through my body almost immediately, and before I know it, we're both fast asleep tangled in each other's arms...

And we don't wake until what we find out is the late hours of morning.

Ryan arches his brow at us from the warming fire someone built in the center of our camp, where he's sprawled out with a cup of coffee in his hands and a smug-ass smile on his face.

"Good morning," he chuckles as I walk beside Cole, whose hand is laced in mine.

"You shouldn't have let us sleep in," I tell him hotly, noticing that our tent is the only one left standing and the camp is nearly empty.

The camp was erected a few yards away from the clearing, tucked in the woods. Ryan tilts his head in the direction of the clearing where Aviva's voice drifts toward us, lifted and sharp.

"Aviva was up at the crack of dawn," he says before taking another sip of his coffee. "Figured if anyone got the pleasure of sleeping in without a kid waking them up, it should be you guys, since my mate is dead set on bossing everyone around this morning."

Cole sits beside him, and Ryan offers him some coffee from a thermos, pouring it into a metal mug for him. I stay standing, crossing my hands over my chest and silently thanking the Goddess that the leggings I packed dried out by morning so I'm not practically bare right now.

"What is she yelling about?"

Ryan shrugs, looking tired. "She's been on a tear all morning, trust me."

I narrow my eyes at him and decide to find out for myself, which I quickly do.

I leave the camp and cross into the clearing just in time for Aviva to say to Jacob, "Fine, then. Anyone who can be spared will be here, guarding this place. You can pick the warriors, or I can."

"We've got the wheat harvest next week," another man I haven't personally met says nearby, and he quickly becomes the subject of Aviva's wrath.

"This place—whatever it is—is a beckon of hell drawing in rogues and hellhounds. We're only thirty miles west of Silverhide right now.

Do you want to harvest wheat or fight off rogues left and right when they realize how close they are to us?"

The rest of the warriors shuffle from foot to foot, but Jacob sighs and nods, saying to the group. "The Luna's right. We'll have to take shifts. Four men, every three days, will guard this place and switch off with the next group."

"Great," Aviva says, eyeing the group for a moment. "Well, then. Pick your four, Jacob. Then we can go home."

She ignores the few grumbles from the group and turns, looking slightly surprised to see me standing there.

I arch my brows at her, giving her a little smile.

"What?" she says, almost shyly.

"Look at you," I tease as we turn back to what remains of the camp. "Being a Luna and whatnot."

"They're not used to a woman bossing them around," she says with a smirk, adding, "but I think most of them are scared of me, so it's not that hard to get them to do what I want."

"You're turning my brother into a stay-at-home-dad."

"He's honestly loving having a respite from his Alpha duties. He prefers... building stuff and goofing off." She sighs, pausing when Ryan and Cole come into view at their perch near the dwindling fire.

I glance over my shoulder at the gaping depression in the clearing. Mud continues to slide into the hole, widening its entrance. Aviva notices me looking back and rolls her lower lip between her teeth, waiting for me to say what we're both thinking.

"We have to find the entrance, don't we?"

"Yep," she replies, running her fingers through her hair. "As soon as we can."

"What are we supposed to do once we're inside?" My powers simmer as the question works through my brain. In all honesty, once the war was over, I didn't touch the barrage of new powers I'd developed shortly after my birthday. I'd ignored them, refusing to train them, to hone them and sharpen them... and now I'm paying dearly for it.

"I knew it wasn't over, you know?" Aviva breathes, both of us still locked on the hole we had to be pulled out of last night. "I couldn't bring myself to relax, even after Lexa was born, and things felt like they were returning to normal."

"I know. I felt the same way. I still feel–feel the same way." I swallow past the lump in my throat and turn to Cole and Ryan, who're calling our names.

Cole obviously notices the slight pinch of my brows because his smile fades, his eyes shimmering with silent concern. I do my best to give him a smile, but it falls flat.

Ryan, however, seems totally oblivious to the concern threatening to turn Aviva and I inside out, and plants his hands on his hips, smiling up at the sun. "I think we have some time to hunt today. What do you think? We could bring a few deer home, I'm sure."

Aviva playfully crosses her arms over her chest. "You mean I'm going to get a few deer, right?"

Ryan beams at her. Goddess, Ryan is totally head over heels, and it's incredible to see. If anyone deserves this kind of love and happiness, it's him. "A few rabbits, too? I could use some new mittens for winter…"

They turn away from camp together, walking toward their pack members, who are starting to pick up their supplies, some of them shifting in preparation for their journey back to SIlverhide.

Cole waits for them to walk out of ear shot before turning to me, his hand ghosting down my back.

"What's going on?" he asks in a gentle, yet commanding, tone.

"I mean, a lot," I whisper, kicking at a pebble with the toe of my boot. "Obviously."

"Misty, can you talk to me–"

"There's really nothing to talk about. We found what we think is a forge and now we… have to do something about it."

"Are you okay?" Cole's words hang in the air before shattering between us.

I turn my eyes to him, praying they're not watering.

"Misty," he says, wincing as he takes me by the upper arms. "It's been months of this, okay? You're not yourself."

I step away from him, shaking my head.

"Things have been hard with Addy, I know. We haven't been sleeping, and I dragged you both here–" he begins.

"It's not your fault–"

"It *is* my fault. This–" he motions between us, "Everything we went through... I didn't–I didn't give us any time to get over it. We didn't work through it. I just forced us into what I thought we needed, a normal life. With a–a house and jobs–"

"Cole–"

"I've been watching your light dim for months now, and I thought coming here would help. I thought you needed to come back to Eastonia to close some unfinished chapter, but I–I think we need to go home."

"No! We can't, especially not now. And you're here for training–"

"Fuck my training," he growls. "I can't put you through something like this again. The first time–I didn't do enough–"

We haven't fought in a very long time. Not since our days in the fortress together, and his palace in Oasia, when things were so, inexplicably horrible, and we only had each other to lean on.

"I hate what we went through, but it's over," I say to him, but the words echo through my mind, my body. "I need to accept that, and I haven't. I have work to do. I have a son, a mate, a life I want to start living again without memories from the war tearing me to shreds, so I'm done." I suck in a breath as Cole watches me closely. "I'm done. We're not going home yet. I have to figure out this forge issue and close that chapter, Cole. And you have to–to do whatever you're doing with *Kyra*."

He steps toward me at the mention of Kyra. "Why did you say her name like that?"

I ball my hands into fists, unsure why I'm suddenly channeling my feelings toward the healer. "No reason."

Cole rubs his temples like he has a headache, squinting his eyes against the sun. His lips part like he's about to say something, to question me further, but Ryan calls out our names.

16

AN OMEN

Aviva

To say I'm relieved to be home is an understatement. Our group is greeted with enthusiasm, especially after it's revealed that we snagged enough deer and elk to see us through nearly the entire winter, and a huge banquet is held in celebration.

Notably absent from the dinner is Misty.

Lexa sleeps peacefully in my lap while my gaze drifts across the pack house.

I sweep past Ryan to a new face in the crowd. Well, not entirely new, but new to the dinner held here every night.

Kyra, wearing a dark green cloak, stands close enough to Cole that I feel a sudden jolt of unease as she reaches into her cloak and pulls out a vial, pressing it into his hands. Cole nods in thanks, but the line between his brows is evident. He looks like he's in pain as he turns away from her, his skin slightly pale and eyes watering enough that I feel myself rising from the bench in an effort to walk over and ask what's wrong, but then he turns back to the conversation he was having with a group of men and their mates seated at another table, and my opportunity is lost.

Instead, I look back at Kyra, who glances around the room before pulling her hood over her head and slipping through the door without anyone–except for me–noticing she left.

Logan wiggles on the bench beside me, picking at his food. I look down at him, watching the way he's looking at a group of boys his age chatting near where their families are seated.

I give him a little nudge, hating the way he flinches. "You could go introduce yourself, you know."

He vehemently shakes his head and looks back down at his plate. I sigh, sliding my gaze to Freya, who was apparently watching the entire exchange between bites of venison, fresh roasted vegetables, and steaming hot bread.

"No Misty tonight?" she asks, adjusting Sam's weight against her shoulder.

I shake my head, drumming my fingers on the table. "Nope. I should go check on her and Addy, I think."

"I'm done, I can do it. I'll fix her a plate–"

"No, I need to talk to her about something, anyway. Thanks, though." I rise, tilting my head in a silent plea to keep an eye on Logan in my absence, and Freya rolls her eyes, throwing me a secret sly smile in return.

I'm still not sure why the Teshkans were so afraid of Logan. He seems like a normal kid, at least to me. He's shy and quiet, but I wouldn't expect anything less from someone who is obviously traumatized and in a new world, far away from everything he knew and loved.

I feel Ryan's gaze on the back of my head as I balance Lexa in my arms and fix a quick plate for Misty then leave, thankful it's not raining, and the moon is big and bright, lighting my way across the village. I weave between the larger buildings, skirting into the woods where the new cabins rest, and hurry up the steps leading into Cole and Misty's cabin at the very second she turns off the interior lights.

I rap on the door, once, then twice, then three–

"What are you doing here?" Misty asks, opening the door a crack, then wider when she notices it's me standing on her porch and not a rogue, or something equally nefarious, that might have followed us home from the clearing.

"You didn't show up for dinner." I hold out the plate, and she accepts it, but she frowns, motioning for me to come in.

"I just put Addy down for bed," she whispers.

"I wanted to make sure everything was okay."

She sighs, setting the plate down on the counter in the tiny kitchen but doesn't turn to face me as she says, "I'm fine, just... I got into a little fight with Cole."

"Oh." I pat Lexa's back, watching Misty roll her shoulders. "What about?"

"Honestly, I'm not even sure. He's worried about me, started blaming himself for how I'm feeling now and I just... I shut him down when he tried to help me. I don't need help. I just need to get a fucking grip..."

"This is going to pass, you know. The feeling like you won't ever get back to feeling normal again."

"I feel like a totally different person than I was a year ago... than I was six months ago. It's gotten worse, Aviva. My powers keep–keep interrupting me. Like, I have a few really good days and feel like I'm finally making progress, and then something feels off, and I have visions, or my powers start nagging at me like they're trying to tell me somethings wrong, and I ignore them constantly, and I've been pretending I'm happy and okay, but he notices." She's rambling, running her hands through her hair over and over again. "Now, this... Kyra thing is starting to get to me. I shouldn't be feeling the way I do. She's not a threat. Cole would never–never do that to me–"

"But you feel in your bones that there's something going on?"

"There's something off about her," Misty says with conviction, finally meeting my eyes.

"There's something off in general," I murmur, resigned. "What can I do?"

"Nothing," she huffs, swallowing hard. "I just need to get over it."

I notice the books stacked near the couch and the notebook splayed out on one of the cushions. "You've been writing again?"

"Trying," she says, wringing her hands. "I figured Cole would be out late tonight with the dinner and needing to catch up with some things at–at the healers cottage–"

As if on cue, Cole opens the door, surprised to see me standing in his cabin with his mate.

He glances between us, slowly opening the door behind him. "Is Addy asleep?"

Misty nods, but her expression shifts like she's trying to hide the pain behind her eyes. I wonder why Misty's having such a hard time talking to him about what she's going through. It's a pretty easy explanation, honestly. Hell, they were at war together. They went through all of that together.

If Misty's issues stem from her overactive powers, that's an easy fix. She just needs training so her powers igniting doesn't pull her pack into her memories of the war.

"I brought you some dinner," Cole says to Misty, who has already turned around, her back to us.

"Is your head feeling better?" she asks.

He nods, and I slowly start backing toward the door, but then he says, "The healer gave me a tonic. It helped."

So, that's what I saw Kyra hand to him at the pack house.

"Goodnight. Uh, Misty, I'll see you in the morning."

Misty turns toward me, furrowing her brow. "For what?"

"Training. Remember?"

"What–"

"We should plan on returning to the clearing in a few days to find the entrance to the temple, so you'll need to be at your full potential, right? Kenna should be here by then to help us."

Cole and Misty stare at me blankly as I wave and dip out before either of them can argue, then I wipe my fake smile from my face and grumble back through the trees.

What I really need is Maddy. She could easily talk some sense into her daughter and son-in-law. Ella, too, might be able to help. Ryatt?

Probably, at least when it comes to Cole. The war was bad, yeah. Really, really bad, but their generation went through... two or three wars and all kinds of other things that would leave the average person in pieces.

But my interest was piqued by Cole's mention of a healing tonic for a headache, and my feet carry me to the healer's cottage without my brain's permission.

I knock on the door, juggling Lexa in my arms as she starts to wake up, confused as to why we're not tucked inside our house.

Kyra opens the door with a confused frown. "Luna? Can I help you?"

"Yes." I edge into the cottage. She reluctantly holds the door open for me, eyeing me curiously as I scan the room. It's empty and smells sharply of herbs. "I heard you have a tonic for headaches."

Her mouth twists into a half smile. "Do you have a headache, Luna?"

"I suffer from them occasionally," I reply, which is a bold-faced lie. I've never had a headache in my life.

I notice a pot sitting on her work table, the liquid inside a murky green. Three vials are tipped upside down on a towel drying out beside it.

"Is that the tonic you made for Cole? I'll just take some–"

"Oh, no," she says quickly, shaking her head. "That's just–just a mineral complex I'm making for some–some of the pregnant women."

I notice the way she stumbles over her words and steps closer to the table, shielding the pot and vials from my view with her body.

"But I can make you something and deliver it tomorrow, if that's all right."

"You don't keep those tonics on hand? Aren't headaches common?"

She searches my eyes, her expression twisting back to something overly friendly and docile.

My senses are suddenly on high alert as she replies, "Normally, yes. But Cole required something special."

"Like what?"

She clicks her tongue, silent for a moment, before smiling and saying, "Oh, you know. Something to perk him up. It must be hard being... *bound* to parenthood and..."

"And his *mate*?" I ask.

Her eyes darken. "Sure. He doesn't sleep much. That's plain to see. His tonics have... a bit of sleeping draft added to help with that. He wants to be sharp to continue his work and study here."

"Does he know they're a sleeping draft?"

"Of course. Do you think I'd drug someone on purpose?"

"What's in it?"

"Oh, Luna, I won't bore you with the details. Apothecary medicine is very complicated." It's an obvious dig. She smiles around her words. "I wouldn't expect someone like you to understand the complexity–"

"Because I'm from Endova?" My words hang in the air.

She grinds her teeth. "You're not a witch, is all."

I smile at her, bouncing Lexa in my arms. "Well, what's in it?"

She stares at me before glancing at Lexa, her eyes remaining dark and her upper lip slightly curled in what I can only describe as disgust. I hope I'm wrong, but my senses are telling that Misty's assumptions about Kyra are true. She doesn't like people from the tribal packs, that's clear.

And Lexa is one of us, isn't she? Endovian blood runs in her veins as it does mine.

When it becomes clear she's not going to tell me, I shrug, backing toward the door. "Well, no big deal. Princess Kenna will be here in a few days, anyway. She can help–"

"Why is the princess coming here?" There's a shred of hesitation in her voice that doesn't go unnoticed.

"She's family. She'll be staying for a while. I assume you're close in age to her, aren't you? You must have gone to school together. It could be nice for you to have another witch around."

She slowly turns to the work table, going slightly pale.

Yes... something's up with this witch.

Misty isn't wrong about that. She isn't losing her mind, that's for sure.

"Goodnight," I say sweetly, giving her a beaming smile that turns to a tight line of grim determination when I leave the cottage and stalk toward home, preparing to tell Ryan he has something he desperately needs to deal with as Alpha of our pack.

But then I hear a voice–a soft, melodic whisper that rushes on the cool breeze coming off the mountains. At least, I think it's a voice. It's calling my name... I'm sure of it.

I whirl toward the sound as it rides on the back of a gust of wind that sends my hair flying off my shoulders in a frenzy before settling again.

"What was that?"

I turn to find Logan standing nearby, looking in the same direction. "You heard that?"

He looks at me, slightly fearful. "Did you see them, too?"

"See who?"

A chill snakes up and down my spine, turning my insides ice cold.

"The two wolves."

My blood runs cold.

"What color were they?"

"White."

17

FORGES

Aviva

I barely slept that night. Actually, I didn't sleep at all. I paced the living wishing for the first time since Lexa was born that she'd stop sleeping through the night to give me something to focus on other than the fact Logan saw two white wolves.

Sure, some wolves have white fur. Like Sarah, for one. Misty, too, is a pale gold, but neither of them have sightless, silver eyes.

Another chill snakes up my spine as I pace across the living room again, rubbing my eyes.

I did my best to convince Logan he'd seen some of our pack members, but I know without a shadow of a doubt that's not the case.

The last time I saw two white wolves was before the war, and I now consider them a warning. A warning of things to come, of trials coming my way, of the threat of death.

Part of me hopes it was just Maddox and Isla paying us a visit, but the creeping sensation in my chest makes me think otherwise.

I don't have powers. I don't have visions. But I see these fuckers when no one else can... until Logan did, just a few hours ago.

A soft whimper echoes from upstairs, and I bolt, tripping in my haste to scoop Lexa out of her bed, which she's been sleeping in now with Logan tucked in the next room, I have no idea why.

I hear my bedroom door open when I fall a second time, and Ryan hisses at me, asking what the hell I'm doing, but I'm already upstairs and darting into Lexa's little bedroom.

She blinks at me as the hall light fills her room, but her smile melts my heart as her chubby hands reach for me. She looks like Ryan when she first wakes up–all disheveled and utterly content. They're the only people I know who wake up happy every morning.

Ryan's shadow passes over us as he stumbles into the room, yawning. "Is she okay?"

"She's just fine," I whisper, feeling at ease again with her in my arms.

"Why'd you run upstairs like you were being chased, then?" His hands rest on my hips, leaning his weight against me and resting his chin on the top of my head to peer down at our daughter. "You've been awake for a while, haven't you?"

"Couldn't sleep," I answer, and it's the truth. Most of the truth.

"What's going on with you?"

I turn toward him, shrugging my shoulder free from my robe and guiding Lexa to my breast. Ryan braces a hand on the doorframe as he runs his fingers through his hair, blinking a few times to clear the sleep from his eyes, and then he meets my gaze.

"We need to talk," I deadpan, and he rolls his eyes to the ceiling.

"Breaking up with me, are you?"

"Will you shut up and just listen to me for a moment?"

He smirks, tilting his head toward the stairs. "I will, but over coffee. These late nights you've been having are starting to wear on me, and I have meetings today to talk about our pack's journey to the harvest festival this fall."

I follow him downstairs, skillfully nursing Lexa while navigating the house. I've found it easy to nurse her while standing up, walking around, whether she's in my arms or tucked in her sling. If I stop moving, she tends to get handsy, pinching my breasts with her sharp little fingernails. Right now, she's delirious with glee from milk and getting woken up by both of her parents and coos excitedly before latching again with renewed fervor.

I wince a bit, adjusting her weight in my arms, and rock side to side as Ryan rummages in the cabinets for the coffee. "What's going on? Something's up, obviously."

"You feel it, too?"

"My beast does, for sure," he says under his breath, straightening up with a brown sack of ground coffee in his hands. He weighs it, sighing and murmuring something about trading for more coffee while in the sacred festival grounds between the three tribal packs, but then his deep, dark blue eyes hold on mine. "What's in that building you and Misty found?"

"We think it's a forge."

He purses his lips as he turns to the wood fired stove, crouching to stoke the still shimmering embers. I continue rocking from side to side as he goes about his morning routine–filling the kettle, putting it on the stovetop, preparing to pour boiling water over the ground coffee beans. He's meticulous about it and makes the same comment every single morning, without fail. "When Ryatt builds his highway to the Deadlands, I'm buying us a real coffee maker."

But right now, he's staring blankly at the kitchen table, turning his empty mug in a circle as he loses himself in thought. "We don't know a lot about the forges," he says absently, thinking out loud.

"No, we don't. What we do know is only legend–stories told around campfires."

"There's a forge in Moonrise," he says.

"Have you ever seen it?"

"No," he replies in a whisper, shaking his head. "Neither has my aunt or my uncle."

"Why not?"

"I'm not sure. I'm not sure if it's accessible, honestly." He sighs over the hissing of the kettle, turning to grab it and gingerly pour the water over the coffee grounds. "You know, my aunt used her powers–used the mask to raise the Firestone castles from their resting places. The castle in Moonrise was under the lake–totally submerged for millennia. But... there's been talk from time to time about unfinished sections of the city–places that didn't rise from the lake. Hidden temples, hidden squares, other places of worship that stayed hidden for whatever reason. I don't know much about the Mystics, but they're the guards of the secrets of the Moon Goddess, and based on what we know about the Firestone witches, they were Her right hand."

I chew my lip, focusing on the way the coffee drips into the glass carafe he covets like it's his prized possession, similar to my feelings about my golden bow. "You think the forge in Moonrise remains underground."

"I think it's in the lake."

"But isn't it active? That's what I've been told. Fire and water don't mix."

"Maybe the forge isn't what we think it is," he says in conclusion. "But you're going to find out, aren't you?"

I lick my lips. "Ryan, I can't ignore this. It's only thirty miles away from our pack. You feel the pull. Misty feels the pull." I hesitate before adding, "I feel it."

His eyes meet mine in the darkness, the sun not yet ready to breach the horizon. "You feel something?"

I step toward him. "It's like I'm being yanked in a direction that's totally unfamiliar to me. Last night, I visited Misty, and she's... something is wrong. Something's wrong between her and Cole, and she's suspicious of our healer, and the forge.... It's too much for her right now. I need–I need her to research *The Book of Whispers,* but I already know she's struggling and can't bring herself to even look at it yet, but it might give us some clues about what the forges were and what they're capable of."

Ryan furrows his brows. "Cole and Misty are having issues?"

"They fought yesterday morning before we returned to Silverhide. I don't know the details."

"I'll talk to Cole," he says under his breath, shaking his head. "Misty has always had a flair for the dramatics but I agree that the war hit her hard. My parents are already aware she's having a hard time–"

"I don't think it's her memories, Ryan. I think her powers are trying to ignite, being pulled toward this–this place, and she's ignoring them, and it's messing her up. Just like when you feel the need to shift into your beast form and fight it."

He rolls his lower lip between his teeth, his hands braced on the table. "She's going to be fine. I'll see to it. I'll make sure her mate understands–"

"I need her to help me find the forge and destroy it."

"Destroy?"

I nod. "Somethings wrong. Everything about this feels wrong. Last night, I was walking home and I heard–I heard voices in the mist. I don't know how else to explain it, Ryan, but I wasn't alone. Logan was there and heard them too, and he saw–" I cut myself off.

I've only ever kept one secret from him. A damning secret that makes my chest convulse when I think about it.

I nearly died a year ago, when Hardan of Navvan called in the rogues, leading to a vicious battle. At the same moment I received my gift from the Goddess, my bow, two white wolves tried to lead me away into whatever afterlife awaits all of us.

I hadn't been ready.

I haven't told him that those same wolves followed us through battle in the desert of Tarsian. I haven't told him that I heard them last night, calling out to me, warning me of what's to come, and that Logan had seen them.

"What about Logan?"

"I think he's different. I think he's more than a shifter." I straighten up, turning my spine to steel as I come to a decision, something final. "Logan needs to be evaluated. I need to speak to him. He trusts me, and I believe he'll talk to me about Emberfyll and what happened there. I think Sarah should come here to look into his mind, too, to paint us a clear picture, to give us an idea why he's here at the same moment all of this is happening. And, while that happens, Misty and I will uncover the forge–together. I need her help and her powers to do so."

"We need to call Ryatt and Ella–"

"And we will, once we understand what we're working with. But we are the Alpha King and Luna of the Deadlands, and the Deadlands are waking up, coming back to life. This affects our pack, our people. We need to know what we're working with and why."

He pours two cups of coffee, stirring in fresh cream and the last pinches of sugar. "What can I do to help, Aviva?"

I breathe, relieved, and feel my mouth kicking into a smile. "Deal with Cole and the healer. I can handle everything else."

And that's exactly what Ryan does. I sip my coffee on the porch while Lexa takes her early nap in my arms, snuggled and cozy in the folds of my robe while Ryan stalks into the village, parting the mist as he walks toward the crop of trees where Misty's cabin rests.

The door leading to the deck opens slightly, and I hear a boyish yawn and grunt as Logan steps outside, rubbing his eyes.

"Good morning," I smile at him. "Ready to go get breakfast?"

He shakes out his gangling arms and rubs his face repeatedly. I get it. I don't like waking up either. "Okay."

"There's some new clothes for you upstairs. Freya made them in the style that's so popular with the boys your age here... I bet you'll make them jealous with your new frocks."

He's trying not to smile, but his eyes shine with unease.

I shrug, turning back to the sleepy village, the first few figures appearing in the mist to start their daily chores or head to the pack house for breakfast. "It's hard making friends at first, but once you do, you'll feel like you belong somewhere."

"But I don't belong here," he says, and it guts me.

"Do you want to belong?" I really don't have it in me to tell him he can't go home, but judging by the look on his face, he's already well aware of that.

"I do," he says quietly and turns back to the house to go change.

And on the horizon, just as the first inklings of sunlight breach the peaks of the mountains, a ripple of energy fans out over the fading stars.

Another person arrives–a family–and just in time, too.

I'm powerless, but with the help of Ryan's family, I can get to the bottom of the mystery of the forge.

I rise from my chair and wave as a family of five appears, the oldest of the children shrieking in excitement as she darts between her parents and beelines for my house.

18

WHO'S KYRA?

Misty

COLE MOVES THROUGH OUR LITTLE KITCHEN IN A HURRY. HE practically jumped out of bed this morning, grunting and bumping into the dresser and the doorframe in his haste to get dressed.

It's not even light yet, and the usual dense morning fog that swirls through the village hasn't yet lifted, but Cole is making so much noise that Addy wakes up in a fuss, his little face twisted as he begins to wail in my arms.

I've been up with him for an hour now, at least. Cole, who's been amazing with divvying up the nighttime wakings so we each get a few hours of sleep, didn't even stir. In fact, when I rose from bed to take Addy out of his crib, Cole rolled over and covered his head with his pillow.

I shouldn't be angry, but I am. He acted strange all night–distant, and quiet. More quiet than usual, I should say. It was like he was in a trance, and after an hour of trying to talk to him when he returned from dinner at the pack house, he'd simply laid down in bed and passed out cold.

I hate to admit that this reminds me of being in the fortress with him all over again–but worse.

I step out of the bedroom with Addy squirming in my arms. "Are you okay?"

Cole opens and closes several cabinets before bracing his hands on the counter, hanging his head. "Please don't yell–"

"I'm not yelling, Cole, I'm whispering–"

He holds a hand out to silence me.

I grit my teeth as unease snakes through me. "What's the matter?"

"I just have a headache."

"A headache?" I swallow, edging toward him. "I can fix that." I reach for him, my powers prickling to life but the second my hand touches his upper arm, he yanks away, raising his hand at me again.

"Don't–"

"Cole?"

"Don't touch me," he growls, turning to look at me over his shoulder. He swipes something off the counter, knocking an empty vial on the floor that shatters at his feet.

My heart's in my throat as he pulls on a jacket. "Are you mad at me?"

"No," he says under his breath but keeps his eyes on the floorboard. He squeezes his eyes shut for a moment, grimacing. "I'm not–mad at you, Misty, I'm hurting."

"Then go lie back down–"

"I can't. I need to work today. I have–I have training to accomplish before we go back to Shadowcrest."

"Fuck your training. What happened last night?"

He looks at me, shaking his head. "What happened in the clearing, Misty? I need to know everything."

"Aviva and I already told you and Ryan everything–"

"What are your powers picking up on? What's in that building underground? What exactly can the forge do?"

"It doesn't matter. We don't know, and… I'm sure Aviva is going to ask for my help uncovering it but–"

"Where is the book?"

"What book?"

"Where's *The Book of Whispers*? I need it."

"Why?"

I've never seen this look on his face before. He's furious... with me. His eyes are nearly black, his pupils so huge and round I can't see the flakes of silver lining his pale gray irises anymore.

"Are you about to shift?" I ask, tightening my grip on Addy.

"Where is the book, Misty?"

"Our bedroom–"

He storms past me. I have all but a second to jump out of his way, the jerking movement causing Addy to cry out.

Cole ignores us both as he retreats from the bedroom, tucking the book under his arm, and leaves the cabin in a hurry.

I look down at the vial, at the drops of amber liquid soaking into the rustic floorboards, and debate chasing him down and asking him what the fuck his problem is, but Addy begins to wail in earnest.

I settle on the couch and nurse him as my mind reels. It's my fault, probably, for being so cold to him on the way back to Silverhide yesterday, but he has to know what it's like facing another issue threatening our safety, our family. He has to know. He told me... he told me he understands. Now he's going to try to fix this himself, isn't he? Because I've given up on myself and my powers....

I turn toward gruff, male voices somewhere outside the cabin, sitting up a little straighter to try to look out the window.

Ryan's voice is clear but strained as he says, "Dude, what the fuck is going on with you?"

"Nothing," Cole replies darkly. "I didn't sleep well."

"You look like fucking shit–"

"Thank you," Cole growls, but his voice is just... he sounds like he's talking to *Richard*, not my brother. "Get the fuck out of my way. I have things to do–"

I feel the tension from inside the cabin. It bleeds from under the door as it carries their voices toward me. I rise, clutching Addy to my chest as I move toward the entrance just as Ryan says, "Go back to your mate and wait for me there. We need to talk. All three of us."

"I have work to do," Cole grinds out, and I feel this weight in my chest—a little yank—that makes it hard to breathe for the space of several heartbeats, but suddenly their voices go silent.

I wait by the door, my heart pounding against my ribs, and then footsteps thunder up the steps and the door opens.

Ryan darkens the doorway looking like he's just been slapped, metaphorically, at least. He raises his eyebrows at me. "What the actual fuck is going in here?"

I gape like a fish, trying to form the words—any words. "I don't know, Ryan. He started acting weird last night. He says he has a headache."

Ryan notices Addy losing his absolute mind and takes him from my arms, patting his back with expert skill as he scans the room. "Aviva said you and Cole have been fighting."

"It's not a fight," I reply, shaking my head. "We're just not—we're both—it's me. Something is wrong with me."

"I don't think so. I think something is wrong, in general, and your powers are trying to take hold, and you're not letting them. You and I are more alike than either of us realize."

"Then what the fuck is going on? It can't be the forge doing this, can it?"

Ryan doesn't answer. His gaze sweeps through the cabin until he notices the broken vial on the ground. He wrinkles his nose. "What is that? It smells… strange."

"I don't know. Cole brought it home last night and said it's vitamins or something."

"Vitamins?" Ryan narrows his eyes at me. "What kind of vitamins? We're wolves, Misty, if you've forgotten."

"How am I supposed to know?!" Frustrated, I throw my hands in the air. Ryan takes a deep breath, his eyes remaining narrowed as he steps forward, easing a now settled Adrian into my arms.

"Go to the pack house for breakfast. Aviva's there with Lexa, and Logan. Kenna, Evander, and the kids just arrived."

Relief washes through me but ebbs away as quickly as it came. "Will you talk to him? To Cole? And find out what's wrong? I think he needs to shift, or something. He's stressed, and I–I think I'm making it worse."

"Do you feel anything amiss in your bond with him?"

"No," I say, and it's the truth. But my brain is in shambles, and I feel like I'm being pulled in a hundred different directions. "No, not at all."

"And he says he has a headache? That's it?"

"He wanted *The Book of Whispers*–the copy I have. I don't know why."

"Fuck me. Okay, just go get breakfast. Chill out for a while. Aviva wants to go back to the forge soon, and you're going with her. I don't have time to be away from Silverhide so close to the end of the harvest, so this adventure is up to you guys. I'll deal with your mate, though."

My throat feels raw as he opens the door, ushering me outside. I'm dressed in simple, cotton pajamas and a bathrobe, which isn't ideal, but Ryan isn't giving me much of a chance to change into something proper. I step into a pair of slippers and trudge behind him into the village where we part ways, with him stalking toward the healer's cottage and me walking with my head down in the direction of the pack house.

Compared to the nightly supper service, breakfast is a quiet affair. Only a few groups seem to stop for plates of eggs and an assortment of breakfast meats–bacon, sausage, and thick slices of honey glazed ham. The smell of birch syrup and pancakes hits me like a freight train as the sweet aroma mingles with the heavy, bitter bite of coffee, and my stomach growls.

I've barely eaten in days, I think. I can't remember the last time I had a real meal.

A squeal of excitement rips through the air as two small figures dart to my stomach, winding around my legs.

Brie and Aris beam at me, jumping up and down with their faces smudged with syrup.

Kenna waves me over to the table where she's sitting with Aviva and Evander, but Evander rises, his face–while characteristically hard, and blank–twists when he sees me… looks right through me, I surmise, and sees the hurt clogging my senses.

I walk toward the group while Evander leans down to whisper something to Kenna. She extends her arms, motioning for me to hand Addy to her, but Evander gently grabs my upper arm and leans in to ask, "Where're Ryan and Cole?"

"The healers cottage across the village."

He lets go and walks out of the pack house.

I sink onto the bench beside Kenna while Aviva's eyes graze my profile. Internally, I feel her knocking on the mind-link, asking if I'm okay.

I nod, unsure what I can do at this point.

Freya passes by our table with Maeve in her arms, bouncing her gently, and Maeve is beaming with her new baby teeth on display. Apparently everyone loves coming to Silverhide, our family drama queen in particular.

"Cole's at the healers cottage, then? I need to speak to him. I was hoping he'd come to breakfast with you." Kenna leans back to check on Brie and Aris, who are making themselves at home with the other kids running amuck through the pack house. "About the results of the tests he gathered here when everyone was sick."

"Oh, you know what that was?" Aviva asks, setting down her fork.

Kenna grinds her teeth. "It's rather concerning, actually. Poison, not a sickness. Likely a contamination event. Do you trade berries with other packs, by chance?"

"Not this time of year," Aviva says, but her voice takes on an edge. "What are you getting on about, Kenna?"

"There were traces of yew berry in all of the samples sent in–extremely high doses."

Aviva rises, shaking her head. "Yew berry? That's–they're trees up in the mountains but very far away, and we're taught, at least in the tribes, to avoid them–"

"Because they're very poisonous to shifters, especially," Kenna concludes. "Just one could bring down a grown male shifter within a few hours. It wouldn't kill him, but at the dose I saw–"

"You're saying our pack was poisoned?"

"Yes, you were."

"How could that have happened without any of us knowing?"

I feel a twisting sensation in my gut. "Kyra," I whisper, turning my attention to Aviva. "You know her feelings about the people from the tribes. It was the Endovian and Navvan settlers who got sick, not any of us."

"Who's Kyra?" Kenna asks, genuinely confused.

We turn to her, both wearing equal expressions of shock. "The healer you sent from Moonrise, the witch," Aviva says, and not kindly.

"I don't know anyone named Kyra, and the healer I sent is named Martha Rose. She's one of my friends from school."

I hold Aviva's gaze. She shakes her head, answering the silent question burning behind my eyes. No one named Martha Rose has set foot in Silverhide.

"What's going on?" Kenna asks, her silver eyes going wide. "Misty? Aviva?"

"Who the fuck is in the healers cottage, then?" I ask, my voice breaking.

19

SHE'S NOT A WITCH

Misty

I snatch Addy from Kenna's arms and break into a sprint, Aviva hot on my heels. Kenna's voice behind us, calling out to her kids, fades as I burst through the doors of the pack house and race across the village.

The healer's cottage rises ahead, but my lungs are burning when I finally reach the front door, which is ajar, and shove my way inside.

The smell of herbs and spices hangs in the air… but that's it. The cottage is totally empty.

"Hello?" I shout, clutching Addy for dear life as dread overwhelms my senses. "Cole?!"

Aviva skids to a stop behind me, panting. "Where are the guys?"

"I have no idea," I tell her, scanning the room. There's a single door along the wall, tucked between two ceiling height bookshelves full of jars and small wooden boxes likely filled with more herbs.

Aviva hisses in frustration and turns for the door, murmuring something about finding Ryan and Evander, and leaves me in the cottage alone.

I step toward the worktable, noticing the fine coating of dust and ash covering its surface. I extend a trembling hand, calling on my powers. My mist expands over the table, but instead of forming the figures of my brother, my mate, and Evander, the faint pale blue fractals of light just flow over the surface, drifting over the table like a wave crashing against a shore wall.

Confused, I lift my hand, spreading my powers throughout the room, finding nothing but magical barriers.

Kyra isn't just a witch. She's a spectacular one.

Wards. She put up wards throughout the entire cottage. The door, especially, off the far wall, is completely warded against my powers of mist.

I lower my hand, my blood thumping and pounding in my ears as an uneasy, absolutely unsettling feeling echoes through my veins.

Addy coos against my chest. I pat his back, my nostrils flaring as my powers try to break through her wards, causing a sizzling, metallic scent to spice the air. It's not working. Everything that I am is telling me I need to find a way through that door.

Because she has Cole in there. I can feel it.

I dig deep, deeper than I've let myself go, reaching for those powers I've kept locked away since the war. Powers I've used only once, when I shattered the Gate of the Gods.

A faint click echoes through the room and her wards fall.

I gasp for breath. Addy whines against my shoulder, sensing something's wrong. I cradle him, tucking him into the confines of my robe as I barrel toward the door, gripping the handle, feeling Kyra's wards burning away as I yank it open.

Cole's on the ground—passed out cold.

"Cole? Cole!" I take a single step toward him before something hard and solid hits the side of my face, and I careen toward the ground with my infant son in my arms. My vision blurs, going black around the edges as I sway, reaching my free hand out to grab anything I can to stop my fall, but I land with a crunch into the side of what I think is a bed frame, smacking my head even harder against one of the posts.

Addy screams. My entire body tingles as I beg my powers to react, but another blow to my head has me face down on the ground beside my mate, clutching our baby to my chest and trying to curl my body around him to protect him from strike after strike.

A snarl erupts nearby and the beating stops.

"Put it down," Ryan's voice booms, his scent filling the room. "Now." Cold, calm fury laces the words–a brutal warning. He's not fucking around.

I sense Evander's sudden presence in the way the air feels like it just dropped ten degrees.

Faint screams and shouts of alarm drift into the cottage from beyond its stone walls, coming in the direction of the pack house. I try to open my eyes, but my vision is still blurry and doubled, and my bloody hair is covering my face, making it impossible to see the scene around me. My healing powers begin to ignite, causing a numbness to coast over my skin, up my neck, as it knits my broken, bleeding head back together.

"Give me the book," Kyra snarls. "I know someone here has it."

"I don't know what you're talking about," Ryan replies sharply. "Back the fuck up and kneel–"

Kyra laughs high and pitched, "I don't kneel for wolves. You'll kneel for me, however, once my hellhound is finished killing off your pack. Give me the book I seek, or you and your filthy, half-breed pack members will die. I'll dance on their bones and make you watch, because that will be all that's left–"

Metal sings at the same moment I lift my head, peering through clumps of my hair at the scene playing out before me. Kyra's standing with a very large, very heavy looking stick with my blood and hair plastered to it. Ryan's only a few feet away but just out of sight.

"WHERE IS THE BOOK!?" she screams.

"Call off your beast," Evander snarls. I painfully turn my head to look at him and find him holding a long blade.

She points the stick at Cole, who looks terrible, his face beaten to a pulp. "He was supposed to bring it to me. He lied, saying it's destroyed. I know it's hidden somewhere, and I'll kill him, his bitch mate, and their child if it's not handed over."

"You're looking for *The Book of Whispers*," Evander drawls, sounding bored. "Why?"

With Kyra distracted, I reach for Cole, my fingertips resting on his cheek. I let my healing powers flow while yanking on our bond, pulling those fine threads binding us together.

What did she do to him?

Kyra only laughs in response to Evander's question, shaking her head. "You must be the Ghost everyone whispers about. But you're more than that, aren't you, *fox*?" She giggles girlishly, a sound that makes my skin crawl. The tension in the air is so thick I could cut it with a knife. "The father of the first Firestone witch born in over three thousand years. What an honor. What a mystery."

I can feel Evander's simmering rage. "Call off your beast."

"No," she replies pointedly. " I will not. These mutts are getting what they deserve. All of you should have perished in the war, you know. Ah, what a dream that would have been—the rebirth of the era of the witches, sans the shifter filth, of course. Tell me, because I'm dreadfully curious, how does it feel knowing that your own daughter will rise as queen and usher in that era herself one day, when she realizes how disgusting and vile you creatures are, especially you, hybrid scum."

"That's enough," Ryan snarls, but Kyra laughs again.

"The Kings of Eastonia don't get enough credit for what they did, how they handled the shifter infestation that the Firestones let happen. And you, Alpha, child from a land of peace and prosperity... you should have stayed there. Your father should have minded his business all those years ago. Your aunt should have never left her gilded castle in Crescent Falls. That's where you all belong. Not here. Eastonia is for witches only, and once I succeed, there will be nothing but witches left, and all the shifters will be dead, or better yet, hell-hounds... our slaves, forevermore."

"Kill her," I rasp, lifting my head a little more. "Ryan, Ev—kill her *now*."

Cole groans. I grasp his shoulder. But Kyra turns to me, hatred in her eyes. "You... where is the book?"

"Get the fuck away from us," I snarl, and she makes the mistake of lifting her stick.

Ryan lunges, tackling her to the ground in an explosion of splintered woods and fabric as they crash through a dresser. Evander grabs me, pulling me upright, his hand caressing the top of Addy's head. Addy is purple with rage from being pinned but otherwise whole.

"Go to the lake. That's where Kenna and the kids are."

"Cole–"

"I'll take care of–"

Ryan stands, swaying, pulling pieces of wood from his chest and arms. "We have a problem."

Kyra isn't lying lifeless on the ground like I expected. She's... nowhere to be found.

"She can spirit?" I gasp, panic erupting through my body.

Evander lets me go and shifts into his wolf form, tearing through the cottage.

Ryan grabs my arm. "Stay here."

"Ryan–"

Cole rolls onto his side, coughing painfully. I drop to my knees as Ryan races out of the cottage, the sound of his clothes shredding echoing toward me, followed by a roar I've only heard once–during battle–when I saw that giant, terrifying beast form of his.

"Cole?" Oh, my Goddess, Cole, look at me?" I clutch his face, tears streaming down my cheeks. Cole's eyes meet mine, and he sighs, bowing his head ever so slightly. "Misty, I need to explain–"

"What happened?"

"You were right about her. She–she tried to poison me. I caught onto what she was doing here. I questioned the sickness that went around and she–I started having headaches that reminded me of what being under the control of Richard's powers."

"You should have told me."

"I wanted to, but I physically couldn't," he breathes, rising to his knees. He takes Addy from my arms and gives him a once over before his eyes meet mine again. "I am so sorry–"

"Don't," I whisper, leaning forward, resting my forehead against his. "Not now. We've been through worse. We're fine."

He shakes his head. "I haven't been honest with you about how I was feeling after the war."

"I know. Neither was I. We're fucked up."

"We're fucked up," he echoes. "I just wanted to protect you. I thought coming back would be good for us both. I was wrong."

I close my eyes, choking on a sob. "We were being called to come back. I understand that now." I look at him, smoothing his curls away from his face, which is now, thankfully, fully healed. "Where is the book?"

"I hid it. She has no idea it's not the original. She thinks the real *Book of Whispers* survived. I guessed what she was after quickly, during our first few days here when her stories stopped adding up. She isn't a healer."

"She's a monster."

A sharp, cold wind thunders through the cottage. Darkness swallows the sky even though it's morning. Chills cover my entire body as I look up, the room settling into total, unnerving silence.

The world seems to stop.

"Oh, no," I whisper, meeting Cole's eyes. "Oh, no, no, no–"

"What?"

"Kenna," I rasp. "Kenna's–Kenna's using her powers right now–"

The ground jerks then shakes violently. Cole grabs me, covering me with his body as books fall from shelves, and jars of herbs and potions crash to the ground. Glass shatters all around us as the shaking grows so violent my teeth clack together.

Through the mind-link, I hear Ryan calling out for Aviva. I hear Kenna screaming in rage and terror… screaming Maeve's name.

And then the world goes silent again, and the shaking ceases.

Cole looks up as the sun begins to stream through breaks in the stone walls, casting speckles of light across the floor, reflecting off thousands of shards of glass.

2 0

DISAPPEARED

AVIVA

SILVERHIDE IS IN ABSOLUTE CHAOS.

I race toward the pack house, still wearing pajamas, of course, but yielding my gilded bow, sending my arrow flying toward the molted beast trying to get inside. Claw marks mar the door–vicious and wide–and the beast, once a wolf, I believe, but now sporting four rows of massive, sharp teeth and multiple eyes, thrusts its entire weight against the door, causing the wall around it to splinter on impact.

My arrow pierces the small of its pack through and through before whizzing back to me. I catch it, prime my bow, and send it flying again.

This hellhound… it's fresh. There's nothing old and tired about it. Magic pours off its body, and blood stains its mouth and claws. People are screaming inside the pack house. People–mostly women and children–who'd been enjoying their breakfast before this creature came over the valley to rain terror on my pack.

If I'd left the pack house only a few minutes earlier, I would have known why Ryan and Evander weren't in the cottage any longer. Ryan had sensed this happening–felt in his bones that something was about to go down, and called on his men, thinking another pack was about to attack. Evander went to the cottage to find Ryan and Cole but found the place empty, but as Kenna's mate he knows the heavy, metallic scent of magic... and he sensed something was off, as well.

So, when Misty and I arrived at the cottage, and I tasted that magic on my tongue... I knew I was too late.

All hell broke loose, and now I'm fighting with a beast dead set on breaking into my pack house and hurting my people. My friends. My family... my daughter, who I left in the care of Freya.

My arrow hits its target, piercing the hellhound through its shoulder, driving deep. It growls, staggering, and turns to me with a terrifying snarl that showcases its pointed teeth.

Panting, I drop my bow, preparing to shift, but then Ryan barrels into my line of sight in his beast form and tackles the hellhound to the ground.

Smoke begins to funnel from the door of the pack house followed by screams for help. I don't waste a second. I turn from Ryan and the hellhound and sprint to the mangled door, trying to yank it open, but it's jammed.

Freya's voice shudders inside, coughing and sputtering.

"Freya!" I shout. "Something's jamming the door!"

"We–We pushed the tables in front of it! Now we can't see anything!"

Fuck. Fuck, fuck, fuck!

I back up several yards and take a deep breath, closing my eyes. I shift, my clothes falling away, and run as fast as I can, lifting off my claws and slam head-first into the door.

The pain is unreal as the door is knocked from its hinges, breaking into pieces that explode throughout the room. Smoke fills my nostrils and blinds me. I try to force myself to breathe but my lungs contract around the smoke.

I let go of a mangled howl as I stagger to my legs. People move around me, clambering for the door, climbing over the tables that didn't end up breaking my fall.

I see Freya in the smoky haze carrying Lexa.

'She's fine,' Freya says into my mind, running toward me.

'Get her out!'

Freya nods, tears in her eyes, as she scrambles for the door, but everyone leaving the pack house is pausing at the smoky entrance, unsure how to maneuver around the fierce battle taking place outside. More wolves have joined Ryan's cause, but this hellhound isn't giving up its fight.

I have no choice but to assist while Freya rounds up the women and children, taking them to safety.

The fire in the pack house spreads quickly. Smoke pours from the entrance, covering the once blue sky in a thick, black haze.

I find Ryan in the fray. He's injured. His left shoulder is completely mangled, and he's favoring his left front leg as he picks the hellhound up by its neck and slams it back to the ground where his men attack, clawing and biting.

I stand back, pacing, waiting for my turn. My adrenaline is running high, and my heart is racing as the seconds tick by. I wait, and wait for the hellhound to try to get up again, but this time, it stays down.

The odd, glowing light behind its eyes slips away, fading to total darkness.

It collapses in on itself, its body turning to ash that's swept away by a breeze carrying smoke and embers from the pack house.

My golden arrow rests on the ground where the hellhound took its last breath.

I'm in a daze as Ryan slowly turns to me, his snout covered in blood. *'Where's Lexa?'*

'She's with Freya.'

'I left Cole and Misty in the healer's cottage. Kyra got away.'

I blink, trying to relax so I can think clearly.

'Evander went to find Kenna. He sent her and the kids to the lake—'

A thundering boom echoes through the valley. The mind-link

erupts with the voices of our family members. Kenna, especially, is screaming in rage and anguish, and suddenly the light burns out of the sky completely, swallowing us in a shadow of... her powers.

Even during the war, I didn't see Kenna in action. I've heard rumors about her powers, of course. She's the daughter of a Firestone witch and Shadowsynger father. That combined is enough to instill a strange kind of fear whenever I think about it.

But during the war, she was acting as a triage nurse. A healer, going from army to army, healing those she could during the main battle and setting up an infirmary in the minutes after the last battle took place.

Now, she's turned the daylight into... darkness. The trees and buildings groan around us as her powers of shadow and darkness spread, and the earth beneath my feet begins to move.

Ryan remains in his beast form, his ears pricked in the direction of the lake.

Kenna screams Maeve's name through the mind-link.

That's enough to get me and Ryan moving.

I sprint after him through the woods, leaving Silverhide behind in a cloud of smoke. The ground continues to shake as we close in on the lake, but just as suddenly as the trembling began, it grinds to an abrupt stop.

I lose my footing, tripping over my own paws, and collide face first with the ground just yards away from the lake shore.

Kenna's powers flicker, sending shockwaves through the area. Water laps aggressively along the shore of the lake as her figure appears on the dock clutching Brie and Aris.

Evander stands at the very edge of the dock, his head bowed, a blade in his hands.

Time stands still as I slowly, carefully, rise to my feet, still in my wolf form. Ryan pants beside me, tucked in the shadow of trees.

'Where's Maeve?' I ask, but I already know the answer. She isn't here.

And neither is Kyra.

Ryan turns to look at the village where a plume of black smoke rises above the trees. *'The kids can't see me like this. I need to go back.'*

'You need to get that shoulder tended to immediately,' I tell him, my heart lurching for more reasons than one.

I look back at the family on the dock as Evander starts to turn to his mate, but he pauses, seeing us in the trees, and looks right at me.

His eyes are dead and dark... and full of murderous rage.

* * *

I stare at the charred remains of the pack house, my heart hanging on by a thread. Six of our pack members are dead—two women, their mates, and two others who were stuck in the crosshairs when Kyra's hellhound attacked the pack.

We still don't know who the hellhound used to be, but it doesn't matter, does it? We'll never know unless we find Kyra, and that's looking less likely as the hours tick by.

Our house is full. Misty and Cole talk in low tones in the corner of the kitchen while Misty brews tea for everyone. Cole looks beaten down and just... wrecked beyond repair. I feel awful for them knowing what they went through less than a year ago and what they must be going through now as a couple trying to keep their young son safe.

Ryan's in a sling, his shoulder barely allowing Misty's healing powers to take effect. He's sitting beside Logan on the couch, who has his head bowed, occasionally glancing nervously at the door.

Brie, Aris, Addy, and Lexa are all asleep upstairs, tucked safely in bed and nests of blankets and cushions on the floor.

Ryan rises from the couch, running his fingers through his hair with his free hand, and walks over to where I'm standing near the door... waiting for news about Maeve.

"I need to do another sweep, meet with some of the men," Ryan whispers to me, sliding into his shoes.

I nod, biting my lip as he presses a kiss to my forehead before leaving the house, the door snapping shut behind him.

I meet Misty's tired eyes, but neither of us have anything to say, not now. Not after this morning. What could we possibly say to make any of this any better.

"Can I go with him?" Logan asks, suddenly appearing at my side. He's already in his shoes somehow.

I nod, exhausted. "Just be careful and stay away from the pack house. It's still smoldering." I reach out on impulse and run my fingers through his hair the same way I do to Lexa when she's falling asleep in my arms. The touch shocks him for a split second before he leans into it, then pulls away, quick on his feet as he runs after Ryan.

I pace to the far side of the house, looking out the windows at the smoky haze still covering the lower part of the village.

"They'll be back soon, I'm sure," Misty says quietly, and she's not talking about Ryan and Logan.

The details of what happened at the lake sting when I think about them. We'd been so unprepared, so incredibly trusting of the stranger who infiltrated our pack and manipulated Ryan's kindness. She also manipulated Cole, who spent months under the yoke of a madman.

I'm sure he thinks he should have known better and is dealing with that guilt, but I don't blame him. Silverhide takes in everyone who needs a place to land.

I hate the idea that that might have to change.

Kenna and Evander watched in horror as Kyra disappeared with their daughter. She'd appeared in front of Kenna, taking her by surprise, and plucked the child from her arms before vanishing in a cloud of mist. Kenna was a single second too late to react, and her powers didn't reach the witch in time.

We have no idea where they are.

So, Kenna and Evander went to Moonrise to tell her parents and get help.

If this had been Lexa, I'd be scorching the Deadlands to find her, leaving nothing but ruin in my wake, and I know Misty feels the same about her son.

"I'm going to check on the kids," Cole says under his breath.

"You should try to sleep," Misty whispers to him, but he shakes his head, holding her gaze for a few seconds before tearing himself away and heading upstairs.

She sighs, pouring more tea, mixing in more sugar than necessary, and I accept a mug when it's brought over, regardless.

We sit on the couch in silence for several minutes. Cole returns and sits on a stool nearby, leaning his head against the wall with his arms crossed over his chest, and closes his eyes.

Only then does Misty turn to me and say, "Logan is a good kid. He likes you."

"He's comfortable here with us," I reply.

"He's going to stay, then?"

"Yep." I sigh into my tea, thankful for the distraction, but still…. This whole situation is weighing heavily on me. "He-uh, he likes Ryan a lot, tends to follow him around when we're all home together. He's been curious about Ryan's camera. They don't have those in Emberfyll."

"Have you talked to him about Emberfyll?"

I shake my head. "I need to, but he's… he's struggling, I assume. He's probably repressing memories of his journey here, and he's still speaking exclusively in Firestone, which means I'm the only one who understands him. He's not ready to talk, and I'm in no hurry to push him."

Ryan arrives home smelling sharply of smoke. "Kenna hasn't come back yet?"

I shake my head.

He nods, his eyes glazed with fatigue. "Okay, this is what we're going to do at first light. Half of my men are staying here to guard the village, and the rest of us are going out to search for Maeve. I already sent scouts to Endova in the event she's there, or nearby, and more to Teshka, but they won't reach that territory until a day from now. We'll–"

"Where's Logan?" I ask, standing.

Ryan gives me a look. "He's not here with you?"

"He wanted to go with you into the village, and I let him."

Ryan straightens, glancing at me, then at Cole, whose eyes are now open and holding on the door.

"I didn't see him at all," Ryan says, stepping back toward the exit.

"I'll go find him," Cole says, but I'm already pulling on my boots.

Something in the back of my mind nags at me, yanking on some invisible thread I've never felt before.

"That little shit," I hiss, whirling toward Misty. "He can shift."

21

CALLED INTO THE FORGE

AVIVA

TWENTY MINUTES IS ALL IT TAKES TO GET FULLY SUITED IN MY Endovian shifting clothes, halter, and knife belt. Misty watches me examine each blade before sliding them into position, metal gleaming in the star soaked darkness. She's dressed similarly, and her eyes hold a silent promise.

We already lost Maeve.

We're not losing Logan, too.

We have no idea why he ran away to, but I'm sure as hell about to find out.

Cole's staying with the kids, and Ryan's staying behind to gather his troops to begin the search for Maeve.

It's probably close to 3:00 A.M when Misty and I set out, following Logan's scent. He doesn't leave the village by the road, however. His scent follows the trail toward the lake.

I stand on the edge of the dock in my wolf form. He was here, but his scent is faint. He was on the move, that's for sure, and as we follow his scent up and over the mountain, past the hot springs, I start to wonder what he was following this way.

Hours pass following the boy's scent. Misty and I stay silent, neither of us speaking through the mind-link until the space around us starts to look and feel all too familiar.

Two miles from the clearing where the forge rests two dozen feet below ground, I stop our progress and shift back to my human form, Misty following suit.

We stare into the darkness of the woods all around us.

"The birds aren't making any noise," she whispers.

"I know," I reply, unsheathing my bow.

I've lost Logan's scent in the soft breeze, but whatever drew him here has to be the same pull both me and Misty are experiencing right now.

We walk the next two miles in our human forms with weapons drawn and a shared, terrible feeling settling into our bones.

Half a mile away from the clearing, we both smell smoke.

Misty lets her powers erupt, covering her body in her mist-like armor. I draw my blades, one in each hand, primed to strike if we come across a camp, or Goddess willing, Kyra.

But when we reach the clearing…

Misty gasps. I have the sudden, overwhelming sensation that I'm about to faint.

What was once a small hole leading down to the temple is now a crater that's absorbed the entire clearing. The trees all around are burnt to a crisp, smoldering with odd looking silver embers that cast the space in an eerie, almost moonlit, glow.

I look down. One step, and I would have fallen to my death, for sure, based on the rock and ruins twenty feet beneath us. More of the temple is now within view… including the entrance, and the pile of ash in the center of the hole.

And a pair of women's boots that look vaguely familiar.

Before I even have the opportunity to ask, Misty raises her hands and lets her powers fly.

The mist filled figures of Kyra, clutching a screaming Maeve to her chest, appear, floating above the gaping crater. She's screaming at Maeve, taunting her, demanding the baby use her powers to get rid of the dirt and soil burying the temple.

"I'll throw you in the forge, you sniveling little demon," she screams, gripping Maeve so hard the baby screeches and smacks Kyra across the face.

Kyra grunts in pain and holds Maeve over the original hole, threatening repeatedly to drop her, but then a small wolf–a pup, by all means, darts out of the wood and launches himself on Kyra with his teeth bared and claws extended.

Kyra, Logan, and Maeve fall into the hole, and the entire clearing erupts in flames of mist as Kyra's scream fades.

"Oh, my Goddess," Misty breathes, hisses against the pull of her powers as they fan around us, showing us the moment Maeve's powers of silver fire ignited the clearing in flames that breach the top of the trees.

The ground around us falls in as her powers show us how the hole widened. It was Maeve, somehow. She did this.

And Logan…

"He killed her," I whisper, anguish lacing each word, as I watch the pup clamp his jaws around Kyra's neck and squeeze, breaking the skin.

Kyra screams, but her voice shudders to a broken cry of pain before she slumps. Silver flames begin to lick up her legs, but Logan shifts to his human form, tearing Kyra's cloak from her body and wrapping himself in it before whirling toward where Maeve's wailing in fear behind him.

"It's okay," he says in Firestone. "You're okay now."

Maeve blinks at him, going silent with surprise, like she under-stands every word he just said to her. She reaches for him, and he picks her up, dusting soot and mud from her cheeks, then looks up at *us*.

But Maeve points to the sky, mumbling something in the language of toddlers no one but their own mother understands, and in a flash of mist, they're gone.

"She jumped. She spirited away with him," Misty gasps, her powers burning out. The clearing goes totally dark again.

"How long ago was this?"

"I have no idea," Misty says rapidly, shaking her head as she takes a step closer to the edge. I grab her arm to stop her from tumbling over as dirt gives way only a few inches away from our toes. "Recently. Very recently. We missed them by an hour, maybe."

I try to mind-link with Ryan, but the connection is hazy, likely because of the conflicting magic in the clearing.

I feel my body gravitating toward the edge of the hole like I'm being pulled toward it by some unseen force.

"What if they're inside?" I ask.

"In the temple?"

"You feel that too, don't you?"

"That pull? Yes." Misty swallows hard. "How do we get down?"

I look back down. Moonlight coasts over the rocks and the scattered ruins of what must have been part of the temple that was crushed inward over the years. "Carefully," I answer, deciding our plan of action. "Very, very carefully."

* * *

THIRTY MINUTES LATER, AND COVERED TO THE NECK IN MUD, MISTY and I look at each other, both leaning a shoulder against an ancient wooden door that's been closed for at least three thousand years.

We have no idea what's behind it. We both know this probably isn't a good idea. We're also well aware that our mates are going to be wondering what the fuck is wrong with us when we go through it to face some other unseen, terrifying force of magic that probably should have stayed covered... but those are problems for another day.

If Logan and Maeve are in here, we're going to get them out. Plain and simple.

"Ready?" I ask in a strained whisper.

"Ready," she says, sounding far more confident than I am, but in my defensive, she crushed the fuck out of me when I inadvertently broke her fall after our plan to get down here went sideways.

We lean away from the door and slam back into it, our combined weight and force almost snapping the door free from its ancient hinges.

"Again," she hisses, choking back a note of pain.

Again. Then again. And… again.

On the sixth try, Misty goes clear through the door's center in a yelp of pain and surprise and lands with a crunch on the other side.

I step through the crack her body left in the wood and squint into the total, all-consuming darkness.

She rises, dusting herself off, mumbling a few curses under her breath before she raises a hand and lets her powers shine like a makeshift lantern, lighting our war.

It's a narrow space–full of dust and stale air. A long hallway leads to nowhere for what feels like a mile before we reach the end of it, and a wide, spiral stone staircase leading down into sucking, empty darkness comes into view.

"I think we're very high up," she says, lowering her hand. "That door might have been off an upper level balcony or something."

I'm not sure I want to go down there, but what choice do we have?

Misty leads the way, lighting our path down deep into the castle until the air becomes so thin we both start feeling light headed and woozy.

Eventually, we reach the bottom of the staircase and find another wide, cavernous, completely dark, and empty place.

The magic pull is far more intense down here, though. So much so that we know exactly what door to pass through and what staircase to take next.

A thick, sulfuric smell breaches us, rendering me even more dizzy. I cover my nose with my arm, squinting into Misty's soft light as my eyes water.

I can barely breathe down here.

"We can't stay long," Misty gags, choking on what little air she can find.

"LOGAN!" I shout, my voice echoing off the walls. Misty's light doesn't reach the far end of the cavern, but we're obviously not in the right place yet, based on what she showed me when we first came here and saw the forge through her powers.

"They can't possibly be here," she says as we continue forward. "Aviva, I'm getting really–" she screams as the floor falls out from under her.

"MISTY!" I jump for her, grabbing her arm at the last second, but it doesn't matter.

The stone pavers beneath us give way, and we careen into empty nothingness.

My life flashes before my eyes. I imagine the moment I locked eyes with Ryan for the first time the day Shoshanna put an arrow through his shoulder. I remember mornings with the girls flipping pancakes, and evenings spent mending my tattered hunting clothes while Mercy worked on her loom. I see my mother in startling clarity, smiling widely at me as I run into her arms while we walk in a field of strawberries blooming.

I see the clearing where Ryan and I slept together for the first time after finally acknowledging our mate bond and feel Lexa wrapping her tiny fist around my finger after she was born and–

I scream in agony when I collide with the floor, the air ripped from my lungs. Misty moans in pain a few feet away, coughing into the total darkness. Pieces of debris hit the ground all around us but miss our bodies by some miracle.

Now we've really done it. We're fucked. Broken—and fucked, leagues below ground where our mates can't find us.

"Wild thing, we've been waiting for you."

I freeze as an unfamiliar, ageless, and genderless voice fills my head like someone screaming in my ear.

"Warrior of the ages, the gods call you. How they gossip about your victories. I believe they're right. Come to me, child of blood and vengeance. The dawn of the Firestones is upon us. Your destiny has been written in the stars, and now it's time to answer to your calling."

"Misty," I rasp. "Misty, who is that? Who's speaking?"

Misty groans, coughing and wheezing. "I can't–I can't breathe–my ribs–"

I roll onto my belly, blinking rapidly to try to clear my vision and... light. Light ebbs in a faint glow from the... *Oh, my gods.*

"Rise, Warrior of the Goddess. Breaker of chains. Commander of Her chosen army. Your time is now."

It's the forge. It's speaking to me, speaking *into* me. I feel its power, unaware that I'm slowly rising, my eyes locked on the wide stone pool in the center of a cave of crystal.

Somewhere behind me, her voice choked and faint, Misty's calling out my name, telling me to wait, to stop, but I... I can't.

"The bow was a test," the voice echoes. *"It only ever had one owner, and it found you again. You passed the test. Come, we've missed you. Come, see who you were in another life, another body. You, an ageless soul."*

Gooseflesh erupts all over my body. My eyes widen as I approach the edge of the forge, expecting fire and heat, but... it's water. Clean, crystalline water. It smells like salt and humid air–like ozone–like the sky after a storm.

"You don't remember, do you? What you sacrificed in another life–"

An image flashes across my mind–a memory I can't claim ownership of–but I know the man, the unfamiliar man, turning to look at me, his eyes wide and resigned as he lifts a battered hand and sword, his body coated in heavy army.

Ryan in another body. Another life... long ago. *My mate.*

An epic battle rages. The last battle. A battle our kind lost, when Eastonia fell, marking the end of the Firestone witches who protected us.

"He promised to find you again in another life. He walked thousands of lives to find you, and you, him. You succeeded at last. Come to us, Angel of Death. Bringer of Justice. Come home."

My legs give out as Misty's scream tears toward me. I slump, my belly wrapped over the edge of the forge as I fall in and down... and down.

OUT OF THE FORGE

Ryan

I WATCH THE LAST GROUP OF WARRIORS FROM SILVERHIDE DISAPPEAR into the night, a few Endovian warriors following them. The forest that wraps around Endova is alive with action–howling, people calling out Logan and Maeve's names.

All over the Deadlands, people and wolves are searching for our missing children and the witch that stole Kenna's child from her arms. It's only a matter of time before we find them, I'm sure. Kyra won't live to see morning if I have any say in it.

I failed my pack as an Alpha tonight. I didn't see the signs in front me that we had an enemy in our midst. James is back in Silverhide cleaning up the mess she made. Cole is tending to the wounded, while I'm here in Endova gathering more troops, and my wife is... somewhere else.

My gaze sweeps over the darkened forest. There's only a few hours left until daylight. I think of my daughter and my little cousins, hopefully tucked up tight with Freya and Mercy watching over them.

Will those kids ever know a moment's peace in this life? Or are we destined to chaos? It feels like it sometimes. It's been one thing after another for years–the Draven coven, the Kane sympathizers, Arcane Umbra and their war that took the lives of my grandparents.

I came to Silverhide to start over, to build a safe, prosperous life for my pack after years of bullying and violence against us in Crescent Falls, only to fall right back into it with no respite in sight.

A shimmer of power skirts across the star filled sky, and I straighten. I breathe deeply in relief as black mist funnels nearby, dissipating to reveal my uncle, the man I've been waiting on for hours.

Ryatt's wearing a black cloak as he steps forward, pulling down his hood. His eyes are sharp and silver in the moonlight and set with vengeance as he approaches me, glancing around to ensure we're alone.

"Took you long enough," I murmur, crossing my arms over my chest. "Where's Kenna and Evander?"

"Evander dispatched the Ghost army. They'll be arriving in the Deadlands within the next few hours so be prepared for their presence." I roll my lower lip between my teeth as he continues, "Kenna is back in Silverhide gathering Brie and Aris. She's taking them to Moonrise for their own safety."

"Silverhide is safe."

Ryatt nods, but the words don't feel that true right now. "No one in Moonrise is familiar with anyone named Kyra, but it's possible that's not her real name. Ella has the Mystics working on this as we speak." He exhales, his eyes holding on the dark woods. "A witch with the knowledge of how to bind a soul to create a hellhound would have studied the dark arts, which is strictly prohibited practice unless they're chosen to study dark alchemy, and those graduates are closely monitored for the course of their careers and lives."

"Kenna studied the dark arts."

"Yes, she did." He sighs, turning to face me. "Your father and Sydney are sending a task force through the borders to the Roguelands to assist with the search, and I've placed wards over the Roguelands and Moonrise, but I need your permission to do the same here."

I furrow my brows. "Why would *you* need *my* permission?"

There's an unfamiliar gleam in my uncle's eyes as he smirks, turning back to the woods. "Because you and I are equals now, Ryan. Two Alpha Kings."

"You have far more political influence than I ever will."

"That'll change… within the next two decades, when Maeve takes her throne."

"Aunt Ella will step down?"

"Of course, that's been the plan since shortly after Maeve's birth, and we became aware of what she was." He doesn't add if she's found, which is my biggest concern right now. Instead, he complains, "I've been accused of creating a political monopoly by placing you here. I don't care, honestly. Eastonia is safest with our family on each throne. I tried to convince Cole to rethink giving up Tarsian, but he was adamant that he had to step down." He grinds his teeth. "Tarsian will be a problem again, I guarantee it, and as Alpha King of the Deadlands with your mate as your commander, you're going to be put in a position that'll give you more power over my territory in the Roguelands as the years pass, and my powers diminish. Maeve will need you."

"And what happens if we can't find her?"

He shakes his head. "It's likely that the witch had no idea what Maeve's capable of. I don't know what the witch wants with her, but Maeve is prone to fits of… fire and other violence, so it's only a matter of time–"

My chest snaps in two. I grunt, gasping for breath as I bend, fighting against a pain I can't even begin to put into words. Ryatt's alarmed voice fades as blood rushes through my ears, pounding in tune with my rapid heartbeat.

"Ryan? Ryan–"

At first I think I've been attacked, assaulted in some way. That my back must be flayed open and my ribs have been torn from my body, but my hand flies over my chest. I'm whole. I'm in one piece but… the mate bond…

"Aviva!?" I scream into the night, taking several rapid breaths before shouting her name repeatedly like she's close enough to hear.

Ryatt grips my shoulder, leaning in and shaking me violently. "What's wrong, Ryan?"

"My mate–she's hurt–I can feel it–"

"Where is she?"

"In the forest somewhere–they were looking for Logan. He ran off–"

"The boy from Emberfyll?"

I can barely form a rational thought. I can hear her crying out for me through the bond. She's in pain. She's drowning and can't find her way out of wherever she is and...

I fall to my hands and knees, closing my eyes and yanking on our bond. Ryatt kneels beside me, frantically grabbing the back of my neck. "Where is she, Ryan?"

"I'm trying," I pant, pulling on the threads binding us. Something's wrong. Something's horribly wrong, and I... I know where she is. I'm not sure how, but...

Cole's voice rips through the mind-link in a shout that splits my head in two, confirming my worst fears. *Misty's in trouble. Aviva–'*

"They found the forge," I shudder, panting rapidly. "It's thirty miles west of here. Take me there."

Ryatt looks stunned, but his eyes narrow as he grips my shoulder. My world goes dark as his powers consume us.

* * *

"Misty!" Cole shouts, pulling on a shirt from a clothing stash left near the hole we dragged the girls out of less than a week ago when they first found the forge. He paces the massive crater still spreading throughout the clearing, frantically looking down at the buried temple.

I can see where they tried to climb down, where they fell and then entered the temple. But my eyes are locked on the pair of shoes and the pile of ash in the center of the hole.

Ryatt licks his lips, his eyes scanning the temple below. "They're in there?"

"They have to be." I take a deep breath, debating my options. Ryatt could easily just use his powers to teleport us down there, but before he can act, Cole leaps. I shout his name, but it's too late.

He lands with a crunch, grunting in pain as he rolls to a stop.

"Goddess, Cole!" I snarl.

"My mate's in there," he shouts, heated. "I'm not waiting."

"Just wait–"

He steps into the temple and disappears into the inky black darkness.

"Fuck," I shout, turning to Ryatt. "Take me down there."

"You have to jump down like he did. My powers are… weak here." Ryatt looks concerned as he scopes out the crater, shaking his head. "Why didn't you tell me about this place?"

"We've had a lot going on," I sneer then turn back to the crater, saying a quick prayer to the Goddess for a soft landing, and jump.

I land feet first, thankfully, with Ryatt following close behind. Even my wolf powers are dim here, like whatever's inside is sucking the life out of all of us.

I race inside, Ryatt hot on my heels, and quickly catch up to Cole. He's shouting Misty's name over and over again, but when we reach a wide, spiral staircase, we pick up Misty and Aviva's scents. They mingle with the sharp smell of sulfur and something else–something that vividly reminds me of Maatua.

I jog after Cole, fighting past the pain in my chest. He shouts in alarm and grabs me before I topple over the edge of a hole in the stone floor.

I look down at the space. Faint light drifts toward us, bouncing off what looks like mirrors, but I realize they're large crystal formations.

"Cole?" Misty shouts, sniffling.

Cole pants with relief as he rests his hands on his knees. "Misty, how do we get down there?"

"I don't know," she cries out.

"Where's Aviva?" I shout down to her. I can barely see her outline in the darkness, but she raises a hand, her powers burning to life but flickering as they illuminate something out of my wildest dreams or darkest nightmares.

On my other side, Ryatt sucks in a breath. "Gods above."

The forge is a huge pool of gurgling water. It roars, sending an echo through the cavern below.

A sinking feeling of dread settles in my stomach. "Where's my wife?"

Misty's face twists with grief. "She–she fell in."

"She fell in?" I say, unsure if the words even leave my tongue. My heart snaps in my chest, and before I can't think, I jump.

I crash to the ground, my body cracking and groaning in protest as I stand and bolt toward the edge of the forge.

I have sudden vivid memories of the waterfall in Maatua. The water smells the same. The air feels the same here, if that's possible.

But everything else is all wrong.

I ignore Misty's scream of alarm as I race toward the forge. I hear Cole and Ryatt drop into the cavern behind me, Cole's voice lifts in mingled concern and relief as he grabs Misty off the ground and hauls her upright.

Ryatt tells me to stop.

I can't. Not now that I'm at the water's edge, looking down in the shining depths for any sign of my wife. I can still feel her. Our bond is still intact. She's alive.

I back up a few feet with every intention of jumping in, but a blinding light explodes from the water, knocking me backward.

Water rushes us, pushing us back against the walls of the cavern and then retreats like it has its own tide. The water rushes back into the forge, but the light grows stronger. Misty throws her powers at it, but they're absorbed instantly.

Somewhere in the distant recesses of my mind, I feel... I feel an odd sensation. Flashes of memories that don't belong to me rush through my head. I can't make sense of anything I'm seeing. Battles rage. A small, delicate house with flowers in the front in the center of an ancient metropolis with towers that spiral to the sky. Fire and death. Blood coated stone pathways. A child running toward me with his arms wide open as I pass through a gate, looking past the boy toward a woman leaning on the doorway.

She's not familiar to me, but I know her.

My wife. My mate.

I snap back to reality the second the light fades, and the forge settles. Eerie silence floods the cavern before Misty begins to whimper Aviva's name.

My heart thuds once, twice, three times… then stops when a hand breeches the water and wraps around the edge of the forge.

Unruly, wet red curls float on the water's surface before Aviva pulls herself from the forge, gasping, her eyes glowing a soft amber in the faint light reflecting off the water and crystal ceiling above it.

I try to move, but I'm frozen with shock as she pulls herself over the edge of the forge and lands on her stomach, choking and sputtering.

Voices skitter through the air, like a hundred people are talking at the same time. Aviva pulls herself to her feet, panting, pushing her hair away from her face but tattoos that burn a bright gold pepper her arms and legs, spreading beneath the soaking wet Endovian hunting dress she's still wearing.

My mate went into the forge.

I'm not sure she's still the woman I know, looking right at me, power glowing in her eyes.

2 3

MADE

Misty

Cole's arms are wrapped around my stomach, his eyes widened in disbelief as he stares at Aviva. She looks like a wet rat right now—completely soaked to the bone with her hair plastered to her face and her knife belt hanging off her waist, but otherwise she's whole.

My powers are a mere flicker of what they usually are, but I feel them simmering to life as the strange, glowing symbols all over her arms and legs start to dim, and the roaring in my ears fades to the point I can hear my rapid heartbeat and Cole's heart behind me.

Ryan looks devastated. Devastated, and shocked—a myriad of emotions I can't even begin to put into words. He shakes his head, mouthing Aviva's name as he reaches a hand toward her then retreats.

Aviva looks terrified as she scans the group, panting hard, her breath coming in shallow rasps. She turns her gaze back to Ryan, and her expression shatters, tears welling in her dark, amber eyes that are finally going back to their usual color instead of gleaming like polished bronze coins.

"Help," she croaks, sucking back a shattered breath. "Ryan?"

Ryatt steps forward and claps a hand on Ryan's chest to stop him from approaching her. "Who are you?"

Aviva blinks, taken aback by his question. "I'm–I'm Aviva–"

"Where were you born?"

"Endova–Endova, in the Deadlands–"

"What was your mother's name?"

She stares at Ryan, silently pleading as she trembles from the cold and damp clinging to her body. "G-Gemma. Why–"

Ryatt shoves Ryan back and steps forward, unsheathing his shadow sword. My blood runs cold as Aviva's eyes go wide with sudden panic.

"Ryatt!" Ryan shouts, but Ryatt points the tip of his sword at Aviva, its pointed tip resting directly under her chin.

"What was his mate's name?" Ryatt asks in a booming voice that echoes through the cavern, bouncing from end to end. "His first mate."

Aviva looks stricken as her teary eyes slide to Ryan. "Hadley."

"Ryatt," Ryan rasps, a broken edge to his voice.

Ryatt's sword gleams in the faint light still pouring from the forge, a wave of deep violet washing from the hilt to the tip where it fades into Aviva's skin.

I have no idea what he's doing to her, but I've never seen my uncle so... so brutal.

"What happened?" Aviva whimpers, shaking so hard her teeth clack together. "What happened to me?"

Ryatt lowers his sword, taking a deep, restorative breath as he turns to us, his gaze sliding from me and Cole back to Ryan. "She's made. We need to go to Moonrise, right now."

"No," Ryan says, shaking his head, his eyes locked on Aviva as she curls her arms around her body to try to find any warmth. "No, she's not going anywhere but home–"

"This isn't up for debate," Ryatt growls, sheathing his sword down his back in a fluid motion that sends shivers down my spine.

"My daughter," Aviva says. "I can't–she needs me–"

Ryatt cuts her off with a wave of his hand. But Ryan looks

murderous as his gaze sweeps back to Ryatt. "We're going home. If you want to fight me on this, Ryatt, be my fucking guest. My wife just nearly drowned. She's not going anywhere but home."

"You have no idea what she's just done–"

"I don't give a fuck," Ryan grinds out, edging past Ryatt. He reaches for Aviva, wrapping his hand around her forearm and hisses out a breath when he feels how cold she is.

Even Cole shifts his weight behind me, his eyes locked on her lips, which are actively turning blue.

Ryatt glares as Ryan gently, ever so gently, pulls Aviva closer into his arms. He whispers something obviously meant for just the two of them into her wet hair before his gaze locks on Ryatt again. "Home. Now. I swear to the Goddess, Ryatt, if you spirit us to Moonrise it'll be the last thing you ever do."

I turn toward Cole, closing my eyes for a moment in an attempt to catch my breath. The last... what? Ten, twenty minutes felt like a fever dream–something conjured by my deepest, darkest night- mares. But Cole's warm and solid as I wrap my arms around his waist and bury my face in his filthy, mud soaked shirt, fighting my own tears.

"Logan and Maeve are–are together," I murmur into the fabric loud enough for everyone to hear. "We confirmed it. Logan–he killed the witch."

I don't look over my shoulder, but I can hear Ryatt's boots as he turns in my direction.

Aviva says in confirmation, "Misty used her powers to show us what happened in the clearing. Logan–he can shift already. He's only twelve. Maeve whisked them away somehow."

Silence settles, broken by the occasional splashing of the water rolling over the edge of the forge as it settles.

I blink a few times to dry out my eyes and glance over my shoulder at the very moment Ryan scoops Aviva into his arms, his gaze still holding on our uncle. "Take us home. We can finish this conversation there. If Maeve's with Logan, she's safe."

"You don't know that. That boy's from a world outside of our own," Ryatt argues, but his tone is softer, fading back to something familiar and far less deadly.

"He went looking for her, Uncle Ryatt," I say, backing Ryan up. "That's the only explanation, and Maeve… she trusts him. We could see that clearly. She's safe, wherever they are. He'll protect her. He killed a witch for her."

Ryatt's silent for several seconds before exhaling deeply, his next words directed to Aviva as he says under his breath, "We'll return to Moonrise, but this isn't over. I need to know everything that happened to you in there, everything you saw and heard."

Aviva nods in Ryan's arms, but my brother tightens his grip on her body. Ryan looks so mad right now, and I understand why. I also get why Ryatt had to question her like that and wants to take her to Moonrise, where he can get clearer answers about her glowing eyes and tattoos.

The truth is plain to me. I can feel it in my bones, my soul. The truth simmers through my powers like a heated warning.

Aviva is different. She didn't come out of the forge the same woman–the same friend–I know and have grown to love like a sister.

Aviva has powers now.

* * *

"She's asleep, and Ryan isn't letting anyone near her," Cole says the second he passes through the door of our cabin in Silverhide. I stand up from the couch with Addy in my arms, absently running my fingers through his thin, nearly white hair.

"Did you get to examine her?"

He nods but purses his lips as he leans his weight against the door to close it. "Barely. Ryan's worried, but I would be, too. She's fine, all things considered. Physically healthy. She's having trouble regulating her temperature, but she nearly drowned and was borderline hypothermic, so that's not a surprise to me."

I scan his face, noticing the lines of fatigue and dark circles under his eyes.

What a fucking day. What a fucking hard two days, actually.

We arrived back in Silverhide this morning but fortunately didn't have to travel the entire way on foot. My powers returned shortly after Aviva emerged from the forge, and then Ryatt got his powers back, and he whisked us here, dropping us off and promising to return at sundown.

But the sun set two hours ago, and Ryatt is nowhere to be found.

Cole runs his fingers through his hair and sinks beside me on the couch, a blank look in his eyes as he gaze locks on the bare, far wall. "Misty, I... I hid the book in the sheep barn. It's still there, up in the rafters."

"You were suspicious of Kyra from the beginning, weren't you?"

He licks his lips, looking down at his lap. "She rubbed me the wrong way at first. I know enough about traditional medicine to know that the sickness that spread here wasn't natural. It would have affected everyone. For shifters to get sick like that–for it to be trans-mittable? It's practically impossible. A few people came to her when the first symptoms began to emerge, and the tonics she gave them didn't make any sense. The herbs she prescribed were wrong–completely. She had no idea what she was doing."

"Why didn't you say anything to me? Or even Ryan?"

He chews his lower up, reaching over to lay his hand over Addy's head. "I guess I'm not over it. Having to–rely on anyone but myself to fix things. I thought I could stop her, and I got close, just like with Richard, and I didn't want anyone getting hurt, so I... I egged her on a bit, trying to figure out what exactly she was here for. She was curious about Ryan, asking me questions about the family, Ryan's powers, your powers, whether Aviva and Lexa had them. She was especially interested in Kenna, but I was vague. She must have over-heard a conversation about Maeve at some point, somewhere, because she began to steer whatever conversations we had toward her." He meets my eyes, giving me a sad sort of smile. "I thought she might have been connected to Richard in some way because of how she asked about the war. I don't think she realized I'd been part of it on Richard's side because she went on and on about him, his genius…. I made a comment about *The Book of Whispers* to see where she'd take it, and I knew for a fact that it was what she was after."

Cole goes on to explain what happened the day Kyra attacked the pack. A few nights before, he'd faked a headache, wanting to know what kind of herbs she'd prescribe. She'd given him what he immediately knew was a sedative. He didn't take it, of course, but visited her again, pretending to be under its influence, and that's when she tried to manipulate him into getting her the book.

"The whispers about the ruins you and Aviva found was the catalyst to her plan. She was planning on just getting close to Ryan, getting between him and Aviva, but I think she realized quickly that wasn't going to work, but then Aviva found the forge, and Kyra thought the book was there until she found out you had it–thinking it was the real copy."

"So that morning you… confronted her."

"Yes. I tried to kill her," he replies, point blank. "I had no idea what I was dealing with, though. Her powers put Richard's to shame, honestly."

And she had a hellhound somehow.

"She was trying to use Maeve to find the forge. I wonder what she wanted to do with it?"

"I think Aviva answered that for us," Cole sighs, relaxing into the cushions. Addy jerks, his arms flaying, before he falls back asleep with a soft coo. Cole smiles gently, the line between his eyebrows finally relaxing, but his eyes are still dark as he says, "Ryatt said Aviva was made. She might have powers now. That's what the forges were used for–to create magical objects."

"I know," I sigh, leaning my head against his shoulder. "Like every special weapon my family keeps inadvertently collecting."

"Now she's part of that collection, and Ryan knows it. I'm supposed to alert him if Ryatt shows up, but I have a feeling he's with Evander looking for Maeve and Logan."

"We have to find them."

"We will. Another search party is going out in the morning. I plan to join them," he says, closing his eyes.

I let my mind wander, thinking about the forges, then the weapons and strange objects that somehow end up in my family's hands... and then I think of Grandma and her stories of Maatua, and the falls, and how she found her powers.

"There's a forge on Maatua," I whisper into the silence. "The falls. It's actually a forge."

We fall asleep on the couch as a family, too exhausted to be bothered moving to the bed, and that night, I dream... I see visions.

I see a little house tucked in the woods in faraway mountains.

24

SHE'S DIFFERENT NOW

Misty

Sometime in the dead of night, Cole took Addy from my arms
and laid him in his crib. I was next and woke up tucked against Cole's
chest as the first rays of warm, morning sunlight drifted through the
window.

Addy wakes up happy every morning lately and is beside himself
with glee when he sees me looking down into his crib, extending my
arms for him. Cole thinks Addy looks like me, but I beg to differ. I
think his hair will be blond, of course, given that both his parents
have fair, light hair but his eyes are starting to change from that soft
blue to a paler, icier gray, like Cole's.

I run my fingers through his hair while he nurses. Cole continues
to sleep, and I let him. I'm dreading starting our day, honestly, and
stepping out into the village to see the aftermath of Kyra's destruction
and wait for news about Maeve and Logan.

I feel awful for Kenna. My heart is shattered for her and Evander. I
hold Addy close as I walk to the pack house on instinct like I have
every morning since we arrived, almost like I've forgotten it's gone,

nothing but ash and embers that haven't quite gone out yet. I'm dressed in jeans and a white nursing tank-top under one of Cole's button down flannels, and my hair in a messy bun that slumps sideways on the top of my head. I pass villagers going about their harvest chores like nothing happened.

Meat is being loaded into the smoking sheds. Carts pulled by wolves are being loaded with wheat to process. The wool shed, which used to be piled high with fluffy, flawless tufts of white, gray, and black is now empty, and as I pass Freya and Andrew's house, I imagine she's been spinning wool every day for weeks now, preparing to trade it at the upcoming harvest festival.

I take my easy life in Shadowcrest for granted sometimes, I realize. Being here, watching a pack being built from the ground up, makes me acutely aware of how easy I have it. I watch a trio of women carrying babies in slings while their toddlers race ahead of them. They're carrying bags of freshly ground flour and baskets full of vegetables and eggs–their shopping trip for the day, not the week, not the month.

Back home, I simply place an order on my phone and drive my lazy ass to the grocery store where the groceries are loaded in the back of my shiny SUV. Here, I'm hoping Ryan has something to eat at his house this morning, at least. A muffin would be nice.

I pass the sheep barn, however, and pause.

I've been neglecting *The Book of Whispers*. I can't decide if that's a good thing or not. I know it's just a copy, but still, the knowledge of Richard wielding it, bending its magic to his whim and sacrificing his own life force to cast his spells, makes my stomach turn.

Maybe we don't need to know its secrets. Maybe they're better left alone, destroyed.

But I'm still a historian, and I'm supposed to be writing our history. I should know what happened before, shouldn't I?

So history doesn't continue repeating itself?

I whirl to the sound of boots crunching over gravel, and I'm shocked to see a man walking in my direction, his hands tucked in the pockets of a very nice, very modern jacket from one of the specialty athletic stores in Crescent Falls that's all the rage right now.

"What are you doing here?" I ask stupidly.

Sydney rolls his lower lip between his teeth as he approaches, squinting against the sun. "I have a small team of warriors in the Deadlands aiding Ryan's forces in the search for Maeve."

I knew that. I'm not sure why I even asked, but still. "Is Sarah here?"

"She is. She's with Aviva right now." He sighs, looking down at his clean boots before meeting my eyes again. "I didn't want her to come, but Ryatt insisted on it, seeing as Ryan refuses to allow her to travel to Moonrise."

"Did Ryan tell you what happened to her?"

"Yeah, he did." He swallows hard but smiles when Addy sneezes loudly before settling back against my chest. "He's getting big."

"We've only been gone a few weeks," I say, smiling despite the heaviness in my chest. I can see the stress and worry behind my brother's eyes, however. Sarah's due soon. They have a full, busy life in Crescent Falls. A full house, a full to-do list....

"The boys are with Mom, of course," he adds, running his fingers through his hair. "Look, I was on my way to your cabin. I need to talk to you about the forge."

"I figured."

"What did you feel in your powers while you were there? Because being around Aviva now is... something's changed."

"She has powers now, Sydney."

He nods, gritting his teeth. "The forge in Moonrise is... tucked where no one, even the mystics, can access it. The other forges, from what we know, are still hidden and unrecoverable, and it needs to stay that way."

"I agree–"

"You destroyed a portal to another realm," he says, cutting me off. "Can you destroy the forge?"

"No," I answer, and it comes from a place deep within my soul. "I can't."

"Why not?"

"Because it's... It doesn't need to be destroyed. Its job is already done."

"I don't understand–"

"The objects. Ryatt's sword, your blade, Aunt Ella's mask and the like... each forge, according to legend, was built to craft specific items. This forge... I assume it made the bow, and Aviva wields it. But she isn't like us–or, at least, she wasn't like us, until yesterday. The forge's job is done. Its power... pretty much dried up after she came out of it, and Ryatt was able to bring her back here from within its resting place. It's just... water now. Like the falls in Maatua."

"You think there's a connection between the falls and the forges?"

"Yes." I have nothing else to add at this point. There's so much we don't know, and again, I'm struggling to decide whether we need to know.

He steps closer, dropping his voice as he asks, "And the book... was that created using a forge?"

Again, that little voice within me, that voice that controls my powers, gives me the answer. "The book was used to create the forges. It's gone now. If the forges are dormant, they can't be woken up. If they're destroyed, they're gone for good."

"So... the magic remains exclusive to our family?"

"Yes, I believe so."

"Good," he says simply, but his eyes tell another story. He's stressed. I'm sure I missed a heated conversation between him and our dad, and possibly our uncle.

He starts to turn away but stops. "She's been asking for you. Are you busy?"

"I was looking for breakfast," I admit.

"There's some up at Ryan's place. Is Cole around?"

"He's asleep." I should probably tell him about Cole's saga with Kyra but decide that's Cole's business. Here I was thinking that I was the only one broken by our experience last year, but my mate is... struggling. I heave a breath and follow Sydney through the village, leaving footprints in the ash.

The pack house is already being cleaned up, what wood and stone can be salvaged stacked and the ground raked of simmering embers.

But there's a gap in the tidy village now. The valley spreads out behind the houses and shops, the furthest peaks dusted with fresh snow—a warning of winter and the end of the ever important harvest.

"Can I hold him?" Sydney asks as Addy gnaws on the buttons on my flannel. I nod, passing the baby to my brother, who smiles and expertly settles Addy on his shoulder. "I've missed this, having a little baby around."

"Does Sarah know what she's having yet?"

"We wanted it to be a surprise, but Cosette is sure it's a girl this time. I think she hopes so, based on the grief she gets from Blake and Liam. Mom, too, would like another girl to add to her collection," he smiles wistfully. "I'm just hoping for a healthy mom when this is over."

"Liam came pretty easy," I edge with a shrug.

"The weeks after that were hard on Sarah. She did it alone the first time... I think she struggles with memories of that, and I struggle with guilt that I wasn't there for her when Blake was born."

"How long until she's due?"

"A month, maybe. She could go anytime, which is why I didn't want her to come, but she convinced me. She's worried about Aviva."

We reach the house and climb the steps to the porch. The windows are open, letting in warm late summer air and releasing the scent of coffee and what I hope are pancakes.

I have memories of visiting Ryan's bachelor house in the old Silverhide territory. He was always throwing parties and always cooking breakfast for the friends who didn't make it home the night before.

My heart warms as I step inside and find him standing over the cast-iron, wood fired stove. He flips pancakes and sausages while talking in low tones to... Evander, who's leaning on the kitchen table with his arms crossed, a mug of coffee steaming in front of him.

I didn't expect him to be here. Kenna came and took her kids back to Moonrise, and he should be out looking for Maeve with his Ghost's, shouldn't he?

His green eyes meet mine, nodding a hello, but my mouth is dry as Ryan thrusts a plate of breakfast in my hands and snaps his fingers in a motion for me to sit and eat.

I glance around the room looking for any sign of Sarah and Aviva.

"They're in the bedroom," Ryan says, pouring more batter in the pan.

I take a single bite of my food before walking to the bedroom and easing through the door, careful not to make a bunch of noise in the event Aviva's asleep, but I find her sitting up in bed with Lexa sprawled between her legs and Sarah perched on the edge of the mattress, looking round and radiant as she smiles up at me.

"Misty!" She struggles to get up in an attempt to hug me, but I meet her halfway. "Goddess, I've heard you've been going through it during your vacation."

"I wouldn't consider this much of a vacation," I murmur, but my eyes slide to Aviva. "Are you okay?"

"I'm all right," she says weakly, giving me a sad kind of smile. "I'm feeling rough."

"It's your powers. Your body's getting used to them being a part of you," Sarah says quickly, pursing her lips. "The rest of us were born with ours and had our whole lives to adjust."

It makes sense. Aviva's pale and struggles to lift her coffee mug to her lips, and dark circles like I've never seen before line her eyes.

"Are you in pain?" I ask.

"No, not really. I'm sore for some reason, but it'll pass." Her voice breaks as she looks down at Lexa, who's trying to grab sunbeams coming through the curtain with her chubby hands.

Sarah clears her throat, giving us both a weak smile. "Sydney isn't going to be happy about this, but I was just telling Aviva that we're going to scry to find Maeve. I think it's our best option. Maeve's powers are strong, which means I'll be able to find her, or get close to it. But it's going to take a lot of energy I don't have to spare." Her eyes scan Aviva's face. "But she does."

"She… what?" I rest my shoulder against the wall, crossing my arms.

Aviva toys with Lexa's feet, refusing to look at either of us.

"Aviva can scry. It's one of her powers—her dominant one, so far. We've decided to try—together. Once everyone has eaten breakfast." She lays a supportive hand on Aviva's thigh. "You need to eat, too."

I stand up a little straighter. Scrying is a very rare power. In fact, only mystics tend to have that ability, and it's rare in their ranks. Sarah's the only person I know who can do it—reading the heavens, finding those vibrations between the realm of living and the dead—and translating it to pinpoint whatever she's looking for, whether it be her car keys—or a person.

"Do you want to do it?" I ask Aviva, noticing her hesitation.

She shrugs, taking a deep breath. "I don't really have a choice, do I? We need to find them."

THREE THOUSAND YEARS

Aviva

I watch Sarah and Misty leave the room. Misty takes Lexa with her, giving me a moment alone. I should be resting right now. If Maeve and Logan aren't found by sunset, I have to put these new, unnatural-feeling powers to the test.

I listen to the soft conversations taking place just beyond the bedroom door. I already know Ryan's on edge and doing his best to handle this situation, but having Evander and Sydney here isn't helping his stress levels at all, I fear.

His wife almost drowned, his uncle wants me locked up in Moonrise until my powers fully emerge to ensure I'm not a danger to myself and others, and Maeve and Logan are still out there, hopefully together and safe.

The door opens a crack before widening, revealing my mate and a large plate of food. The scent of blueberry syrup fills the air, bringing back memories of making this exact breakfast for my sisters, but that... causes my mind to drift back to the tangle of new memories.

Memories of the countless lives my soul has walked in different bodies trying to find the man now setting the plate in my lap, telling me to eat.

We haven't spoken much since we came home. Ryan's just been fluttering around me like a little bird, his concern punctuating the air between us.

"Do you want more coffee?" he asks, but his eyes barely meet mine, and it kills me.

"Are you afraid of me?"

Ryan looks down at his feet, sighing deeply. He moves toward the door and closes it, clicking the lock into place, drowning out the voices beyond. "No, I'm not afraid of you. I'm... I'm worried for you, for what this means for you."

"It doesn't have to change anything."

"It changes everything," he says, meeting my gaze.

"Between us?" My voice breaks. I'm still his mate, and he has no idea what I now remember... how long we actually went without each other. I'm not sure how to make sense of what I saw while buried beneath fathoms of water in the forge, but I have to try. I have to try to make him understand, somehow.

"Not between us, no. But... for Lexa. For any other children we might have who inherit your new powers."

"These powers aren't new," I whisper, and the tension reaches impossible heights.

He edges toward the bed with her eyes narrowed as I drag my fork through the syrup, unable to take a single bite.

"What do you mean?"

"Do you want to know what I saw?"

He hesitates before nodding but doesn't sit down on the bed. He remains standing, his feet braced apart like he's preparing for impact.

My mouth moves but no sound comes out as I try to put into words what falling into the forge felt like.

Finally, I find my nerve, and begin, "I couldn't stop, Ryan. I was being physically pulled into the water. Like I was bound by some invisible thread, and I realize now it was you, tugging on our bond, but not–not really you as you are now."

He shakes his head, not understanding. I realize at that moment that everything I know and feel from lives in the past are something he'll never be able to experience with me, and that's crushing.

"We were together before. Fated mates. It was in the time of–of the Firestone witches and their downfall. We fought in the first wars…. You were a–a commander of some kind, and so was I."

Ryan slowly sits down, but his gaze doesn't break from my face.

"We had two sons. One was older–ten or so. He–he died when our village was attacked. That was the catalyst to you joining the Firestone army even though our pack was very rural, and we were happy there… separated from the larger cities in the Deadlands, in Novana."

"Novana?"

"That's what the Deadlands used to be called. Its missing name. No one in our time remembers it." My voice is barely above a whisper now. "The enemy rounded up our people. You watched them kill our boy in cold blood and couldn't stop them. They took you from me–both of you. I left our son behind–our baby–and put together my own forces, all women because that's all that was left, and we marched to the Firestone castle of Endova."

We gaze at each other. Yes, Endova was once a sprawling, beautiful metropolis, and now only the village remains, unaware of what's buried beneath.

"We were separated for ten years, Ryan. The war raged and raged. I never gave up on you. I trained. I trained myself and my warriors until we were killers of the coldest variety. We toppled factions of the enemy. We fought to find our mates again, and I was rewarded by the Firestone Queen for my service when they believed the war had ended. It was a ritual. I walked into the water with my favorite weapon–my bow–and when I came out, I was remade. I was… what I am now." I extend my palms face up, letting amber light dance through the lines, showing him my light for the first time.

"I was nearly fifty when the final war, the Deciding, they called it back then, began," I whisper. "I'd given up hope of finding you. The empire of the witches and shifters was massive, and you could have been anywhere, but I thought you were dead because I knew that, if you were alive, you would have fought until your last breath to find me. In the end, that's exactly what happened."

"During the battle–the final battle–when the Firestone armies were losing and waging their last stand, I saw you in the fray. You-you turned to look at me. You were raising your sword to strike an enemy, but when you saw me, you stopped. You were so beaten and weak, Ryan. You'd been enslaved for decades then escaped only to be forced to fight once more on the Firestone side, and even then, you looked for me. We found each other on the battlefield in the last seconds of our lives."

The Kings of Eastonia, the enemy, had won. They used the full might of their stolen treasure–*The Book of Whispers*–to decimate the Firestone armies. The last of the old gods who once walked beside us retreated–the Goddess Herself–and in the moment her queens laid down their lives in a last ditch effort to protect their people, using the last of their magic to bury their cities and their memories deep underground in the promise a new queen would rise with Firestone blood and take back what was rightfully hers, I raised my bow.

"I killed you," I whisper, tears falling down my cheeks. "As the world crumbled, I whispered a promise on my arrow that I'd find you again, and pleaded with the gods to give me a chance to be with my mate once more. Just once. I killed you because I couldn't stand the idea of anyone taking you from me, and you died quickly while the rest of us died in anguish."

Ryan's eyes are dry, but his expression is severe. I doubt he believes me, but I keep going. "Our son who lived, our baby, was sheltered away in Veiled Valley, which didn't fall during the war. He grew to marry the princess and became the father of the first Shadowsynger King, who's sword Ryatt now carries, once belonged to you–changed, and remade in the ancient forge in Moonrise before the fall."

Ryan takes a heavy breath, trembling as his hands slide into mine.

"I looked for you in every lifetime. For three thousand years. In lifetimes short and long, I waited for you, and I didn't find you again until now. We were separated by the veil, or by age, or by distance... until now. We're getting the chance I prayed for without realizing it."

He closes his eyes, leaning toward me. I press my forehead against his, sniffling.

"The forge feels like... being stuck between planes of existence. It's cold there, empty. But there are stars like I've never seen. She was with me."

"The Goddess?"

"No. She sent a messenger. Your grandma."

Ryan squeezes his eyes shut.

"She guided me back and told me to tell everyone how much they miss them, how they watch over us from time to time but are mostly enjoying their eternal rest together in peace, without any family calamities to stress them out."

Ryan laughs, but his eyes finally spill with tears.

"I'm not so changed," I say after a moment, cupping his cheek. "I'm just... I'm what I'm supposed to be now. I have my bow; I have my mate. And now, we have the time that was taken from us."

"Did you have to kill me though?" he teases, breaking the tension between us.

I smile, choking back either a laugh or a sob. "You looked on the verge of death already. I think I was doing you a favor."

He laughs again, but I'm still feeling utterly undone. "Do you believe me?"

"Of course," he says, leaning back to take my face between his hands. He swipes my tears away with his thumbs, pressing a tender kiss to my forehead. "I believe you. Always." There's a brief pause before Ryan, whom I love deeply, but who also fails to linger in any serious moment for too long, says, "So, the Shadow Sword is techni- cally mine, huh?"

"I wouldn't bet on Ryatt giving it to you, if that's what you're asking."

"I'm his like... great, great, great, great, great, great grandfather or something, then?"

"I think it goes further back than that," I smile.

"He's gonna be fucking pissed when I tell him."

"Maybe you shouldn't," I reply, feeling suddenly uneasy about anyone knowing about this.

"I'll think about it. Just… eat something, please. Sarah's already figuring out how she plans to test your new powers and I really don't like it, but it sounds like you already made up your mind, huh?"

I nod. I want Maeve home, of course. She's vulnerable but also extremely dangerous with her powers not yet trained. And, honestly, I want Logan back. I want him home, with us, where he belongs.

Ryan kisses my lips before telling me to eat once more and disappearing out the door. I eat as much as I can, barely tasting the food, and lie down, falling into a deep, deep slumber that makes my bones like jelly when I wake up again several hours later.

It's nearly nightfall and no news about Maeve or Logan has reached Silverhide, which means it's my time to shine.

I pull myself out of bed and dress, my breasts achingly full of milk, and go to find Lexa, but the second I step out of the door, I realize the house is full… again.

Misty and Cole sit on the couch looking forlorn. Sydney paces with his arms crossed. Sarah speaks in quiet tones to Evander in the kitchen.

And Ryan turns to me holding our daughter, smiling faintly.

"Are you ready?" he asks.

I reach for Lexa, nodding.

SCRY ME A RIVER

Aviva

"No one needs to worry about me," Sarah says confidently, cradling the swell of her belly as she leads our group through the woods toward the lake. "I'm not going to go into labor right now, I promise."

Sydney grumbles something under his breath in response, the words drifting on the warm breeze making the leaves dance above our heads. Ryan's hand is on my lower back–a warm, solid presence. Lexa's asleep in her sling on his back, and when I look up at the two of them–with Ryan wearing a traditional Endovian sling and his face cast in uncertain shadows–I feel a prickle of regret.

Part of me believes I shouldn't have told him about what I saw in the forge. The past lives I walked through, the wars, the downfall of our kind... and most importantly, the fact that in another life, we lost our children and were separated for decades, only to find each other again in the very last moments before we both died.

It stings to think about, though it doesn't affect our lives now. I'm not sure I believe it fully. I'm not sure I want to.

History repeats itself, doesn't it? Why would I be shown those lives if I wasn't being warned about times to come?

A shiver runs up my spine as we reach the lake. The stars are out in full, shining down on us from the heavens. I catch a glimpse of a shooting star moving so swiftly I blink, and it's gone, too fast for me to even make a wish.

Misty and Cole hung back tonight. They went home to their cabin to rest for however long this takes, because if I find the kids, we're leaving as soon as we know where they are.

Sarah stands on the shore and takes a deep breath, smiling as she says something to her mate, who looks like he'd rather be anywhere else, doing anything else, than standing beside his heavily pregnant wife while she begins to summon her strange powers of sight and manipulation.

"Why can't you just do it?" Ryan says, his voice heavy and stern.

Sarah glares at him and points to her belly, frowning. "Scrying takes an insane amount of energy that I don't have. I nearly passed out scrying for Misty, and I wasn't pregnant yet at the time. I can't, and even if I could, I could only give us the general area... plus, everyone knows Aviva has a special connection to Maeve somehow."

I go rigid when Sydney, Ryan, and Sarah look at me expectantly like they want me to agree, but I shrug, toying with the pockets of the dress I pulled on before leaving the house. I think of being led into the forge by the Firestone witches in my vision—those incredibly beautiful women with features I've only ever seen displayed in two people I know currently. Tall—incredibly so for a woman. Dark, lush hair. Alabaster skin that seems to glow on its own and those eyes like polished sea glass.

Firestone witches weren't like the witches alive today. No, they were something else. Something else entirely... and back then, they chose me to command their armies, just like Maeve commands the use of my lap for naps.

Sydney crosses his arms over his chest, checking his watch and casting Sarah a look. "Are you sure about this?"

"As long as Aviva's sure," Sarah replies, turning expectant eyes to me.

I nod. What choice do I have?

Ryan licks his lips and gently takes me by the elbow, turning me away from his brother. He dips his head, sighing before saying, "You've never used your powers before. I'll be here the entire time. I'll pull you from the lake if need be."

"I know," I whisper, reaching for his hand and squeezing. "But I'm not going in the water. I'm going to try it Sarah's way and use the water as a conduit–or whatever."

Ryan exhales deeply, his eyes shining with silent concern, but he doesn't try to stop me when I turn to Sarah and walk on steady feet to meet her at the lake's edge.

"You'll feel it," she explains. "Just dig deep and pull."

"It's that easy?"

She nods, smiling softly as she steps to the side to give me some space. "Think of Maeve and Logan. Call to them. Ask the in-between for their location, and it'll show you."

"The in-between?"

"You'll know when you see it," she says, a hint of mischief laced through each word. "Go on, then. I'm excited to see what you can do!"

Sydney huffs his disagreement, and Ryan widens his stance like he's preparing to jump to my aid, but I step closer to the shore until the water laps around my toes, slinking past the leather straps of my sandals. There's a cold bite to the water this time of year that doesn't go unnoticed, but I push past my discomfort and take a huge breath, then I close my eyes and try to–well, I don't really know what I'm trying to do, trying to reach, I guess. I think of Maeve.

I extend my hands over the water, breathing deeply, trying to clear my mind of the chaotic tangle of thoughts fighting for dominance. I imagine the moment I met the strange baby for the first time. I imagine holding her in my arms. I imagine her perched on my hip while the warm, salty water off the beach in Maatua swirls around us, and she laughs, reaching for the waves.

Something flickers in my chest.

"That's it," Sarah says in encouragement. "You almost have it."

I'm not sure how she knows, but I'm beyond being able to question her about it. My mind stills, my memories sliding away, and when I finally open my eyes again I see fields of wheat—and Logan.

It's the day I walked him to the hills overlooking the village, when he talked to me for the first time, opening up enough I could sense how broken and lonely he was. How he longed for his family even though he knew they were gone. How he knew he was alone, and now a strange lady with wild hair and propensity for killing things was offering him a lifeline and her mate, a big, scary brute of a man wanted him as much as she did—

I gasp as the lake roars to life with voices I can't decipher.

I almost give up out of fear, but I can't stop now, not when my mind is racing through the world all around us, through the stars, over rivers and streams and high into the mountains where villages dot the valleys.

"Keep going, Aviva," Sarah says over the roaring in my ears.

I feel it. Them, the kids. I see a small village tucked far away in the distant mountains. A burbling stream, a barn, several sheep, and a pen full of pigs. A stone house rises before me, its windows glistening with light as a family settles down for dinner. But the house fades from view at the very moment I catch a glimpse of Logan leaving the barn, creeping through the shadows toward the house.

I gasp as my powers cut out. My eyesight returns at the same moment the water of the lake recedes and grows calm again.

Sarah's at my side looking owl-eyed and excited as she clutches my arm. "You saw them, didn't you?"

My heart races as adrenaline ghosts through my body. "I think so, yes. I saw Logan, for sure." I struggle to catch my breath as I turn to Ryan. "He's in a village somewhere up north, I think. I know the mountains. I could get us there."

Ryan scans my face before nodding, his eyes slightly glazed. I bite back a wince as he looks down at his hands before curling them into fists and turning toward the trail back to the village.

I'm like him now. I have powers.

Why do I feel like he thinks of me differently now that I do?

* * *

"Is she asleep?" I ask as Ryan closes our bedroom door. I bring my knees to my chest, curling my arms around them as he steps into the darkness and pulls off his shirt.

"Yeah, she went back down pretty easily. She's had an… interesting few days."

"I–I don't want to leave her again."

"I know you don't." He breathes, giving me a soft, understanding smile that doesn't touch his eyes. "This mess is temporary. Soon it'll be the harvest festival and by then, our family will have returned to their homes, and everything will go back to normal." He sits on the side of the bed with a grunt, hanging his head like he's stretching his neck. His broad, solid back muscles flex with stress, and my heart sinks.

"I'm so sorry, Ryan."

"There's nothing to be sorry for–"

"You brought your pack to the Deadlands to escape–to put some distance between you and your–your magical family, and now your mate has powers, too."

He looks at me over his shoulder. "Aviva, that's not what I'm thinking–"

"But you have to be," I edge, tucking my knees a little tighter against my chest. "It's what I'm thinking. I'm thinking I've changed, and there's no going back to the way things were before."

He scoots back, wrapping an arm around my shoulders, forcing me out of the fetal position. He lays us back against the pillows, our eyes on the ceiling.

"I'm not worried about that. I love you. I love you more every day that passes, and that won't change. It won't change when you start getting wrinkles and gray hair. It won't change when neither of us can walk any longer, and our pack puts us out to pasture so Lexa can rule."

I snort a laugh.

He continues, his tone a little lighter than before, "I'm not worried about us. If what you saw is true, this is your second chance as much as me finding you was mine. Whatever comes, we'll face it. We'll complain and curse the whole way, but we'll do it. And we'll get the kids back. Logan will come home, and everything will be fine."

I draw lazy lines over his chest, watching the moonlight play over the ceiling.

Ryan sighs, curling his fingers around mine. "There's something I want to talk to you about."

"What is it?"

"Logan," he says, rolling his lip between his teeth. "Logan should stay in the pack, I think. He's comfortable here, and there're boys his age to play with, to learn with. He can shift already, which is incredibly early, but we can train him, get him used to shifting. I–I think he should stay with us."

I lift my head to look at him. He has his eyes closed, however. "Shouldn't he be with a family?"

"Aren't we a family?"

"Yes, but… shouldn't he be given new parents? A new mom and dad to love him?"

His silence is the answer I hadn't known I'd been longing for, that for some reason, Logan dropped into my life, and I had an instant connection with him but couldn't understand why.

"I feel like he was meant to be here," Ryan says. "With us. Don't you?"

"Yeah, I do."

"I think we're supposed to be his parents."

Another pregnant pause makes the air go still around us.

"What do we know about teenage boys?"

"Enough to know we have hell ahead of us when he starts getting comfortable enough to push boundaries, and Goddess forbid, liking girls."

I don't bother to fight the smile starting to spread across my lips. "It should be his decision."

"We'll let him make it. And we'll leave the mystery of Emberfyll and its people to Ella and Ryatt. I have no interest in that as it stands."

I nod, laying my head against his shoulder. I curl up against him, drinking in his scent, his warmth.

He presses a soft kiss to my temple before we slip into sleep at the same time, sharing dreams of a peaceful, quiet life.

With our kids.

THREE HEART BEATS

Misty

COLE DOESN'T TELL ME I SHOULD GET SOME REST, AND FOR THAT I'M eternally grateful. I pace the cabin, watching as he organizes and takes inventory of his medical kit. I remember the day I found out he was a physician. It had been a shock. My arm had been torn to the bone by a rabid, cursed wolf, and this man—this stranger who I thought was evil—sewed me back together again.

That feels like a lifetime ago. Maybe it was, honestly. Sometimes I wonder if our weeks in Richard's fortress actually happened or if it were a fever dream. But the glint of lantern light on the sharpened edge of a scalpel pulls me back into reality as he drops it into a pot of boiling water.

"Are you going with us?" I ask into the silence.

Cole's mouth twitches with something unsaid. He shakes his head, glancing at me over his shoulder. "No. I'm going to stay here with Addy and be available to anyone who needs a healer."

I wait for him to tell me I should try to get a few minutes of sleep, but he doesn't. Instead, he turns to face me, leaning his weight against the counter with a sigh as his eyes pitched closed and he runs a hand over his face.

"I'm sorry, Cole."

"There's nothing to be sorry for–"

"This isn't what you expected it'd be. Coming here, to Silverhide, where it's supposed to be simple and quiet." I wave a hand around the rustic cabin for emphasis. "You thought this would be a much needed vacation for us, and instead, I unearthed a fucking–a fucking forge."

"I'm used to this," he says, laughing a bit. "I imagine this isn't the last time a plan of mine goes awry because of your powers."

I look down at my hands, which I've been ringing for the past hour. I've picked my nails to the quick, going over the plan in my head over and over again, and I'm exhausted. Exhausted, and ready to just… be done with it all.

"The Mystics in Moonrise have a way to get rid of powers. Some witches elect to do it from what I've heard. It's not easy or comfortable but I could–"

"No," he says sternly.

"But–"

"You're not doing that."

"I could. It would make things easier for us."

"How would giving up a part of who you are make anything easier for us?" He steps toward me, frowning, his eyes narrowed. "Have you lost your mind?"

"I have," I admit, trying to keep my voice down while Addy slumbers in the center of our bed only a few feet away. "I have lost my mind. Entirely. I left it on the battlefield the moment I watched you fall flat on your face–dead–because of me!"

He exhales sharply, nostrils flaring. "Misty–"

"I'm lost. Okay? I feel like I've been barely surviving for the past year. I just wanted us to have a chance. I wanted us to have a life where everything was perfect, and we were happy, and–and we come here and get thrown into the fire again. I'll always be hunted for what I am. Someone is always going to want a piece of me–of us–of our children—and I'm so tired of it, Cole. I was tired of it back then, and I'm tired of it now." I close my eyes, covering my face with my hands. Memories of the war sprint back to the forefront of my mind. Cole's glazed, heartbroken look when he'd rejected me to force me away. The dead look in his eyes those first few weeks in the fortress. Georgia's fear. The nameless faces and screams from the day the university was attacked.

"It'll happen again," I rasp, lowering my hands to look at him. Cole is closer now, having taken several steps in my direction, his face lined with concern. "I know it will. As long as I have power—as long as my family has powers—someone will come for us. They'll challenge us. We will always, always, be at war."

Cole reaches for me. I flinch away at first, and he hesitates but then pulls me hard against his chest, crushing me against his solid warmth. His scent wraps around my senses, squeezing tight, weighing down the turmoil and fear clogging my mind. His hand drifts up my back to my neck, holding me in place. I choke on silent sobs, torn between letting it all out and holding it in so I don't wake up our son.

His grip on my body tightens. "You saved my life last year. I'm not talking about the battle, either. That night, at the party in the tunnels under the campus… when I finally got a real glimpse of you? You gave me something to fight for. And then you had him." He takes a shallow breath. "You brought our son into the world, and it was the most miraculous thing I'd ever seen. You did that without using an ounce of your powers. You brought me back from the dead and gave him life."

I shake my head as tears slip free, soaking into his shirt.

"You've never given yourself credit for what you did," he whispers into my hair. "Not once. You didn't give yourself a single second to grieve your grandparents. You didn't go back to who you were before."

"I can't find her."

"She's still there," he sighs, swaying ever so gently like he's rocking an infant to sleep. "I see her in your writing, the interviews you've conducted. That's what you should be doing, Misty. That's your real power, and it always has been. Knowledge."

Something finally clicks in my brain—something I've been waiting for, desperately reaching for, and missing by mere inches.

I start to pull away, to look up at him and blubber whatever apology I can think of, when heavy footsteps sound on the front porch.

I'm not surprised by the intrusion. Aviva and I are meant to be waiting for Kenna and Evander to arrive so we can go get the kids and bring them home.

But when my brother walks through the door, his face drawn and drained of all color, my heart immediately sinks.

Cole straightens, gripping my arms as he scans Sydney's face. Sydney's mouth moves, but no sound comes out. I've never, ever, seen him look like this, and real fear rushes through my veins.

Cole, however, takes a steady breath, stepping away from me and sweeping his medical kit off the counter, ignoring the pot still sanitizing the precious tools I can't even begin to name.

"When did her labor start?" he asks Sydney in his doctor voice—so calm and cold it could cause ice to form on the windows despite the unseasonably warm night.

"It hasn't—I don't understand," Sydney says, unable to catch his breath. "There's just—too much blood."

Cole brushes past me and grabs Sydney by the shoulder. They run off into the night, turning to shadows against the silver glow of moonlight. I grip the doorframe wondering what the hell I'm supposed to do now. Seeing Sydney like that was so incredibly unsettling that it's impossible to think past. I turn back into the house and quietly gather Addy into my arms, wrapping us both in a blanket before turning off the stovetop and shoving the pot of boiling water to the far back of the stove. Then, I dart into the night as fast as my feet can carry me, trying my hardest not to wake Addy up.

Sydney and Sarah were supposed to be staying in one of the empty, newly built cottages in the village square, but it's empty.

By some miracle from the Goddess Herself, I whirl, catching a glimpse of Freya hurrying out of her house with a basketful of linens. She sees me, sighs with relief, and waves me over.

"Where are they?" I ask hurriedly, catching up to her in a few quick steps.

"Ryan and Aviva's house," she says, setting the basket down and motioning for me to hand Addy to her. "Let me take him. Lexa's already with Mercy."

"Have Kenna and Evander arrived yet?"

She shakes her head, looking pale as she adjusts Addy's weight in her arms. "No, they haven't." She takes a deep breath. "Did you know she was having twins?"

"Sarah?"

Her nod is solemn and shakes me to my core. I pick up the basket and sprint to the house, panting, my legs burning with the effort of running up the stairs leading to the porch. A low, guttural moan echoes toward me before my feet have even landed on the porch, followed by the sharp cry of a newborn.

Relief floods my body, but it's brief. Sarah cries out, and Sydney– he's desperate. I can taste his emotions as he says, "I don't have enough power for this. Why is she bleeding so much, Cole?"

I shove through the door. Aviva's standing in the kitchen looking pale as she ravages the cabinet, but her eyes light up when she sees me with the basket of linens. "Thank the Goddess."

I glance at the living room where Cole, Sydney, and Ryan are blocking my view of Sarah... and maybe it's a good thing. Ryan turns to look at me, his shirt stained with blood and his arms cradling a bundle–a blanket.

His eyes are heavy with worry.

"Hold onto her leg," Cole says without an ounce of emotion in his voice. He hisses out a breath, his shoulders rigid as he kneels. I can't see what he's doing, but Sarah groans weakly, and I feel my healing powers ignite for the first time in... a year.

"The second baby is stuck," Aviva whispers before passing me with the basket. I watch her set it on the ground beside Cole. Ryan hands her the first baby. Aviva cradles the infant, making small, sad shushing sounds as she turns back in my direction.

I'm frozen in place. My powers simmer beneath my skin, but my legs refuse to move. I watch the scene as if in slow motion–Cole trying to deliver the baby. Sarah's leg slumping at his side. Sydney leaning over her, begging her to wake up while his healing powers skitter over the leg he's holding onto for dear life, barely enough to breach her skin.

"Is she all right?" Aviva shows me the first baby. "Misty? Misty–"

I snap out of it and look down, smoothing the blanket away from the baby's face and chest. The baby squirms, her face twisted in fury and confusion. She lets out an angry whine before bursting with life–her wails filling the house.

The men aren't even looking in our direction. Aviva hurriedly wraps the baby back up in the blanket and fumbles with her shirt. "She needs milk, right?" Panic flares behind her eyes.

I nod, in a haze, torn between Aviva and Sarah. "What happened?"

Sarah lets out a weak sob, but Cole grunts with effort, and then the second baby makes her entrance into the world.

It's a silent one.

"No," Sydney rasps, clutching his mate's leg. "Sarah? Sarah, look at me!"

The world stops spinning as my feet carry me across the house. Cole is desperately trying to save Sarah's life, but the bleeding won't stop. Sydney holds his daughter. She's very small–and quiet. Born in a beam of moonlight against a sea of stars.

It's not fair. None of this is fair.

I fall to my knees next to Cole. He's in over his head. Two empty vials of precious tears–likely the very last in existence–lie beside the top of Sarah's head as she takes a shallow breath, her skin a mottled gray.

I realize what happened. Sydney has healing powers like I do, but not nearly as strong. His powers are a flicker in comparison, but enough to save a single life.

He saved the first baby, didn't he? Not realizing how bad things were going to go in a matter of moments?

I brush Sarah's hair away from her face, clutching her cheeks between my hands. Powers I refused to acknowledge—the same powers Grandma used to save an entire kingdom—shoot out from my palms.

The entire house erupts in pale blue light for a heartbeat… and I'm alive again.

2 8

BABY GIRLS

Misty

"Briar," Sarah says weakly, sweeping her thumb over the perfectly pink baby girl's cheek. Sarah smiles softly, her eyes still glazed with exhaustion and her hair damp with sweat. "And this one–" she reaches for the second baby, another girl, nestled in a traumatized Sydney's arms. "Celeste."

"Those are beautiful names," Aviva says gently, laying another warm rag over Sarah's forehead.

I'm watching from afar, my trembling hands cupping a mug of calming tea that's doing nothing for my system. I was a teenager when Sarah came into Sydney's life. I remember whispers about her falling ill but didn't understand how horrifically sick she'd really been until now.

Sarah is a Mystic. She's different. It takes so much more energy to heal her. Healing her sucked my powers dry, and I feel… shockingly empty right now. It was like running a marathon and then getting hit by a bus, but she's alive, and so are her twins.

Sydney accepts another cup of tea from Ryan with a weak nod. He looks like death itself, unable to look anyone in the eyes. Ryan pours a heavy dram of whiskey in Sydney's mug and claps him on the shoulder before walking over to where I'm gripping the kitchen table for dear life while Cole stares out the window in silence.

None of us have ever seen anything like that. Even Ryan, the king of saying something totally inappropriate and lighthearted during times like these, has nothing to say except, "The midwife will be back from Endova in a few hours. My scouts caught up to her and are escorting her back." He sighs, running his fingers through his hair. "Bad timing, I guess. She was heading into Endova to help with a birth there."

Aviva appears, looking shaken but somewhat recovered. "They'll be fine in Endova without her. She was only assisting their new midwife." She debates sinking into a chair beside me but decides against it, glancing out the window instead. It's still a few hours until morning. A few hours until we're meant to leave to get Maeve and Logan.

I feel Ryan's gaze sweeping across our battered group. He clears his throat, leaning against the wall beside Cole. "Aviva and I will go to get the kids. I think it's best you stay here, Misty."

"Why?" I ask, my throat quivering like someone took a rake to my vocal cords.

"You saved Sarah's life. Cole got the babies out, but Sarah and Briar would be dead if it hadn't been for you. I'd feel better leaving knowing you were here with them in the event she needs more help."

I look down at my hands still gripping the mug. I take a sip of the tea, then swallow the entire heavily sweetened liquid down, wincing at the taste. "I can barely think straight. She... Sarah needed all of my powers to heal. It'll be a while–"

"We have one more vial of Isla's tears," Aviva cuts in. She looks at Ryan, her lips pressed in a thin line.

Ryan nods solemnly. "We do. If she needs it, give it to her. Meanwhile, rest, eat something, and be prepared to step in if things go south again."

"What about Sydney?" I ask as Aviva turns, steps back into the kitchen to fetch the kettle, and pours more tea.

"Sydney's fucked up right now," Ryan sighs. "But… we don't have a lot of time. Finding the kids and bringing them home is the priority. Evander is supposed to meet us here in a few hours. He's bringing back up–a few of his Ghosts–but I don't want to wait."

"What are you suggesting?" I ask, prickles of unease coursing through my body, or maybe that's just the tea thawing my frozen muscles.

He scans his wife, who's trying to thrust a cup of tea into Cole's hand. "Aviva and I will go on foot. It'll take longer than having Sydney or Kenna take us there, but we can't wait any longer, and I think Sarah could use Kenna's help, as well."

I lean back to peek at Sarah, who's still lying on a nest of blankets on cushions near the fire in the living room, her head tilted back against the couch and her eyes closed. Sydney's head nods with fatigue. He's barely able to keep his eyes open. There's no way he's going to be able to carry anyone to the distant mountains.

I look up at Cole. He's watching the sky, the stars. His eyes are glazed in thought, and he looks absolutely beaten. He's wearing one of Ryan's shirts, but I can still see the remnants of blood staining his hands. Maybe I'm just imagining that, but still. I'm processing how quickly this happened.

He needs me right now as much as Sarah does.

"Okay," I say after a moment, nodding. "I'm staying."

Ryan nods, squeezing my shoulder in passing as he moves toward the living room. He crouches, checking on Sydney, before rising and disappearing into his nearby bedroom. Aviva starts pulling her weapons down from the rustic hangers lining the wall near the front door.

"I just mind-linked with Freya. The babies are fine with Mercy, but can you nurse Lexa for me while I'm gone?" She looks over her shoulder at Sarah. "Mercy's brewing some raspberry leaf tea for Sarah. She needs to drink it–drink anything, honestly. Her milk hasn't quite come in yet."

Ryan returns with a bundle of supplies and sets it on the table, adding, "When Kenna and Evander get here, have Kenna notify Ryatt about what happened so he can get in touch with Mom and Dad."

I nod along with their instructions, keeping a mental checklist. I sip my tea, watching them move through the house. Aviva disappears into the bedroom and returns wearing one of her Endovian shifting dresses and begins looping her weapons belt and halter over her small, muscled frame.

Ryan returns from upstairs with a strange backpack that's obviously meant to be worn in his wolf form. He starts stuffing supplies inside of it, his face washed in determination.

Silence hugs the cabin when they leave long before the first light of day. Aviva knows her way around the Deadlands and has apparently traveled into those mountains before to hunt in her youth. Still, I'm anxious. Maeve has been missing for days now, and our only consolation is that she's with Logan, and he's keeping her safe.

"You need to eat something," I whisper to Cole while rummaging through the cabinets. I find some bread, cookies, and other dry goods. Everyone here eats their hot meals as a group, and it's far too early for breakfast.

Cole breaks his gaze away from the window for the first time in over an hour and walks past me, crouching beside Sarah and gently taking her vitals. He's still in doctor mode. He's come home like this a few times after his shifts in the hospital… and I know it probably has to do with stress or feeling like he failed. I say nothing until he walks back over to the table and sits down, running his hand through his hair. I pour him a fresh cup of tea and sit beside him, both of us listening to the soft, rhythmic breaths of the family sleeping in the living room.

"You couldn't have saved her," I tell him, reaching for his hand. I squeeze his fingers, and thankfully, he squeezes back.

"I realized that pretty quickly; when she started bleeding like that." He chews his lower lip. "It was the babies that broke me, I think."

"Sarah's not the average shifter," I remind him. "Her body's different. Her biology isn't like ours. She's not a witch, nor a wolf. She's something else."

"I know." He looks down at our joined hands. "This is… important work we're doing here. What I'm doing here. Ryatt and Isaac keeping the border open between Crescent Falls and Eastonia means… more people like Sarah living in Crescent Falls eventually. People who need something else when it comes to medicine and healing. We're wholly unprepared for it in Crescent Falls."

"But you'll be prepared," I edge, giving his shoulder a little nudge.

"Maybe you should take up healing," he sighs, meeting my eyes for the first time all morning. "Your powers are… comparable to Isla's tears, and those are in shorter and shorter supply these days. They'll be gone soon, and you're the only other person who has powers that potent."

"My tears aren't like hers. My healing power is in my light. I don't know how to harness that for… commercial use."

"I think we need to figure something out… for people like Sarah and her kids. For our kids, probably, if they have powers like yours."

I haven't given much thought to whether Addy will grow to have powers. Some people in the family wonder if our powers will weaken in the coming generations, especially in couplings like ours. Cole is a shifter. He doesn't have gifts. Sydney has a few, but they're nothing in comparison to his mates. Aviva was normal until recently, and Ryan… Ryan is a beast, he doesn't have light or healing gifts.

I think of Kenna and her family. Evander is a hybrid fox-wolf shifter. That's a gift in itself. Kenna is a Shadowsynger and Firestone witch, the most powerful being in our worlds other than her parents. But even Ella's powers don't hold a candle to Ryatt's. He's a scary guy—a freak of nature.

And Maeve?

She has enough power to destroy our world if she wanted to, and she's only a baby.

There was so much stock put into whether or not I'd have powers. The public speculation around our family only grew as I got older. It was an enormous burden to carry, so much so that I buried my gifts as deep as I could to live as normally as possible… and for a while, I was able to.

Selfishly, I hope Addy doesn't have powers. I hope he can have a normal life where all he has to worry about is shifting. I love that we live in suburbia, in a safe pack with my brother leading us so we can just… raise our kid. We can order a pizza when we're hungry instead of hunting. I can drive to the nearest department store instead of shifting and worrying about where I'm going to find clothes before picking up my groceries.

But I know I can't live like this forever. I was given these gifts for a reason. Aviva was made by the forge into something no one understands yet for a reason–a reason that may come in the future, when our family is needed again. When we have to rise up to protect ourselves, and our people, our kingdoms.

Sydney groans, which breaks me out of my own thoughts. Cole rises and walks to him on silent feet, their whispered conversation lost over the sound of boiling water I'm using to make oatmeal. Cole walks back to me holding Celeste while Sydney stumbles to the bathroom in search of a shower.

"Look at you," Cole smiles. "You're perfect."

I stand and look down at the baby girl in his arms. She has white hair–a lot of it. So does Briar, her sister, younger by ten minutes. "She looks like Sarah."

"I know." Cole's eyes meet mine, and I have a split second of vision showing me a glimpse of our future, our future girl. She'll come as easily as Addy did, born into Cole's loving hands… in our house this time because I will–again–ignore every sign of labor.

"When we have a daughter, I want to name her Josephine," I whisper, stroking Celeste's cheek.

"Why?"

"I've just loved the name for as long as I can remember. There was a book I used to read repeatedly about a girl named Josie who went on these grand adventures, and I… wanted to be like her because she was strong and funny. So, when it's our turn again, I'll have a little Josie of my own."

Cole kisses my forehead as the first light of morning breeches the top of the mountains, painting the valley in pale pink and violet... and the dark shadows cast by Kenna, Evander, and his Ghosts arriving.

29

———

DON'T LOSE YOUR HEAD

AVIVA

THE FOREST SHIFTS FROM ENDLESS SHADOWS TO AN ASSORTMENT OF pale gold as the sun rises. I'm sprinting in my wolf form, Ryan not far behind in his. There was no reason for him to shift into his beast, thank goodness. He's actually slower in that form than his wolf, but we've covered serious ground in the two hours since leaving Silverhide.

Forty miles, in fact. A new record.

Panting, I reach the far edge of the forest that weaves through the tribal territories of the Deadlands. Behind us, the packs of Silverhide and Endova are just waking up for the day. Ahead of us, the sun hasn't even begun to touch the towering mountains to the far west, where my new powers showed me a glimpse of Maeve and Logan.

I'm still getting used to the prickle of energy that wasn't there before. It's now the air I breathe—the blood rushing through my veins—the rhythmic thump of my heartbeat.

I'm changed; for better or worse, I don't know. All I know for sure

213

is that we have another twenty to thirty miles to cover this morning, and we can't stop now.

Thick, angry black clouds swirl over the distant mountains, casting a cold shadow over the sweeping plains ahead. The sunrise can't even touch the sky here. The clouds absorb the light, swirling with fury and the promise of hell once we reach the base of the mountains.

Wind whips through my fur, sending chills down my spine. *'Have you been able to reach anyone in Silverhide?'* I ask Ryan through the mind-link as he races behind me, his large wolf leaving massive paw prints the rain-soaked ground.

'No. I think we're out of range, but Sydney and Cole both know where we were planning on going. Kenna could get close and catch up, I'm positive. We don't need to hang back and wait.'

I agree. We need to get the kids. We need to close this chapter and move on. Ryan can't be out on adventures right now, not with the upcoming harvest and a new pack house to build. I need to be with Lexa and helping the women with the rugs, tapestries, and fabrics we plan to trade at the harvest festival.

A single day away from our pack right now could be the difference between a successful harvest or a brutal winter where food and commodities are scarce. We can't gamble our time any longer.

'I don't like the look of those clouds,' Ryan says as we skirt the edge of the forest under the cover of the trees.

'Me neither. I'm looking for a more direct route into the valleys there. There must be a village or something. I doubt these people live alone in the middle of nowhere, completely cut off from a pack or town.'

'You'd be surprised, Aviva,' he replies as I leap out into the glistening, neck height grass. *'Many people want exactly that. Hell, I moved my pack over a thousand miles away to achieve some peace and quiet... and then I met you.'*

If I were in my human form, I'd be throwing him a smirk. Instead, I growl, then dart through the grass, smiling to myself as he grunts and complains about my speed through the mind-link.

It's miles and miles of this—wet grass. Cold wind. An endless, open shadow the sunrise can't breach. Neither of us ate breakfast this morning, and by the time we reach the base of the mountains, we're starving, wet, and freezing cold.

I finally allow us a small break. We seek shelter beneath a crop of gnarled trees with a cliff face behind us, giving us a respite from the brutal wind spinning down the mountain tops. Neither of us shift. It's warmer in our wolf forms, for sure.

'Have you been this deep in the Deadlands before?' I ask him.

'No, not this far west, at least. I guess Moonrise is actually pretty close, if you think about it.'

'On the other side of the mountains, yes. The mountains are the place where the Deadlands, the Roguelands, and Moonrise converge, from what I've been told and seen on the maps.'

This place is a barren wasteland until it touches the border with the Roguelands, but the mountains above us are wooded–not thickly, but enough to block our view of any roads and trails leading into the valleys several hundred feet above our heads.

It's impossible to believe anyone could live up here. Ryan's thinking the same thing because he says, *'We need to prepare for anything. If these people are aggressive, we'll have to take the kids back by any means necessary.'*

'I know,' I reply, sighing through our bond. *'Let's hope it doesn't come to that.'*

Without another word, we set off again, beginning our climb. It starts out rocky and steep, the two of us picking our way past the cliffs and boulder fields then following a creek into one of the valleys. Day comes without any light. Rain falls in a torrent, sending rocks skittering down either side of the valley. There is no village here, no trails, no roads.

So, we try the next valley, and the next, until we're miles deep in the unending mountains. Finally, toward midday, we breach another mile or so stretch of thick forest and come upon a dirt road.

'Shift back,' Ryan says, lifting his snout to the sky. Over the rain and heavy scent of ozone, another scent–something spiced with smoke– clouds my senses at the same moment he picks up on it.

I obey, shifting back into my human form. Ryan stays in his wolf form, lying down on his belly on the muddy road so I can fish a heavy leather cloak from the backpack strapped to him, the straps fitted to his wolf form. Rain slides off the leather, and inside the cloak my skin immediately begins to heat. I slip into a pair of sandals he packed for me–something I won't be too sad to lose if I have to shift abruptly, and we begin to follow the road deeper into the mountains.

I didn't expect to have to go this far, honestly. I've been searching for that strange feeling–that tug I feel with Logan, but to no avail. Ryan walks beside me, and it's obvious he's thankful for the rest and my slow pace, but within an hour, we come across the first people we've seen on our journey...

And they're not happy to see us.

Ryan snarls as three men and four wolves dart in our direction down the road. Sheets of rain fall over us, making my view of their positioning hazy. I pull my gilded bow from my back, the metal singing as I prim an arrow and point it at the man leading the charge.

He's young. In his early twenties perhaps, like me. He halts, wide-eyed, as my arrow points directly between his eye-sockets.

His companions are all men. I don't know about the wolves, though. They pace around the three men blocking our way up the road, their gums pulled back over their teeth which gleam in the faint dark-blue haze given off by the storm.

Ryan takes a single step, growling and hissing aggressively, and the group backs off just enough that I risk lowering my weapon and pulling back my hood.

They're surprised to see a woman, it seems.

"Who are you, witch?" the leader–the young man–asks, and not kindly.

"I am not a witch, first of all. Secondly, it doesn't matter who we are. I'm looking for two children. A boy, about twelve, and a toddler girl."

The men glance at each other, shrugging.

"Where is the nearest village?"

"Why should we help you?" One of the other men sneers, edging in my direction.

Ryan doesn't like this and growls in warning, which stops the man.

"You have no reason to help us other than kindness," I say because it's true. "We've traveled a long way, and we're tired and wet to the bone. I haven't eaten breakfast, and neither has he." I jab a thumb in Ryan's direction. "He gets a little cranky when he hasn't eaten."

The men eye Ryan wearily.

"How many miles until we reach the nearest village?"

"Ten, give or take."

"And what are you doing out here so far from your pack?" Their leader watches me take a step toward them, my hands still gripping my bow.

"We're hunting," he says.

"Ah, well, we haven't seen anything but rabbits, so hopefully you're not that hungry," I reply, but I'm feeling more than a little uneasy, especially as the man's eyes drift from my face to my breasts, which are full of milk and aching.

"We can escort you back to the village, if you'd like," he drawls, giving me a half-cocked, sly smile. "There's a bunkhouse. It's not much, but it has beds." He runs his tongue along his lower lip in a motion that makes my stomach twist. "It'll cost ya, though."

I arch my brow. Oh, this is going to be fun. "What is your price?"

He walks in my direction with a pep in his step, looking me up and down like I'm a prize that he's just won. "Spend a little time with me, sweetheart, and I'll take you there for free." He reaches out, twisting one of my wet curls around finger, giving it a tug.

I laugh cruelly but don't swat him away. "You shouldn't have done that."

"Done what? Touched you? The places I could touch you–"

Ryan loses his fucking mind, and I know within seconds, all three men and their wolfish companions will be dead.

The backpack holding supplies explodes in ribbons of leather. Ryan's vicious, terrifying beast replaces his dark-brown, blue-eyed wolf. I don't even flinch, but everyone else is screaming, running for their lives, I assume. I can't see them anymore. Ryan is chasing them up the road, and I sigh, clicking my tongue and shaking my head as I gather what I can from his destroyed backpack and carry our camping gear in my hands, walking at a snail's pace to catch up with my pissed off mate.

I follow Ryan's massive paw prints through the rain and mud. Eventually, the mud begins to mix with blood, and I sigh, sweeping my hand over my wet face. It doesn't take long to find the first bodies. The wolves attacked him, it seems, because they're definitely dead and in pieces.

I roll my eyes and step over the carnage, careful not to get any blood on my shoes, but I finally reach Ryan and he's… not alone.

The three men are dead, that's clear. Pieces of them litter the road—a few arms, a few legs… a head.

But it's the five or so men standing with my mate that catch my attention. They're holding weapons—knives and longswords, but not threatening Ryan in any way. In fact, they're staring at the bodies with smiles on their faces and expressions of mingled relief and joy.

I stare at the men, who finally notice my approach.

"This thing yours?" an elderly man—likely my father's age—asks, pointing at Ryan, still in his beast form and coated in blood.

"Ah, yes. That's my mate."

A few of the men exchange glances, but the old man raises his brows, shrugs, and motions to the mess Ryan left on the road. "We've been chasing down those bastards since last night. Your, uh, mate took care of a pretty big problem for us, miss."

"Aviva," I tell him, giving him a graceful nod.

He narrows his eyes. "What'd you say?"

"Aviva, that's my name."

"You wouldn't be Aviva of Silverhide, would you?"

"I am."

A few of the men glance at Ryan in sudden surprise.

The old man approaches me, and to my immense surprise, lays down his sword and kneels in the bloody mud, bowing his head to me. "Then you'd be Queen of the Deadlands," he says, looking up at me. "Correct?"

"Sure, I guess," I glance at Ryan, who's still too worked up to shift back. "Uh, listen, we're looking for two kids. A boy and a toddler girl. They're on a farm somewhere in these mountains and–"

"The Graston farm, yes. They found a boy a few days ago. We've been meaning to help him back down the mountains but this storm–"

"The girl," I rush out, grabbing his arm and helping him upright. "Is she with him?"

He scans my face, sighing. "The one that can burst into flames? Yes. She's with him, and you owe them a new barn, I'm afraid."

3 0

A WITCH AND A PUP

AVIVA

RYAN LOOKS HILARIOUS IN THE TOO-TIGHT CLOTHES BORROWED FROM some rural villager half his height and weight. He glances at me with a scowl, rolling his eyes and cursing under his breath. "Don't look at me, Aviva."

"I can't help it. Your whole ass is out," I giggle, wiping tears from my eyes. Goddess, I wish I had his camera with me.

He reaches down to pull what had once been trousers down over his thighs while shooting me another glare. He had to cut them into shorts to fit. The shirt isn't any less revealing, but at least he's not naked... or worse, in his terrifying beast form. He's too exhausted after being in his beast form to shift into his wolf, which would have been easier than this, but I'm enjoying myself thoroughly at his expense.

A few of the men from the village titter behind us while I walk a few paces behind my mate who's turning a deep red in the face and sulking as we walk up the rural road, passing a few shops and cabins where people peek from their windows as we pass. The man leading

221

our sorry looking group—the elderly man who showed no fear at all when he saw Ryan and thanked us for killing the rogues on the road—turns his head to look at me and then turns around completely, walking backward. "This is Mountain Crest," Alpha Roan says, splaying his arms wide. "There're not many of us, but we make it work."

I glance around, but it's hard to see past the clouds and drizzling rain. "How close are you to the nearest… large pack?"

"Oh, miles upon miles," he says with a smile. "We prefer it that way. I doubt Mountain Crest is on any of the maps you've seen, Luna." He winks, pointing into the mist rolling off the mountains. "Moonrise is only a hundred miles west. There used to be a river that ran between Moonrise and these mountains. Once, I'm sure, there was a prosperous trading network between those witches and the people of the Deadlands, but that river has been dry since the Great War."

"That would make sense," Ryan says, tugging his shirt down over his bulging abdominal muscles. "The temple ruins are a straight shot south through the valley below us."

I wrack my brain for memories of hunting trips from my youth. "Yeah, a river makes total sense. There're huge swathes of what I believe were once wetlands all through the tribal pack territories."

Alpha Roan smiles and nods, replying, "The Deadlands weren't so dead a few thousand years ago. But I don't mind the quiet."

"Who do you trade with?" Ryan asks.

"No one. We have everything we need right here."

The road comes to an abrupt stop. Alpha Roan walks to the right, and we follow. I steal a glance at Ryan, noticing him going a bit rigid as he shifts his weight in his too-small clothes.

The Alpha notices his discomfort and smirks, "We don't make 'em that big in Mountain Crest, I'm afraid."

"Apparently not," I laugh, which awards me another sharp look from Ryan.

A few minutes later, we walk out into a large field of grass. A few sheep bleat at us, and Ryan stiffens when a group of semi-feral pigs snort past, curious but skittish enough to give our group a wide berth. I wince when the outline of what was once a barn comes into voice, burnt to an absolute crisp.

Ryan sighs under his breath, mumbling something about getting that fixed.

A two-story house comes into view. Shadows move along the porch before a young woman in homespun pants and a wool sweater comes down the stairs with her arms crossed.

"Nellie," the Alpha says with a little bob of his head.

"What's this?" she asks, turning her blue eyes toward me then to Ryan, narrowing them into cat-like slits.

Ryan grinds his teeth as he sizes the woman up, but then a man comes out on the porch, something in his arms.

"Maeve," I rasp, gasping with relief as I start in her direction. She bounces in the man's arms, her chubby fingers reaching for me with enthusiasm, but the man tightens his grip.

"Henry," Alpha Roan says, shaking his head. "I let you know we were coming and had the family of the kids."

"How do we know for sure?" Henry–tall, broad, with dark red hair, narrows his eyes just like the woman currently blocking my path to Maeve.

Nellie must be his sister by the looks of it.

"I'm Alpha King Ryan of the Deadlands," Ryan says with marked annoyance, "And Maeve is my cousin."

"And the boy?" Nellie asks, still unconvinced. "Who does he belong to?"

"He's ours," I say as firmly as possible, losing my patience. "Where is he?"

Henry cries out and drops Maeve. I lunge past Nellie, who whirls toward her brother in alarm. Maeve lands hard on her butt, scowls, and stands on unsteady feet before reaching for me. I scoop her up, close enough to see the bright red hand print on Henry's forearm that he rubs and coddles.

"He won't come inside the house," Nellie says under her breath, eyeing her brother's arm before watching me walk back to Ryan. I stand at his side while he reaches for Maeve, stroking his palm across her cheek. "He's been out in the woods for two days now."

"He only comes by the house to check on the baby," Henry cuts in, tugging his shirt sleeve down over the enormous blister starting to form on his forearm.

Alpha Roan watches the entire exchange with an amused smile. He's a strange man, but his presence is calming, especially since Nellie and Henry look like they want nothing to do with us.

"Well, that's settled," the Alpha says. "So, the little one is a witch, is she not?"

"She is," Ryan says, but his eyes narrow as he meets my gaze. He gently takes Maeve from my arms and hikes her up on his shoulders. She fists his hair with a delighted squeal, kicking her legs.

He's not going to say what kind of witch she is, however. I can see the uncertainty in his eyes–feel it through our bond. He doesn't trust Nellie and Henry and has conflicting feelings about Alpha Roan.

"I'll go find Logan," I whisper, turning from the group, but Alpha Roan starts walking in my direction without invitation to join me.

I hear Ryan mention something about the barn as his voice fades, replaced by Alpha Roan's boots squelching in the wet grass.

I risk a glance over my shoulder, and he gives me a short smile, motioning for me to wait. I slow my pace until the old, but spry, man catches up, then we continue into the mist.

"I need to apologize for Nellie and Henry," he says, bending to pick up a long, sturdy stick. "They're like that with everyone."

"Like what?"

He shrugs, tapping the stick against trees as we cross from the field into the woods. "We don't have many kids in Mountain Crest. It's not necessarily a problem seeing as how removed we are. Having kids means having more mouths to feed, and winter is already hard on us as it is. Nellie and Henry grew up alone with their father, farming. When their dad passed, they basically removed themselves from the pack. Neither have been to pack meetings in months."

"Does that bother you?"

"It bothers me that Henry's preventing Nellie from venturing off to find her mate," he says under his breath. "There're a few other packs around–all small and contained in the mountains. We've had some issues with a nearby pack. It's new and mostly men. Your mate killed a few of them on the road, actually, which I'm thankful for but will likely be dealing with the fallout. Henry is protective of Nellie and doesn't want her traveling on the road."

"So she's just… alone?"

He nods. "I suppose."

To be honest, the drama of Mountain Crest doesn't involve me, therefore I don't really care but… "Do you know about the Harvest Festival? In the Deadlands, the tribal lands?"

He closes his eyes against some memory. "Oh, Luna, it has been decades since I stepped foot on the plains of the Deadlands–"

"Why don't you travel with your pack to the Harvest Festival this fall? It's in a month. You'd have plenty of time and an opportunity to trade some wares for things you need over winter. Plus," I say, smiling at him, "Nellie might find her mate, and so could Henry. He wouldn't be so cross with a mate warming his bed."

"And is your mate no longer cross?" he jokes.

"I'm the one with an attitude," I laugh, liking this guy. But, I'm supposed to be looking for Logan. I pause in the shelter of a large tree and funnel my hands around my mouth, calling out his name. My voice echoes, bouncing from tree to tree, and then I wait.

The birds go silent. Even the mist settles back against the forest floor as if in anticipation of a fight. For a moment, I feel a prickle of unease and reach along my back for my bow. Alpha Roan watches me with interest as I take a single step out from under the tree.

A crashing sound rushes toward me, then a short, pained yelp. My fingers leave my bow with a sigh as the outline of a small wolf darts through the mist, unsteady on his feet.

I've never seen a wolf pup before. Everyone comes into their wolves by twenty-one, sometimes a few years before, but never as a child.

But Logan is the exception, and I should probably find out why–

eventually. Right now, however, he throws himself into my arms, knocking the wind out of me.

"Never seen a pup before," Alpha Roan laughs as I struggle with Logan's weight in my arms. "Rather scruffy and cute, I think."

"And heavy," I say, my voice strained. "Do Nellie and Henry have some clothes he can wear?"

"I'm sure we can find something more comfortable for your mate as well," the Alpha sighs, reaching out to roughly scratch Logan behind his fluffy ears.

* * *

NIGHT FALLS AGAIN IN THE VILLAGE OF MOUNTAIN CREST. I STARE AT Logan and Maeve, both fast asleep in a bed in Alpha Roan's house in the center of the village. His mate, Gloria, smiles softly at me as I quietly close the door and run a tired hand over my face.

Ryan's voice drifts from downstairs. He's talking to the Alpha about getting supplies here so the village can rebuild the barn Maeve destroyed.

It's damn lucky she didn't burn the farm house down or kill anyone, which reminds me how desperately we need to get her back to her parents.

"She's a Firestone, isn't she?" Gloria whispers.

I freeze, slowly looking at her. Her soft brown eyes narrow in a gentle expression, taking my silence as my answer.

"The legends always said they'd return. I never thought I'd meet one in my lifetime," she sighs, smiling to herself. "She's a sweet little thing."

"She's a danger to herself and others," I reply, unable to help it. "Her mother should be here soon, any minute now."

"You're welcome to stay as long as you need," Gloria replies then goes silent for the space of several heartbeats. She reaches out and lovingly squeezes my forearm. "And you could use some food and rest." She motions to my swollen, aching breasts–full of milk. "How old is your little one?"

"Too young for me to be gone like this so often," I painfully admit.

She purses her mouth in a sympathetic smile and tilts her head toward the stairs. "I'll put some tea on–"

The house trembles, a gust of energy flowing through the gaps in the wooden walls. I turn toward the window as the metallic taste of magic fills my mouth, then sigh. "Kenna's here."

3 1

IT'S FINALLY OVER

Misty

"Everyone's okay," I tell Lexa and Addy, laying them out in the center of Ryan's bed, side by side. Both babies scowl up at me–Lexa, for not being her mother, and my own son for showing another baby attention.

Lexa's face scrunches. She puffs her cheeks out in the threat of a wail while Addy picks up on her energy and begins to whine. I cover my ears, taking the deepest breath I can handle, and scoop both screaming infants into my arms for the hundredth time in the last two hours.

"They just won't sleep," I say, rounding the corner into the living room where Sarah is still camped out with her new babies, and Sydney is pacing like a madman in front of the windows, looking for any sign of Kenna, Ryan, Aviva, and the kids.

Sarah's fast asleep with her brand new twins resting in a floor cot nearby, but Sydney has free hands, so I thrust Lexa against his chest without saying another word.

"Freya's supposed to be coming up to help," he says under his

229

breath, still looking worse for the wear, but he has some color returning to his cheeks, finally. "And Mom's coming, apparently. I'm not sure Sarah and the girls can travel home like this."

"So we'll have help?" I ask, my voice strained. This is far too many babies to handle, and I'm starting to feel a little claustrophobic as Addy roots against my chest.

Sydney nods. I don't ask about the logistics of how Mom's getting here, whether she's bringing Blake and Liam or if they're staying behind in Crescent Falls with Dad, but I don't have the chance to, anyway, because my mate ducks through the door with Aris riding on his shoulders.

Aris is the spitting image of Evander but with dark hair like Kenna. It's wild to see, honestly, and reminds me that babies do, in fact, grow up. Aris's head bobs, and he blinks rapidly before rubbing his eyes.

"Where's Brie?" Sydney asks, tilting his head toward Aris, who is desperately trying to stay awake but failing miserably, his head nodding as Cole comes to a stop with a sigh.

"She's asleep in our bed back at the cabin," Cole says to me, then turns to Sydney, motioning to Lexa with his elbow. "Freya's coming to get her any second now." Cole looks back at me with a soft smile. "I have some news."

Sydney straightens from the wall, glancing between us. "What? Are they back?"

"Not yet," Cole says, gently lifting Aris, now fast asleep, off his shoulders and cradling him like an infant against his chest instead. "But they just made it in range of the mind-link. I just spoke to Ryan, and they'll be home in an hour or two, Kenna's resting her powers for a moment."

Sydney and I heave sighs of relief. Both of us have exhausted our powers over the past day and a half tending to Sarah, who needed a lot more than the herbs and tinctures the midwife could supply to heal. My powers are barely a flicker. I couldn't shift if I tried, and the mind-link is practically useless right now.

I turn to my brother. "We'll take Aris back to our place. If you need me, just let me know."

"I will," he says, exhausted, bouncing an increasingly irritated Lexa in his arms.

"Jacob and Andrew are going to come up to help get Sarah and the girls back to the cottage you were staying in. She needs a real bed, and you need sleep, Sydney," Cole adds, cocking his head to the door. "Everyone's going to be okay now. You can shut your eyes for just an hour, and it would still do you a lot of good."

Sydney looks like he'd rather sit here and stare at his mate to ensure she's still breathing but nods along nonetheless.

The sun sets on Silverhide for the second time since Ryan and Aviva left yesterday morning. It's a quiet, calm night. The first hints of cool weather descend on the pack as shadows creep over the fields and valley beyond.

I wait for the rush of energy Kenna creates when she jumps from place to place, but after laying Aris down beside Brie, and finally getting Addy down for bed, the air stays still and unbothered.

So, I wander around the cottage, bouncing between checking on the kids and checking in on Cole, who's been scribbling like mad in his notebook, likely recounting Sarah's birth into his written memory. I've had the notebook rebound twice since the war ended, adding new paper each time. It's huge, and notes are constantly falling out of it, but it's a reminder of the Cole I love to remember—before I really knew him. The Cole who kept notes about me during those weeks under his care in the fortress.

"You know what?" I ask, moving in his direction to where he's seated on the couch, sprawled out with his notebook on his lap.

"What?" He looks up at me as I move in on him, settling on his legs.

"I think," I begin, smiling as I adjust my position to fit more comfortably with him despite the fact he's making no moves to give me some space on the couch, "I think we should stay here for a few more weeks, until after the Harvest Festival."

He arches a brow and sets his notebook on the coffee table. "What changed your mind?"

"You."

"I'm more than ready to go home–"

"I don't think that's true. I think we have unfinished business here, in Eastonia. I think you need to learn what you can from the midwife, and then visit Endova, and spend some time in Moonrise at their hospital–"

"And what about you?"

I tilt my head toward his notebook. "I need to finish writing about the war. You were right about that. It's what I wanted to do before everything happened–be a historian... so, I might as well start now, before I get so busy as Dad's record keeper at the castle that I forget."

He pulls me toward him. I lie down with my head on his chest, and he pulls a blanket over us. Within minutes, I'm drifting off to sleep with my cheek squished against his ribcage, his heartbeat the lullaby that finally settles my nerves.

But what feels like seconds later, I hear Cole say, "Are you all right?"

It's pitch black in the cabin–full, undeniable night. Brie says sleepily, "I think Mama's here."

"You can feel her coming?"

"Yeah," Brie yawns, and Cole begins to sit up at the very moment I feel that shift in the air, like a knife through the fabric of time and space.

I slide off Cole and gather Brie to my chest, patting her on the head, whispering encouragement as I help her with a flannel jacket I packed with me from Crescent Falls. It hangs off her tiny, almost five-year-old body, but it's a bit chilly out, and she's refusing to stay inside.

"Daddy said he was going to meet her over the mountain and bring her back," Brie whispers on the front porch, gripping my hand while rubbing her eyes with her other hand. "Then we can go home."

Inside the cabin, through the open door, Cole's packing up his medical kit in the event of another emergency, but I feel... calm.

Everything is fine. Everyone is coming home in one piece. I can feel it.

A shadow descends through the moonlight, casting a torrent of dark mist across the ground. The mist snakes around the trees, gathering at our ankles, but Brie doesn't flinch. She stares, owl eyed, at the moonlit landscape and patiently waits for her parents to appear.

I watch her curiously, smiling to myself at her show of strength and maturity. Brie's a tough kid, a smart one, too. But the second figures appear walking in our direction through the shadows, she frowns and huffs a breath.

Kenna walks up to the porch under the cloak of moonlight, carrying Maeve. Kenna beams at Brie, her lips parting to say something to her oldest child, but Brie cuts her off with a wave of her little hand and points an accusatory finger at Maeve.

"That was naughty, Maeve," Brie hisses, wiggling her finger. "You can't disappear like that. We've talked about this."

I blink, taken aback, then make the mistake of meeting Kenna's eyes. Kenna purses her lips in an attempt to not laugh as Brie continues reading her little sister the riot act, and all we can do is watch and agree with every word the little future Luna says.

"Don't do it anymore, okay?" Brie concludes, and Maeve flashes her a two-toothed grin before breaking out in peels of giggles.

"Well," Kenna says tiredly, shaking her head. "That's settled, then. How's Sarah? The girls?"

"They're great. They're just fine," I answer but squint past her into the moonlight as four more figures appear, their bodies cast in shadow.

Ryan and Evander are easy enough to spot given their height. Evander steps forward and scoops Brie into his arms, showing more animation and emotion than I've ever seen from him... ever. "Did you take care of everyone for us?"

"Yes, Daddy," Brie says, sounding almost bored. "I'd like to go home now. My dolls are waiting for me."

"The house is taking care of them, remember?" Kenna smiles.

I picture their strange castle in Veiled Valley with its mysterious magic that makes the place come live, like a spirit lives within its walls.

Evander sets Brie down, turning to talk to Cole, who asks if everyone made it back all right, but I notice Brie staring into the darkness.

I follow her gaze to where Aviva's standing beside Logan, her arm wrapped protectively around his narrow shoulders.

Logan is staring right at Brie, his eyes narrowed and brow scrunched in confusion. Brie takes a huge breath and plants her hands on her hips.

All of the adults stop whatever hushed conversations were taking place and watch the odd stand-off.

"Did she hurt you?" Brie asks Logan, but he just blinks at her. "Did the witch hurt you?"

"Honey, Logan can't understand you," Aviva says apologetically. "He doesn't know how to speak our language yet."

"He should learn," Brie says, matter-of-factly, tapping her foot on the step.

"He will," Kenna laughs but glances around at other adults. "Be nice, Brie. He kept Maeve safe for us. We owe him for that."

"Who is he?" Brie asks, pointing at Logan this time.

"He's family now," Evander says, nodding at Logan. He just stares, leaning into Aviva's body like he's trying to disappear, but his eyes are still locked on Brie. He finally drops his gaze and turns toward Aviva, hiding his face from the group gathered on or near the porch. While Kenna and Evander gather up their kids to immediately take them home and Cole assists, I watch Ryan and Aviva talking in gentle tones to Logan.

Eventually Ryan and Logan walk away, heading toward their own home, but Aviva hangs back, her face washed with confusion.

"Are you okay?" I ask, and she nods, but then shakes her head.

"He just asked how he knows her," she says, turning to face me.

"What do you mean?"

"He asked why he knows Brie. He said he's met her before but then got really confused. I had Ryan take him to bed. It's been a long day of travel, and he doesn't handle jumping well."

I chew the inside of my cheek in thought as we stare out over the sleeping village. "He couldn't possibly know Brie, could he? He was what… seven when she was born, and he's not from here at all."

"He's just tired," Aviva concludes, but I can tell she's lost in thought as well. Moonlight reflects in her eyes as a hush falls over the valley, broken by the soft rustling of the wind through the trees.

Aviva and I look at each other.

"Do you feel that?" she asks.

"Yeah," I reply, taking a deep breath. "It's over. We can finally just… move on, right?"

She sighs, crossing her arms, blinking up at the stars. "Now what?"

32

TIME TO GET TO WORK

Misty

I SINK TO THE EDGE OF THE BATHTUB AND TEST THE WATER, STEAM rising in ribbons that dance around my wrists. The lavender and honey scented soap wafts through the air, which is still and dark, mingling with the comforting, candle-lit darkness all around me.

Kenna and her family left three hours ago. Aviva went back to her house. Sydney and Sarah are tucked up and recovering in a nearby cottage, being tended to by the midwife and Cole, so I'm alone.

Addy is asleep in the bedroom only a few yards away, exhausted. I don't blame him. The last time I felt like this–this worn to the bone–was right after the war when Cole and I closed ourselves in my old dorm room for an entire week just to rest, recoup, and come to terms with what we'd just been through–and somehow survived against all odds.

I pull my shirt over my head and shimmy out of my pants before tying my hair up and sinking into the water, groaning softly at the heat. The warmth works through my muscles, untangling knots from the stress and uncertainty of the last several days–the last several weeks, in fact.

I can feel my healing powers working beneath my skin. What they're doing, I have no idea, but soon I'm totally limp and relaxed, leaning my head against the side of the tub as the relaxation turns to utter fatigue.

I just want to sleep. I want to sleep for days and wake up with a new outlook on life. Tomorrow morning, the sun will rise, and it will be a new dawn, a fresh start. At least, I'll continue to tell myself that, over and over, until it finally feels like the truth.

I hear the door opening and closing sometime after midnight. The water in my bath has gone from hot to barely warm when Cole's cautious footsteps ring through the house as he searches for me. Finally, he opens the bathroom door and takes a breath, smiling softly as he says, "How long have you been in there? The bubbles are gone."

"A very long time," I reply, feeling suddenly heated as his gaze rakes over my naked body. "I couldn't sleep?"

"Are you tired now?" He steps into the snug bathroom and closes the door behind him, reaching for the buttons on his shirt.

"Not yet," I whisper, watching his skilled fingers undo each button. He shrugs out of the shirt and tosses it on the ground before turning to where I'd hung a towel. He unfurls it, motioning for me to step out of the tub.

I obey but with a sigh of complaint. The air is chilled. The weather has definitely started tilting toward fall. No more warm nights or mornings without the threat of frost on the grass. It's almost time to go home, honestly. There's less than a month until the Harvest Festival.

I step into his arms, letting him wrap me in the towel.

But he doesn't let me go. I take a shallow breath just before his mouth meets mine in an exploratory kiss–like he's not sure where my head's at and whether I want this kind of attention right now, but I can feel him burning just as brightly as I am when my lips part, and his tongue sweeps in to caress mine. I close my eyes, leaning into his touch. His hands rove down my back, dragging the towel with them until I'm naked before him. His hands cup my ass, lifting me up. I wrap my legs around his waist, murmuring, "Addy's in our bed."

"I know." He turns and sets me on the counter, splaying my legs wide while leaning in with his hands braced on either side of the mirror. I reach down for his belt, pulling it free and tossing it on the ground with his discarded shirt. His mouth finds mine again in a hungry kiss that has my toes curling in anticipation.

I drag the heel of my hand up his length, loving the way he shudders and curses under his breath. "I missed you today," he whispers against my lips.

"We were together all day," I remind him with a smug smile.

"I missed this," he growls, his tongue darting out and sweeping over my lower lip. "That's all I've been thinking about all day."

His mouth travels across my cheek, to my jaw, where he peppers my skin with heated kisses while I desperately shove his pants and boxers down over his waist. He sucks in a breath when I fist his cock, pumping up and down in slow, rhythmic strokes.

He licks and sucks my neck where his mark is scarred on my skin, turning my insides molten. I splay my legs wider, whimpering as heat begins to pool at my core and every touch becomes too much.

"Please," I whisper into his hair, closing my eyes as his hands leave the wall and grip my thighs, pulling me to the end of the counter. In one hard thrust, he buries his cock inside of me, and I resist the urge to scream in pleasure.

My nails leave marks down his back as he moves inside of me, his mouth never once leaving my body. He steadies me with a hand on my back, his fingers digging into my skin as the other hand gropes and kneads my breasts.

We needed this—this moment where we are the only thing that matters. Our mate bond pulls tight as he pushes me toward the edge of release, every stroke of his cock hitting places that have me biting down on my lip so hard I nearly draw blood.

But then he pulls out, dragging me off the counter and whirling me around. I catch a glimpse of our reflections in the steamy mirror. Me, flustered, pink, my eyes heavy with lust, and him, wild and unburdened, looking at my body like it's a meal, and he's been starving his entire life.

I gasp when he grips my hips and enters me from behind. He groans loudly, not bothering to hold back. One of his hands snakes up to grip my neck, forcing me to watch in the mirror as he devastates my body in the most delicious way.

I am incapable of thought. Pleasure of the highest degree blinds me to everything else in the world. He leans forward, covering my body with his, pushing back my hair to tell me how much he loves me, how good I am and how good I feel and I'm… overcome.

I cry out, gripping the counter as my legs begin to shake. He thrusts into me hard at the very moment my inner walls clench and throb against his cock.

"Cole!" I rasp, gasping for breath as my vision blurs, and my body shimmers with pleasure. He pours himself into me, his hands planted on either side of the counter like he's shielding me from something–or someone. I feel safe and whole in his arms. I always have. I hate that I'd forgotten that for so long, that he was all I needed to heal.

He pulls out slowly, breathing fast. We look wild when I catch our reflections in the mirror again.

"You're in heat," he whispers, his voice clipped as I turn around to face him.

"How can you tell?"

"I'm your mate. It's something I just… feel."

I reach up to stroke his cheek. He already knows I'm not on any contraceptive tonics–not since we left Crescent Falls.

Maybe we should have been more careful, but the only thing on my mind, and apparently the only thing on his mind based on the fact he's still fully, unwaveringly, erect is… doing this again.

I take a deep breath. He does, too. Then his mouth is on mine again while I drag him to the ground and ride him into oblivion.

* * *

I WAKE UP WITH A START TO SUNLIGHT BEAMING THROUGH THE OPEN curtains. Music floats in through the closed bedroom door, but I'm totally alone—and starving. A few sounds of panic wane when I realize Addy isn't in bed and then hear him cooing somewhere nearby.

I slide out of bed, wincing at the slight ache between my thighs but smile at the memory of last night, when Cole and I went three rounds before finally dressing and climbing into bed.

But that must have been… hours ago, right? The sun is high in the sky, signaling noon, and my breasts are so full of milk I might actually explode.

I pull on a robe against the chill in the air and race into the main part of the cabin where Cole is on the couch and Addy is in his lap gnawing on his forearm while Cole scribbles in his notebook again.

"Good morning," he says brightly, smiling.

I snatch Addy out of his arms and pull up my shirt. He latches immediately, thank the Goddess.

With a sigh, I sink onto the couch beside Cole, who watches us with a soft smile.

"It's afternoon, you know."

"You needed the rest. I woke up to you topless and Addy enjoying free rein when it came to milk and figured we could give you a break for a few hours." He rises, setting his notebook down. "I grabbed some breakfast earlier and brought some back for you. Do you want coffee?"

"Yes, please," I breathe, leaning back against the cushions. Outside, I can hear the villagers of Silverhide going about their day—doing chores, feeding animals, and whatnot.

But the pounding of hammers echoes through my head.

"What's going on out there?"

"Ryan has some guys starting construction on the new pack house. He wants it done by the time snow falls, so they're working quickly. I might go help, but Ryatt is here and wants to talk to us."

"Ryatt's here?" I lean forward. "Why?"

"I don't know. I saw him talking to Ryan, and then he disappeared again. Ryan said he'd be coming back later and to expect a family meeting of some kind, but he brought your mom with him. She's with Sarah and the babies right now."

I smile despite the severity of our rough summer here and everything that happened. My mom doesn't have powers–like Cole. She's normal, but her gifts of caring for us are the greatest powers of all.

"I'll go see them after I've eaten something. Oh, don't fall asleep yet, you still have the other side–"

Addy yawns widely, smacking his lips as his eyes roll back in his head, but I settle him on my other breasts regardless, helping him latch and start massaging out the milk.

Cole sets a cup of coffee and a plate of eggs, potatoes, and bacon in front of me while Addy nurses himself to sleep. I reach for the table on the side of the couch and grab my own notebook and the copy of *The Book of Whispers*.

I can feel Cole watching me with interest as he tidies up in the kitchen.

I choose to ignore him, for now, knowing he's curious why I'm flipping through the pages of the book, which is written in a language none of us understand–even those who read Firestone.

"It predates the Firestones, but the symbols are similar," I tell him absently. "It's like the first written version of their language."

"So you're breaking the code?"

"Well, if Luke wasn't up in Celestoria doing Goddess-knows-what at the university up there, I'd call on him for help, but I've been putting this off for too long, and I need to get to work." I meet my mate's eyes. "I want to know how, and why, the forges were built, and I think the book will tell me that."

"But the book was made by a forge, wasn't it?"

"I'm pretty sure whoever wrote these spells threw it into the very forge that Aviva and I found. I think it's the same forge that made her bow. I think it was the first of the forges."

Cole leans against the counter as I turn back to the book, smiling to myself as my pen glides across my notebook, working out the roping symbols and deciphering their meanings.

"I love you, Misty," Cole says, turning back to his chores.

I feel the corners of my mouth twitching into a smile. "I love you, too."

33

NO GOING BACK

AVIVA

A CALM HAS FINALLY SETTLED OVER SILVERHIDE. THE SHIFT IN THE energy after we brought the kids home was palpable almost immediately.

Now, it's late afternoon. The sun is warm and bright, but the threat of rain hangs over the mountains where dark clouds simmer over the peaks. I walk toward the house where Sydney and Sarah are resting with their girls but stop when Maddy steps out of the house, her face bright and cheeks pink with excitement. She spots me and stops, smiling widely, and motions me over before reaching up to pull her long, dark red hair into a bun on the top of her head.

"How are they?"

"Oh, they're just fine," she smiles, smoothing the fabric of her yellow shirt over her midsection. "They're just beautiful. I'm so happy for Sarah and Sydney."

I look up at the second story windows, which are open to let in some of the last warm, early autumn air. "Do you think they'll be able to travel home soon?"

"Sydney is a little worried, of course, but Sarah's ready to get home. She wants to be in her bed, which I totally understand. Ryatt's been bouncing around all day, but he's supposed to come to take us all back to Crescent City. Sarah doesn't think her powers can spirit us home on her own."

I nod, sighing as the clouds begin to creep toward the sun, casting long shadows over the village center.

"I was just about to go up to your house to love on Lexa for a while." She smiles, lovingly squeezing my arm.

"Please do," I reply, taking a shallow breath. "I'm trying to find Logan right now, but he seems to have disappeared."

"I saw him running around with a few of the boys from the village about twenty minutes. They looked like they were heading to the creek." She turns from me, walking in the direction of my house on the far edge of the village. Behind us, hammers split the air as the first level of the new pack house rises, at least a dozen men working around the clock to have the first version of it built by the time the snow flies.

I squint at the sun again, trying to gauge how much longer we have until that happens. It's been exceedingly warm so far, after all.

I tuck my hands in the pockets of the flowy, dark blue dress hanging from my shoulders and turn back toward the creek following the road out of the village. Within minutes, I hear the tell-tale sign of little boys splashing in the creek and spot Logan a few yards away from where the other boys are knee-deep, looking for frogs. Logan has a long stick in his hands, jabbing it into the water to overturn rocks. He looks up as I approach but doesn't stop his little game.

"What are you up to?" I ask in Firestone.

He shrugs in a very teenage way. "Nothing, really."

"Can we talk for a minute?"

He looks up at me then glances at the other boys. Eventually, he nods, tosses his stick into the water and follows me through the village. I walk with him in silence up to the lake, sitting down on the dock with my toes dusting the water. A few other people dot the lakes edge fishing or having picnics, but otherwise we're alone.

I haven't had much of a chance to talk to him since we got home. He was exhausted, and honestly, I think a little traumatized after what he went through with Maeve.

"How are you doing?" I ask.

He lies down on his back, his face tilted toward the sun. Freckles dot his nose and cheeks, the sun casting shadows over the sharp planes of his cheeks. He'll be a handsome man when he's grown up, I can already tell.

But it's hard to imagine what ten or twenty years from now might look like. Logan's silent for a while. He crosses his arms over his chest and sighs deeply before asking, "Is there anything that can be done about that baby?"

I smirk. "You ignored my question."

"I'm fine."

I take him in, noticing the healing burns on his hands and forearms.

"Maeve is very powerful, but she's young. The family has been discussing how to go about her future training."

"She burned down a barn just by sneezing."

"Well, consider yourself lucky you don't have the same powers. They seem rather inconvenient."

He keeps his eyes closed, but his mouth twitches into a smile.

"Seriously, Logan. What you did for her—for us... you didn't have to go after her like that, rescue her."

"I picked up the scent of the healer and thought it was odd that she went into the woods, so I followed."

"You shifted."

He opens one eye to look at me before closing it again. "I did."

"You're only twelve. That's very young to come into your wolf powers."

"Not in Emberfyll."

I look at him, hoping he's going to say more, but the ghost of a smile on his lips fades to a tight line. His expression sags, and I know that's it. It's painful for him to think about his homeland, let alone talk about it.

"One day, when you're grown, you can go back," I tell him. "One day, when you've time to train and hone your skills, you can return. You were a prince there, weren't you? Your parents were an Alpha and Luna–"

"There will be nothing left by then," he cuts in.

"Can you tell me what happened?"

Logan doesn't move. He lies in silence for what feels like several minutes before he sits up and takes off his shoes to dip his feet in the water, like me. He grips the edge of the dock, his eyes locked on the dark blue surface, and says, "I don't understand."

"You don't understand what I asked? I know my Firestone isn't perfect–"

"I don't understand how everything went bad so fast," he says under his breath. "I went to bed one night, and the next morning, my mother was hurrying me to a boat. Dad met us there. I'd heard rumors of war and sickness but I didn't think about it so much. It didn't seem real."

Because he's a child. Of course, that wouldn't mean much to him. I resist the urge to lay a hand on his shoulder as he continues, "I don't remember the journey on the boat."

"Where were you going?"

He shakes his head. "I don't know. There's islands around Emberfyll, but we'd been on the water for days, maybe… two weeks. Mom was sick, and Dad wouldn't let me see her. I knew it was sickness that killed off those packs in our territory without him having to confirm it. And just like the morning we left, one night I went to sleep, and then I woke up in the water, alone, with nothing but water all around me and darkness. No stars, no moon, just water."

I lick my lips in thought.

He says, "My uncle was a bad man who hated us, but he was the Alpha King, and he had an army on his side. He was never supposed to be Alpha King. My dad was, but he banished my dad and his loyal-ists. That was before I was born."

"Is your uncle still the Alpha King of Emberfyll?"

"If the sickness didn't get him, yes, but I remember my parents would talk in the evenings about me... about how there were more and more people who wanted my father on the throne because of me, his heir. They called me a promise of Emberfyll's future when things felt so dark and hopeless."

I reach over and squeeze his hand. He doesn't move.

"Ryan and I talked, and I think you should start training your powers. Train like our warriors do."

"It doesn't matter–"

"It does, Logan. You're twelve, but you can shift. You'll have nine extra years of experience in your wolf form by the time you turn twenty-one. One day, you can go home. You can fight for your people —for what's left, if you choose."

"And until then?" he asks, looking up at me.

"You'll have a home here with us–with me, and Ryan, and our pack."

He slides his hand away from mine. I try not to wince at the rejection.

"Logan–I'm not saying you need to call me mom, or anything like that, but you're old enough to know and understand that our people, our rulers, they know nothing about Emberfyll. It's not on any maps, even the ancient ones. All we know is that the sea off the coast of Tarsian is full of magic–full of chaos and demons meant to keep us away from something. You survived it, and I believe you're the only one who ever has... which should mean something to you. That means you could go back when you're ready, and you've trained for it. And we will help you."

He swallows hard, his eyes on the water. "And the girl?"

I blink. "Who?"

"The little girl with brown hair. How does she factor into all of this?"

I shake my head, unsure what he's trying to say. "Brie?"

He nods, his eyes distant and hazy as he absently rubs his chest.

"Brie is... Maeve's sister," I tell him, tilting my head. "She's five–"

"She called for me to find Maeve," he whispers to himself, and then rises, and walks away.

I watch him go, staring after him in confusion.

* * *

"I wouldn't take it personally," Ryan says, moving around the kitchen table with Lexa strapped to his chest, fast asleep. He pours Ryatt another cup of strong coffee before moving on to my mug. "He's a kid."

"He's a teenager," Ryatt says around the rim of his mug.

I frown at both men. "He's not a teenager yet."

"Well, you grew up with sisters, so you know practically nothing about teenage boys, or boys in general," my mate adds, lifting a brow in my direction. "They're weird and ornery."

"This has nothing to do with him being… weird," I reply, scoffing a bit.

Ryatt chuckles, crossing his legs as he leans back in his seat. "You made the right call by telling him he can't go back until he's grown up."

My head snaps in Ryatt's direction. "Did I? Because it seemed to really upset him," I growl.

"Even I have no idea what's past the sea, nor does anyone from Tarsian. When word about Logan's arrival reached us, Ella had the mystics look into it, and they came up with nothing."

"I find it hard to believe the Firestone witches didn't explore the ocean that bordered their kingdom back in the day," Ryan says from the kitchen.

I agree, but Ryatt doesn't seem that convinced. "I don't think they could," he says before taking another drink. "I think they were barred from it, which is where the lore about the monsters and demons in the water came about."

"You think there's some kind of… barrier between here and Emberfyll?" I ask.

"I think there's another veil," Ryatt replies, setting his mug down.

Ryan turns to look at us. "That's impossible. Your own mate took down the veil."

"Around Eastonia, yes." Ryatt taps his fingers on the table, checking his watch. He's supposed to be leaving with Maddy, Sarah, Sydney, and the twins soon. He offered to take Misty and Cole back to Crescent Falls as well, but they declined, deciding they're going to stay until after the Harvest Festival.

"Whatever it is, it's going to prevent him from returning. But, he's here, and being looked after by our family now. That puts him in a position to go through warrior training and the best schooling we can offer."

Ryan and I look at each other. I turn back to Ryatt, "You don't think he's too young to start training now?"

"I think it would be good for him. He needs to learn our language and customs, as well. When he's sixteen, he can come to Moonrise to train with the royal army. Until then, do your best with him here."

Ryatt stands, quietly thanking Ryan for the coffee, and says he'll be back for the festival, and leaves.

Just like that.

Ryan purses his lips as I sink back into my seat, hanging my head in my hands. I feel him come up behind me and lay a hand on my shoulder, squeezing. "We'll make it work. He's a good kid."

"He wants to go home," I whisper.

"He can't. Not yet."

UNITY

Aviva

Fall

THE AIR IS CRISP AND SCENTED WITH SMOKE AS I WALK THROUGH THE maze of brightly colored canvas tents. Lexa, dressed in furs to stay warm and beaded booties I worked tirelessly on the past few weeks, looks around, turning her head side to side like a little owl, taking in every new sight and sound.

This is the largest Harvest Festival I've ever been to. So large, in fact, that the festival stretches for over three miles. Just two days ago, this sacred place was nothing more than a grassy field. Now, it explodes with life, color, and the promise of a comfortable winter where food and supplies will be far from scarce.

We pass a tent selling apples covered in sticky, hardened sugar. I drop a few coins into an elderly woman's hand in exchange for the treat, letting Lexa paw and mouth it while continuing our exploration.

I've been Luna of Silverhide for just over a year, and Queen of the

Deadlands for just as long, but I'm not used to being recognized by anyone outside of Silverhide and Endova. Since we arrived two days ago with our pack, however, I've been stopped repeatedly, fawned over, and often blessed by weathered hands.

People stare at me as I walk by, sometimes whispering to their companions and pointing, giving me a wide berth, but others are braver, willing to reach out to touch me, to talk to me.

Still, I feel like an imposter. I'm sure the feeling will pass with time, just like the odd sensation of the new, so far untrained and likely undiscovered, powers in my blood.

"Where'd you get that?" Ryan asks, plucking the apple on a stick out of my hand and taking the biggest bite imaginable. Lexa squawks at having her snack taken from her despite the fact she doesn't have any teeth. "The juice is the best part, see? Isn't it better?" Ryan holds the apple out for her to lick and gnaw at the raw apple beneath the layer of sugar, smiling as Lexa's eyes go wide and she bounces in my arms, her mittens sticky with sugar as she grasps the apple with her iron grip. "She's going to be bouncing off the walls," he laughs, meeting my eyes.

"Good, then she'll have a nice, long nap afterward." I adjust her weight in my arms and scan the dozen or so tents we spent two days setting up near the center of the festival. Our pack takes up residence here, trading and selling their wares.

I step to the side as a cart full of rolled furs and stacks of cut leather passes, pulled by two wolves. A young woman wearing traditional Teshkan robes steps past, carrying two bundles of fabric under her arms as she leaves Freya's stall. I let out a deep breath as I watch the gathered crowd and our pack members. It seems like I've been holding my breath for weeks.

"We'll make it through winter and then some," Ryan says, following my gaze with a sigh. "I'm not sure how we pulled this off with everything else we had going on this summer."

"The Goddess took pity on us," I whisper loud enough for only me to hear.

A trio of men from one of the newly settled packs in the Deadlands walk over to us to speak to my mate about grain or something, I have no idea because I turn and walk to the largest tent in our camp. Unlike the others, there are no stalls attached to sell goods. I pull back the flap and step inside, sighing against the rush of warmth and the smell of astringent.

Cole leans on the side of a worktable with two small children wiggling side by side on top of it as he checks their ears. Their mother watches with fascination, eyeing the otoscope, which I doubt she's ever seen before.

"Hey," Misty says. Her tone rushes as she brushes past. "What are you guys up to?"

I turn to her, watching as she packs a bag with her notebooks and several pens.

"Just killing time before the ceremony tonight," I reply, nerves I've been trying to tamp down all day creeping back to the surface of my subconscious.

"Want to come with me? I'm finally getting some time with the warriors from Teshka today. There's a few Tarsian warriors who married into the pack after the war who I'm interviewing today, too."

I glance at Cole and the line of parents and children waiting to have exams and nod, switching Lexa to my other hip. "Sure. Where's Addy?"

"He's with my mom. I have no idea where she is." Misty laughs, tucking a strand of golden hair behind her ear before flinging her bag over her shoulder. "Let's go!"

The sun begins to set on the festival as I walk from tent to tent with Misty, watching and listening as she interviews warriors who fought in the war, writing down their stories. Lexa falls asleep in my arms at one point, but I know the rest will be short lived.

As time ticks by, and the stars come out to play, my nerves grow stronger, my heartbeat more rapid, and it becomes almost impossible to focus as I go back to the Silverhide camp in search of my mate.

People are clearing out of the festival to gather at the ceremonial hill for another night of speeches, celebrations, and a few weddings. It's usually my favorite part of the day while at the festival, but this feels different... because I will be the one standing on the hill calling to action an entire generation of people to join a cause that died centuries ago.

"Are you ready?" Ryan asks in our private tent, which is big enough for a few bedrolls and our personal belongings.

I have no mirror to look in, no idea what I look like right now, but I can tell based on the look on his face that I must be pale and nervous.

I twist my curls around my face and smooth the fabric of my dress–Endovian made for shifting. It's simple. Something I'd wear day-to-day while hunting.

I am queen of this land, but I wear no precious jewels or fine fabrics. My feet are bare, my skin exposed and freckled from a long summer in the sun where my hands grew more calloused from hard work and the repeated use of my bow.

I will never change, even with new power in my blood.

"Yes," I reply, swallowing back my nerves. I grab my gilded bow and slide it along my back, following my mate, my Alpha, out of our tent.

I catch a glimpse of Maddy in the crowd as we make our way to the hill. Several of our extended family members came to the Dead-lands for the festival. Maddy loves it, and she's currently wrangling Lexa for us, which I'm grateful for, but the second we reach the top of the hill I spot Ryatt and Ella waiting in the shadows.

Ryatt's eyes burn like liquid silver as they meet mine. Ella holds Maeve, who smiles widely at me, reaching for me as she leans out of Ella's arms.

Something deep within my soul tells me to take Maeve, so I do. She clutches my leather dress, sliding her fingers into the loops around my shoulders and hangs on as I turn toward the crowd.

I scan the line of brides awaiting the ceremony under tonight's full moon, their mates waiting nearby. I look at the Alphas of the new packs and the patriarchs from the tribes, one being my father, who gives me a nod and a small smile, just for me to see.

I'm reminded of who I once was. A fiery, arrogant girl who wore shells in her hair and slept outside most nights to hide from her demons.

Now, I'm a queen. A warrior queen, and the day has come to call upon my army to prepare for whatever the future holds, whatever *her* future holds.

I smile down at Maeve as moonlight dusts over us. She looks up at me with her strange, blue-green eyes. They shine like sea glass, shimmering with power that seems unreal if not totally impossible.

She's the only one of her kind.

And it's my duty–my Goddess given destiny–to protect her.

"We've gathered here to mark the five hundredth harvest." My voice booms over the crowd. "And what a prosperous year it has been for our people of the sacred Deadlands. Look around at your neighbors, your loved ones, your friends. Look at those who fought in the war, who stayed behind to care for the sick, the injured, and the orphaned. Tell me, what do you see?"

Murmurs float through the crowd. Excitement simmers, creating tension as tight as my bow string.

"I know what I see. I see a strong kingdom. A kingdom that has stood the test of time–stood against the terrors of a world run by kings of stolen magic and the old gods of death and despair they worshipped, anointing themselves in the blood of the enslaved, our blood. Our ancestors' blood. Those days are over."

Shouts of joy ring out through the crowd. I feel Ryan's pride through our bond.

"On the rise of this full moon, I challenge you to look around and see what we have built, and most importantly, why." I adjust Maeve's weight, swallowing hard. "We've heard the legends, the prophecies passed down from our ancestors to the youngests' ears around our fires, in our homes, in our temples. We know our history. We are descendants of the survivors who did not bend their knee to the wicked kings and their ungodly magic. But we must not be complacent, not after what we went through last year."

The tension rises as howls and shouts ring out through the crowd, nearly everyone nodding in agreement. In the distance, a drumbeat begins—thrumming like my heartbeat.

"We have always been a land of equality—our women just as fierce as our men." Women shout their agreement, and I smile. "That will never change, but change is coming. We hear it in the wind, don't we? We see it in the land—in the trees and the mountains. The prophecy came to fruition with the birth of this child." I step forward until moonlight illuminates Maeve entirely. "The Firestone's will rise again, and we will, too."

A thunderous applause echoes in my blood as people stand and shout for Maeve, our future queen.

"And we will fight for her!" I shout. "We will fight for the Deadlands! We will not allow another false god to reign terror on our lands or others!"

I'm trembling, my untrained powers desperately trying to ignite, but I hold them back.

Lowering Maeve back onto my hip, I also lower my voice, looking down at the brides, at the women and young girls in the crowd.

"I am not just the Queen of the Deadlands. I am the commander of its army—the army will be built to lie in wait for when we're called to fight for the Goddess and Her people. An army of warriors. An army of *women*. Who will stand with me?"

A hush rolls through the crowd. It's so silent I can hear the numerous fires in the city of tents crackling. No one moves for what feels like an eternity. Soft whispers of shocked conversation drift through the chilled autumn breeze, and that little voice in me that's been warning me all day snickers.

No one will stand to fight with me. Not the mothers clutching their infants. Not the brides in their dresses. Not their mothers, sisters, aunts, or grandmothers.

But just when I give up hope, a girl of what I imagine is only eight stands and walks through the crowd, which parts for her.

She holds up a hand. "I will fight."

The brides watch her, and then, one by one, begin to rise.

All across the crowd, women rise. Some hold babies. Some rest an arm on the swell of their pregnant stomachs. Some clutch their mates' hands.

And the hushed silence is replaced by a roar of unity–the roar of my army.

3 5

HER STORY

Misty

Crescent Falls

I TOSS MY KEYS ON THE COUNTER AS I COME THUNDERING THROUGH the kitchen, sweat lining my brow. "Cole? COLE!"

"I'm upstairs!" he calls out as I sprint around the corner into the hallway where the foyer opens up, spilling wintery sunlight through the bay windows overlooking the curving staircase. Snow falls in thick clumps, covering the ground. Two suitcases rest near the front door, but upstairs, I hear Cole talking to Addy and the sound of zippers closing.

I trip on each step in my haste to get upstairs, carrying a bundle of papers in my arms. A few notes come loose, floating through the air behind me as I rush into our bedroom.

Cole turns to me with another suitcase, arching his brows. "I didn't think you'd be back until this afternoon–"

"I finished it," I rasp, breathless, thrusting the stack of printer paper into his full hands. All two-thousand pages, front and back, stare up at him, and he looks down in shock.

"How?"

"I just–I just got it done," I pant, glancing at Addy, who's happily gnawing on his fist in his playpen. "I just… something clicked. It's done. I owe Dad a shit ton of printer paper and ink, but it's finished–I–"

Cole takes the papers from my hands and sits on the edge of the bed, thumbing through them one by one.

I stand in total silence, my heart beating out of rhythm. This is all I've done for three months. Writing. Writing. Writing until the tips of my fingers were raw and my laptop was pleading with me to give up.

I conducted dozens–no, hundreds–of interviews this summer. I traveled to Veiled Valley three times to meet with their strange, ageless historian to learn all I could about the old kings, specifically King Kane and his predecessors. I traveled all over until I'd gone through six notebooks, each of them spilling with sticky-notes, napkins, pieces of leather–whatever I could get my hands on to write our history down.

And now it's done.

Cole smooths his hand over the title page where my name is printed in bold.

He looks up at me, smiling faintly. "There's no title."

"I have no space in my brain to name it. Not yet. But it's not just about the war last year. It's about–about everything–everything from the beginning. What Aviva now remembers about the fall of the Firestone witches, how the kings came into power, the veil, how the Goddess played into the use of the water to bring the magic into Maatua so someone could find it again and harness it to help Eastonia. Then, of course, the war. Our story. Stories of the warriors and the families they had to leave behind. The order members who got trapped by Richard's magic–" I suck in a breath. "It's all in there. Everything is in there."

He blinks up at me. I'm sure I'm red in the face. I nearly drove my car into a ditch three times driving back from the castle in my haste to show him what I'd done.

I wring my hands, smoothing out my aching muscles as he rises and presses a kiss to my forehead. Addy sees this and chuckles, which makes me smile.

"I'm so proud of you–"

"Don't be proud yet. Dad and Ryatt are discussing my options for publishing, of course. I'm tempted to take my name off it."

"Why?"

"Because it doesn't feel like it's mine. It's our history, yes, our story woven between the pages, but this is the story of everything as we know it to be true. It doesn't belong to me. It belongs to everyone. It'll be free. No one has to pay a dime to read it, but I doubt most people would want to…. It's long, and dry, and boring but–I did it."

Cole stares at me, his gray eyes slightly glassy. "You did it."

I take a deep breath, laughing at myself for acting so insane, but I haven't even begun to process what this means.

But, I don't have much time because we're supposed to catch a boat to Maatua this evening to celebrate Solstice with the entire family.

Three hours later, I'm standing on the bow of a ship watching my mate talk to a group of our fellow travelers. Cole has a knack for making friends everywhere he goes these days and dropping into his doctor role the second he thinks someone looks too pale or worn out. Right now, he's giving the mother of a child who just threw up over the railing some tips about treating seasickness while I hold our son, who's actively tangling his grubby fingers in my freshly blown-out hair.

Addy's six months old now. We left Silverhide three months ago and traveled for a few weeks, spending some time in Moonrise, then Veiled Valley, then coming home for a week or two before traveling to Tarsian for Georgia and Declan's wedding.

All the while, I've been glued to my laptop, but now I'm watching the shoreline of Crescent Falls drift away as the sky fills with stars.

A day from now, we'll be in Maatua, soaking in the hot sun and watching the tide roll in while the kids hunt for seashells and track sand through the beach house that once belonged to my grandma and grandpa.

Cole saunters back over to us with his hands in his pockets looking smug. I roll my eyes. "Do you always have to do that?"

"This is the life you signed up for when you married someone who wanted to become a doctor."

"I was forced into this, if you want to get technical," I remind him with a cat-like grin.

Now he's the one rolling his eyes as he leans against the railing to watch the waves rushing against the ship. "It could be worse. I could be the Alpha King of Tarsian."

"That's true," I laugh, blowing out my breath. I honestly can't imagine how different our life would be if he'd chosen to stay in that role, to rule, be the Alpha he was born to be.

I'm glad he gave that up. He didn't want it—never did. We'd be spending our nights in the company of his advisors and dealing with conflicts instead of eating take-out and watching whatever new reality show is premiering.

I smile to myself. "I talked to Sarah today. They're already in Maatua."

"Oh, yeah?"

"I think Cosette drove them out of the house a few days early. I know the kids drive her nuts."

Cole laughs, shaking his head. "What do you think she does in that big house when she's alone? When Sydney, Sarah, and the kids aren't home?"

"I think she sits in the atrium in the quiet," I smile. "I know I would."

Cole reaches out to lay his hand over my belly.

"Am I showing?"

"Not yet. Don't worry."

"It better not be twins."

"There's just one in there." His eyes are heavy with pride and excitement I'm still trying to feel. Our marathon that night in Silver-hide did, in fact, produce another baby, but I'm only three months along. I'm not feeling sick, thank the Goddess. In fact, I feel totally fine.

"Are you still planning on keeping it a secret for a while?" he asks.

I sigh, turning back to the water while Addy tugs on my earrings. "Well, your mom already knows. So does your sister. Only because they can keep a secret."

"Your mom will tell the entire world the second she finds out," Cole laughs, and I nod.

"She can't help it. She won't be satisfied until she has a hundred grandkids running around."

"What if we told her as a Solstice present?"

"What about the other presents we got them?"

"Just add it on. You know they'll be ecstatic for us." He ropes an arm around my shoulder, turning us toward the door leading into the ship. "Your cheeks are red, Misty."

"Well, it is winter."

"Let's go inside, get some dinner."

I follow my mate into the ship, letting my mind wander, finally allowing myself to bring up old memories.

I huddle Addy close–the baby neither of us expected. The baby that unraveled Cole's heart and stitched him back together again in the end. The baby forged by force and hardship, who ended up being the love of our lives.

And then our girl, because I know it's a girl this time just like I knew Addy would be a boy. She's being born into a different world than Addy was, then I was, honestly. She'll know peace and safety. She was conceived out of the purest kind of love and so desperately wanted it brings tears to my eyes when I think about it.

Because she wouldn't be here if I hadn't fought for Cole, and if he hadn't fought for me, neither of them would.

Our room is a suite, of course, thanks to my dad. While my mate does make a decent living as a resident doctor at the hospital, I still tap into the family funds. I don't care, honestly. I definitely paid my dues during the war even though Dad titters and groans when his credit card statements come in, and I smirk when Cole opens the door to our suite for the night and takes in the finery of it all.

Next year will be a year of change, but in a good way. Josie will be here in the spring, most likely, if not the early weeks of summer. Cole and Sydney's fancy pediatric clinic will be done with construction around that same time, and Cole will be done with his residency and moving on to private practice, which means no more late nights at the hospital and days away from his family.

Later that night, in bed, with Addy sleeping in a little crib on the far side of the room, Cole strokes my fingers, drawing lazy circles over the back of my hand while the ship does its best to rock us to sleep. We've been talking about my book for an hour in hushed whispers.

"What are you going to write next?"

"Nothing for a long time. My fingers are like an old woman's, I can barely bend them."

He chuckles softly. "When you're ready to get back to it, I am."

"I'm sure Dad will have me busy with pack history," I sigh. "And Wellington wants me to teach a few of their entry level history classes, but I haven't given them an answer–"

"What are you going to write for you, Misty?"

I think about it for a long time. I think about it still as Cole falls asleep waiting for my answer.

I think I've always known what story would come next–the story I left out in the book I just finished.

The story that started it all.

I imagine her again, walking up those front steps in that little skirt and her sorry excuse for a suitcase. I think about the secret she kept for so long, and the trails of those early days as a breeder.

She had no idea what the future would hold for the family she started, for her two children and the four grandchildren that came after.

Her story is the most important because Isla's story both started, and ended, the wars that plagued our kind and paved the road to a future of peace for generations to come.

"I'm going to write her story next," I whisper to the darkness, to the stars blinking high above the boat and the water all around us. "And it's going to be a fucking bestseller."

WHAT THE FUTURE HOLDS

Misty
Ten Years Later

SUNLIGHT FANS THROUGH THE KITCHEN WINDOWS, HIGHLIGHTING THE frost coating the glass. I blink, shielding my eyes as the sun drops below the tree line and the light in the room shifts, fading to a deep gold that paints the kitchen table and the mess my children left behind in their haste to get to school this morning.

It's a quiet late afternoon. It's my favorite time of day, actually. The house is still and silent–the calm before the storm... which is running up the driveway right now, pushing and shoving toward the front door.

The door swings open, the chilly late afternoon air carrying two small voices through the foyer and hallway.

"Mom! MOM!" Addy's voice echoes over the sound of heavy winter fabric dropping to the ground, probably in a wet heap. "MOM!"

"I'm in the kitchen!" I call out, smiling to myself as I stick my coffee mug in the microwave. Two sets of footsteps thunder in my direction, and then I'm surrounded by blond hair and overlapping, excited voices.

"Addy pushed me off the bus!" Josie whines, pointing an accusatory finger at Adrian, who scowls down at her.

"I did not! She fell off because she was messing around!"

"You PUSHED me!"

"All right, all right!" I rush out. The microwave beeps, and both kids look up at me, suddenly remembering they're hungry.

Two plates of chicken nuggets later, I'm dialing for pizza delivery when the garage door rolling up sends a hum through the house. Addy looks up from his homework, his blond curls dancing around his face. He has light gray eyes like Cole. He's made in Cole's image, actually, his son through and through.

But where Adrian is quiet, stoic, and serious... Josie is none of those things. She's boisterous and loud, always chatting and unable to stop moving, even in her sleep. She leaps out of her seat at the kitchen table, her math homework falling to the ground. Her bright, nearly white blonde hair falls out of the braid I spent ages perfecting this morning as she races toward the garage, screaming, "DAD'S HOME!"

Addy rolls his eyes but hops out of his seat, racing after his sister to bombard their dad with attention.

This is our usual routine. The kids come home from school, go a little nuts, settle down to do their homework after an hour of prodding, and sometimes pleading, and then Cole comes home and ruins the quiet vibe. Still, he comes around the corner with both kids hanging off him and presses a kiss to my lips–and today it's not a quick peck.

I have the sudden urge to slide my hands over the kids eyes when Cole leans into the kiss, deepening it, my cheeks flaring with heat, but then he pulls away and says, "Hey."

"H-Hi," I stammer, blushing deeply. "Nice to see you, too."

He narrows his eyes, giving me a secret, sly smile. "Are the kids ready?"

"Ready for what?"

The kids have already scurried back to the kitchen table to rush through their homework, but Cole sets his briefcase down on the kitchen island, shaking his head as he laughs, "You forgot, didn't you?"

"Forgot what?" I lean on the counter, crossing my arms over my chest. "It's not our anniversary for another couple of weeks."

"Solstice break isn't until next week," Josie says pointedly, tucking her hair behind her ears.

Cole arches a brow at her as she playfully narrows her light blue eyes–identical to mine–mimicking his expression. "Kids, go pack an overnight bag. You're staying at Grandma and Grandpa's house tonight."

"Really?!" Josie leaps out of her chair and jumps up and down then runs out of the kitchen with Adrian hot on her heels.

Quiet settles throughout the kitchen. Cole runs his fingers through his hair and fixes me with a look. "You haven't checked your phone all day, have you?"

"You know I have a deadline next week." I smirk, rolling my eyes. "Why are you being so secretive?"

"Misty," he laughs, leaning toward me. He cups my cheek, swiping his thumb over my skin with a sigh. "Happy birthday, sweetheart."

My lips pop open in a laugh but promptly snap shut again in confusion. "I forgot my own birthday?"

"You've been writing non-stop for weeks," he says with a tender smile. "I did tell you happy birthday this morning before I left for work–"

"I was barely awake," I murmur, and he laughs again.

"The flowers I sent to the house?"

I step out of his arms. "I thought those were an apology for getting the kids so riled up they didn't go to bed until ten last night."

"You need to start reading the card," he smiles, pressing a kiss to my forehead. "Go get dressed. We're going out."

* * *

TWO HOURS LATER, DRESSED IN A SPARKLY BLACK DRESS I'D BEEN SAVING for a special occasion, I clutch Cole's arm as we speed toward the penthouse restaurant in the tallest building in Crescent Falls. The elevator jolts to a stop, and we step out, greeted by a hostess almost immediately who offers to take my coat.

The place is washed in dark red and lush gold, creating a luxurious, and expensive, ambiance that's a stark contrast to the brightly colored walls and finger-smudged surfaces at our home, where I'd planned on ordering a pizza tonight... on my own birthday... which I completely forgot about.

I'm normally not this careless. In my defense, I've been rather busy.

"I think a celebration is in order," Sydney says as he pours four glasses of champagne, raising his glass. "To my baby sister's thirty-second birthday. I honestly didn't think you'd make it this far."

I playfully glare, and Cole hums with laughter beside me, but Sydney remains standing, his glass still raised.

"In all seriousness, happy birthday, Misty."

Sarah beams across from me, "Happy birthday! And congratulations, by the way."

Cole presses a kiss to my temple. I squirm, blushing harder than I ever have before. "Don't congratulate me yet," I grumble into my champagne.

"Why not?" Sydney drains his champagne and sinks into his seat, throwing a lazy arm over his mate's shoulder. "Your book is already the talk of the kingdom. I'm sure people will be lining the streets to get their hands on it next month."

For the thousandth time in the last... five years since I decided to do this, to write the story of our grandparents, I'm wondering if I made the right decision.

"Grandma Isla would be the first in line to buy it," Sarah smiles, her violet eyes holding my gaze.

"I know she would," I reply, my lips tightening into a smile.

Dinner moves on, the conversation flowing through my upcoming publishing date, the family's plans to meet in Maatua this year for Solstice, and what our brother, sister-in-law, and cousins are doing in Eastonia.

A chocolate cake is brought out with thirty-two candles, of course. I make a wish, the same wish I make every year.

That my family remains safe, and at peace, and that our grandparents didn't die for nothing.

When we reach our house again, it's very late. The kids are tucked up and hopefully asleep at the castle with their grandparents and their cousins–Sydney and Sarah's children–and we're… alone.

But even after another birthday celebration with Cole that left us tangled and breathless in our sheets, I can't sleep, not with the full moon creeping through the windows casting moonlight across my face.

I wrap myself in a robe, slipping my feet into slippers, and head downstairs. On instinct, I peek into the kids' rooms. I know they're spending the night with my parents, but this is my usual routine when I feel like this–when I feel this tug. When I feel her call–and answer.

The heated covered porch off the kitchen beckons to me as I step outside and shake out one of the blankets I left out here earlier today. I sink onto the wicker couch and cover my legs with the blanket, closing my eyes for a moment as the crisp air mixes with the electric heater near my feet.

'*Did you have a nice time?*'

'*I did,*' I answer, rolling my neck. '*I forgot it was my birthday today.*' I smile at the memory. '*We've all been so busy lately and… it just slipped my mind.*'

She laughs softly–a sound I desperately miss. '*Time moves quickly when you have young children. I blinked, and Ella and Isaac were teenagers, and I was closing in on my forties.*'

'*How's Grandpa?*'

'*The same,*' she says with a knowing smile in her voice. '*He's wondering when things are going to get interesting again. He believes the new road system your aunt and uncle are completing in Eastonia will bring them some… interesting situations.*'

I hum a laugh, shaking my head, not daring to open my eyes. '*We haven't been to Eastonia in a few years, honestly.*'

'Are you still afraid?'

'Yes,' I answer. I could have written a book about everything we know, and don't know, about Eastonia, the supposed birthplace of our kind and the ancient magic still lurking untouched beneath its forests, lakes, and sand. I could have written my story–told the truths that have weighed heavy on my heart for the last decade.

But her story needed to come first.

I swallow hard, my powers prickling over my skin. *'Grandma,'* I say into the ether tugging us together for this single moment in time, *'Can you tell me if everything will be okay? That the kids–all of them–will have it... easier than we did?'*

Grandma sighs. *'No, honey. I don't know. All I know, all that's written in the stars, is that change is coming.'*

I open my eyes and turn to her but find nothing but an empty wicker chair coated in moonlight and a whisper of her blue light fading back into the stars.

I return to the house shortly thereafter and slip into bed beside Cole. He curls his body around mine, slipping back into sleep with a comforting sigh.

All is right in the world tonight. The stars are out to play against a cold, winter sky. Downstairs, our Solstice tree is still half decorated. I need to go grocery shopping. I'm supposed to volunteer at their school for the Solstice market....

I open my eyes to waves brushing against the shore. For a moment, I think I'm in Maatua... but it's all wrong. It's too quiet here. No luxury beach houses line the coast. No surfers speed across the waves ahead of me and behind me, nothing but... destruction lines the base of the rolling, scorched hills.

I turn back to the water, confused, in time to see a young woman with light brown hair pull herself out of the surf, cursing in fury.

She angrily shoves her hair out of her face, panting and spitting water before screaming in what I can only describe as rage and anguish.

"LOGAN?! MAEVE?!"

She falls to her knees, sinking her hands into the wet sand and hangs her head.

Familiarity rushes through my system. I know those soft curls starting to spring loose from her salty hair. I know the brown eyes and rosy cheeks as she lifts her face to the sun and screams.

My heart hammers. This is a vision. I'm seeing a glimpse of a future I don't understand.

In my current reality, this woman is only *fourteen*.

"Brie?" I rasp, but then I'm pulled out of the vision, dropping back into my body, my bed, with my mate's arms wrapped around my waist in a loving embrace.

37

HE'S BACK, BUT NOT TO STAY

Aviva

"Line up," I whisper against ten-year-old Lexa's ear. "Breathe in… release." An arrow splits the cool spring air in two. A soft squeak whispers toward us as a squirrel falls from its perch on a nearby cottonwood tree. I squeeze her waist in silent congratulations while she beams, her dark-blue eyes wide and round. "Good job." I grin, giving her a pat on the back. "Go get it."

Lexa takes off in a blur of red curls and homespun textiles in soft creams and browns that match the melting snow. In the distance, over the shadowed mountains, plumes of gray smoke stretch toward the first inklings of the sunset.

Lexa bounds back to me, squirrel in hand. I tie it to her belt and help her put her b aow back in her halter while seven-year-old Nora puts the finishing touches on the snowman she's been building for the last hour.

"Nora, come on!" Lexa calls out, motioning for her little sister to hurry up, but Nora has never listened to anyone in her life.

I smile as the girls start to bicker back and forth. It reminds me of my little sisters, who aren't so little anymore. Shoshanna married during the last harvest festival and now lives in one of the new packs that settled nearby, and Lora is seventeen and in warrior training. They dote on their nieces whenever they visit, but it's been a quiet winter. Now, spring is fast on its way.

I shift, taking a moment to find my footing in the slush beneath my paws. Lexa helps Nora onto my back before climbing up, wrapping her arms around her little sister's waist while Nora clutches the halter strapped around my chest.

I carry my girls back to Silverhide against the warm light of the sunset, climbing over the mountains and dropping back into the village, which has grown immensely over the past decade.

The new pack house rises before us, smoke funneling from its chimney carrying the smell of dinner. Yes, we all still eat in the pack house. Yes, we still farm and hunt to get us through the winters, but the road leading into Silverhide is now paved, connecting us to the other packs that settled in the Deadlands from the Roguelands, Crescent Falls, and beyond.

We reach the house tucked in the outskirts of the village, and the girls jump off my back, racing up the steps. I shift back to my human form just in time to hear Lexa exclaim that she got a squirrel and walk through the front door to her jumping up and down, holding it up for Ryan to see.

Ryan, crouching to help Nora out of her boots, smiles at Lexa. My heart squeezes every time Ryan interacts with our girls. He was meant to be a girl dad. I'm also happy he was just as done as I was when Nora was born because she was just as big as Lexa.

Even now, the top of Lexa's head brushes my shoulders at only ten years old. By next year, I'm sure I'll have to look up at her when I'm scolding her for not picking up her room.

"Daddy?" Nora grunts as she pulls off her wet socks, tossing them on the floorboards with a splat. "Can we go to the pack house now? I'm hungry."

"Yeah, yeah, but we're waiting for somebody. Go get some fresh socks on." He takes the squirrel from Lexa's hand to inspect it before handing it back to her. "Be sure to take this down to the pack house so the cooks can use it for supper tomorrow."

The girls start for the stairs, but I turn to Ryan, tucking my hair behind my ears. "Who are we waiting for? We're already late for dinner."

The bathroom door just around the corner of the kitchen opens, and heavy footsteps sound just out of sight, but the girls scream with joy and surprise.

"Oh," I manage to say, pushing Ryan away and tearing toward the tall dark-haired young man exiting the steamy bathroom in fresh clothes, his curly hair brushed back away from his face.

Logan picks up the girls and squeezes them tight, pressing a kiss to each of their foreheads.

"When did you get here?" I exclaim, my hands on my hips.

Logan glances at me, looking slightly guilty as he sets the girls down and tells them to go change. I feel Ryan come up behind me as Logan runs his hand over his freshly shaven face. "Uh, an hour ago."

"He just dropped in," Ryan says with a hint of amusement in his voice.

Logan purses his lips as he looks down at me, his eyes shining with guilt. At twenty-two, he's finally grown out of his boyish looks and his lanky frame. He's a man now. Tall, muscular, and scarred.

He notices me staring at the healing wounds on his knuckles and tucks his hands behind his back. I lick my lips and give him my best attempt at a motherly look of disapproval but... I've never truly been his mother. I've come about as close as possible to that role, but in truth, we only had four years with him before he shipped off to train to be a warrior in Moonrise under Ryatt's direction. He'd been sixteen then, and four years later, he returned for a summer before practically disappearing off the map.

That was last year.

A prickle of displaced anger rises in my chest, but I quickly banish it and step forward, wrapping my arms around him in a hug.

He leans down, resting his chin on the top of my head. "I'm sorry."

"You should be," I murmur into his shirt. "You asshole. It's been a year since we've heard from you. You were dead, for all we knew."

"You knew I was training with the Ghosts," he says as I pull away.

I glance up at Ryan, noticing the far off look in his eyes as his gaze sweeps over the scars and broken skin on Logan's hands. Ryan looks like he's about to say something, but the girls thunder back downstairs, begging to be taken to the pack house before they starve to death.

Thirty minutes later, I'm sitting at my usual table while Ryan does his evening rounds and the girls play with the other village children.

I pile their empty plates with a sigh, scanning the room until I find Logan standing with the group of boys—now men—he used to be friends with as a kid. Some of those friends went to warrior training in Moonrise when he did, but he was the only one who didn't return. Now, most of his friends have found their mates and have begun to start families like most twenty-two-year-old shifters do... but not Logan. He sticks out, honestly. His arms are crossed over his chest, and his face is cast in shadow as he chats quietly with old friends, but I notice the dark circles under his eyes and the aura of darkness around him.

"He's so grown up now," Freya says, sitting down with a bottle of currant wine. She pops the cork and pours me a glass, then turns to Mercy, who's braiding her youngest daughter, Moira's, hair.

"I know," I whisper, lifting my glass to my lips. It's sweet, but the aftertaste is more bitter than I remember... or maybe that's just the sour taste in my mouth.

"I heard he's a Ghost now," Mercy chimes in with a smile. "What an honor for Silverhide having one of our own be a part of that legion of Ryatt's army."

Freya nods, but I'm not smiling.

"I begged him not to join," I say under my breath.

"Oh, come on, Aviva," Freya smirks. "You're a commander, and you didn't want Logan to be a warrior like you? He worships the ground you walk on. You were a mother to him."

"I tried," I sigh, and Freya frowns, noticing the hurt in my voice. I don't need to tell her that I worry about Logan constantly. I've been worrying about him since the day he walked into our lives, but more so now that he's a man, and can… try to go *home*.

I told him once that this is what he needed to do, didn't I? If he wanted to see Emberfyll again, to fight for the home that was taken from him? I gave him the guide to make that happen but… he was so young then. I didn't think he'd actually do it, and I didn't realize how badly it'd hurt to watch him go.

Ryan comes over, pressing his palms on the table. "The girls want to stay with you tonight, Mercy. Gabriella told them Jacob finished building the doll house, and they want to play with it."

Mercy smiles, rolling her eyes as Moira jumps off her laugh to join the older girls. "Sure, but they're going to bed by nine."

Ryan shrugs, pleased with a night off from our kids, it seems, because he throws me a wink before walking away.

Mercy gets up with a sigh, gathering her plate. While I had two kids, Freya and Mercy didn't stop in the baby-making department until recently. Freya has four boys, with the youngest being only a year old, and Mercy and Jacob have six kids now, including a set of twins. Gabriella's a year younger than Lexa, and she's Lexa's best friend.

I watch Mercy walk to her mate, the two of them gathering up the hoard of children now having a sleepover at their house on the other side of the village, and walk out into the night.

But I remain at the table even after Freya takes her leave and the pack house grows quiet. Only a few groups remain at the long tables, but a shadow passes over me as I pour myself a second glass of currant wine, and Logan sits down across from me.

He takes the bottle, drinking deeply from it, and sets it down.

"Gross," I point out, giving him a look.

"It is gross. I hate currants."

I crack a smile despite myself, but he's looking at me, trying to read the expression I'm doing my best to keep hidden. "I should have written."

"Why didn't you?"

He flexes his jaw. "I've been traveling for a while, tracking a band of rebels in the Roguelands. I... we were undercover, and it was diffi-cult–" He cuts himself off with a sign, reaching for the bottle. I watch him take another drink, my eyes darting to the injuries–new and old–dotting his hands.

"You don't owe me an explanation. I'm not–not your mother–"

He covers my hands with him. "That's not why."

"Then where have you been?"

"Trying to find answers," he admits, and judging by his tone, it's difficult for him to say it. "I–I need to go back. To Emberfyll. Being part of the Ghosts gave me an opportunity to do that."

I pull my hands away, my eyes narrowing in confusion. "What do you mean?"

"The Kings of Tarsian are putting together an armada along the coast of Tarsian. There's been... signs of boats trying to reach our shores."

I feel like standing up in shock but freeze instead.

"Pieces of boats," he amends, swallowing hard. "I asked Evander if I could be stationed in Tarsian to aid the kings and their Alphas on the coast."

"So you've been in Tarsian–"

"I'm going to Tarsian," he says, his eyes holding mine. "Tomorrow."

I shake my head. "How long will you be gone?"

"Six, seven years... it depends on my contract and whether–whether–"

I bite my lip to stop from saying the words on the tip of my tongue, but they come out anyway. "Whether or not you can get on a boat and go back?"

He looks down at his hands. "I have to try."

I'm being selfish. I know I am. He's an adult now. He can make these decisions for himself, but... he's family. He's family, even if he doesn't see it that way. I feel a sudden jolt of anger at Evander, and even Ryatt, for allowing him to do this, but if there's really boats washing up on the shore of Tarsian, Logan's been the only survivor to ever wash up, and that was a decade ago.

Ryan starts walking toward us after lurking nearby, giving me a moment with our semi-adopted son. Logan notices his approach and straightens up, saying, "I should go, I think. I'm supposed to be at the border first thing in the morning–"

"You'll stay the night," Ryan cuts in with a sigh, nodding. "Stay the night, have another shower, eat a good breakfast, and then go." He pauses before adding, "We want to hear about it, Logan. Everything you've done."

Logan glances from Ryan to me.

"Because we're proud," I admit, even if it hurts knowing we're about to lose him again.

And for all we know, it'll be years before he's back.

If he comes back at all.

38

A DECISION HAS BEEN MADE

Sarah

"It isn't that serious," I tell Blake and Liam as they blink at me, their faces dappled with mud and their knees stained with grass. "But I've had enough of the fighting. You're too old for this, especially you, Blake." I fix my oldest son with a look I've had fourteen years to perfect.

Blake, now a teenager, purses his lips and frowns. "He's been harassing me all day—"

"You were supposed to be helping me clean the garage," Liam, thirteen, bites out.

I feel the tension beginning to boil between them and clear my throat. "Both of you, enough."

"Mom—"

"You're both already grounded," I edge, crossing my arms under my chest and arching a brow. "Do I need to add another week to your sentences? Or are you ready to behave like good little wolves and finish the chores Cosette laid out for you?"

Liam grumbles under his breath. Blake mimics my stance,

crossing his arms. We're eye level at this point, and Liam isn't far behind in the height department. Still, Ella and Maddy taught me their tricks when it came to perfecting the motherly glare, and both boys simmer down the second I narrow my eyes.

"Go finish cleaning out the garage," I grind out. "Without fighting."

Liam huffs, turning away and stomping out of my office on the first floor of our manor in Shadowcrest, but Blake makes no move to follow his brother.

I sink back into my chair and open my laptop. "Blake, I expect more from you. You're the oldest."

"By a year," he says under his breath, perching on the armrest of one of the twin chairs in front of my desk. He blinks up at the ceiling for a moment looking like the younger version of his dad. Liam takes after me in a lot of ways–the blond hair, the violet eyes. But Blake is Sydney reincarnated, right down to his all-business personality and general distaste for authority other than his own. He sighs, picking at the hem of his dad's old Wellington sweatshirt. The faded ink on the letterhead catches the late spring sunlight as silence settles through the room, but I can tell by his fidgeting that something is on his mind.

"What's up?" I ask, closing my laptop with a sigh.

"Did you and Dad talk about warrior training yet?"

"We've been discussing it, yes." I run my tongue along the front of my teeth. "When you come into your wolf, you'll be able to train. There's not much we can do before then."

"That could be two years away."

"Or longer," I tell him, resting my arms on my desk. "I didn't come into my wolf until I turned twenty-one."

"Well, Dad was sixteen."

"And you're fourteen. We don't want to rush you–"

He finally meets my eyes, that same endless, dark blue as Sydney's. "I want to train in Moonrise when I turn sixteen."

"Well," I say, rising, knowing the real fight is coming. "As a prince and your dad's heir, Wellington is… where you'll go, most likely."

He scans my face for weaknesses, for any cracks in my armor. "I don't want to go to Wellington. I want to go to Moonrise and do real wolf training, not whatever they do here."

"You are fourteen," I remind him. "We'll have this conversation in two years–"

"I'm like *you*, and you know it."

I freeze, resisting the urge to close my eyes to take a second to gather my bearings. "Have you–have you had another vision?"

He shrugs, looking down at his fingers before tucking his hands in the pocket of his sweatshirt. "No, but Liam's in the garage right now doing the chores I was supposed to be doing," he says matter-of-factly, going as far as to shrug like manipulating his little brother's mind is an okay thing to do.

"Knock it off," I whisper. "Blake, I'm serious. That's dangerous–"

"Then send me somewhere that can teach me to control it," he tells me, his cheeks flaring with frustration.

Footsteps sound in the hall outside my office. Blake continues to hold my gaze in challenge, however. While he looks like his dad, the man currently walking through my office door, Blake's mind is… like mine. His powers started showing themselves last year, starting off as nightmares that turned to visions, and now…. "Knock it off," I repeat firmly, and Sydney halts in the doorway, glancing between us.

Blake clicks his tongue, shaking his head as he stalks out of the room without so much as looking at his dad. Sydney watches him walk down the hallway before turning to me with a confused look on his face. "What was that about?"

"He's using his powers to manipulate Liam into doing his chores for him." I sigh, leaning on the side of my desk and thumbing the paperwork stacked on the edge just to do something with my hands. "He admitted it."

Sydney rests his hand on the top of the armchair Blake just exited, tapping his fingers. He stares at the floor in thought for a moment, but I already know what he's thinking.

What are we going to do?

"We need to consider letting him spend the summer in Moonrise. He's right." Sydney says after a moment.

I shake my head even though I know, deep down, it's the truth. "He's just a kid. Training with Mystics is… serious. Strenuous and intense, and I don't think he's ready."

"If he's breaking into Liam's mind, then he's ready." He meets my gaze. "Sarah, I know you're not ready, but he is."

"I barely understand my own powers. I don't want him to… hurt himself, you know?"

"He could hurt others if we don't do something."

I look down at my desk, closing my eyes against the rush of emotion tangling my thoughts. Sydney approaches me, wrapping an arm around my waist and pulling me toward him. He's right. The emergence of Blake's powers is something we've known would happen but have ignored for years. We're busy enough to ignore it, seeing as we have five kids and a full life, but our kids are growing up, and with that comes the powers our family is known for.

"Where are the girls?" he asks as I pull away to wipe my eyes.

"At Misty and Cole's. Noah's upstairs taking a nap," I explain, trying to smile past the nerves.

"I'll pick them up later, okay?"

I nod, chewing my lip as he starts to turn for the door, then pauses.

He sighs, dragging a hand over his face before turning back to me. "Dad called today."

"Oh? What about?"

"I'm not really sure. He wants us to come to the castle tonight, with the kids. He sounded strained, so I'm under the impression whatever he needs to meet with us about isn't just a family dinner."

I nod, noticing the lines of stress around his eyes.

"I'll go talk to Blake," he says, then slips out of the room. Upstairs, Noah's sleepy voice calls out for me.

* * *

MADDY EXCITEDLY GREETS THE KIDS AS WE STEP INTO THE CASTLE LATER that evening. Blake and Liam immediately head upstairs to the massive family-style room on the third floor where they were told in the car they could play video games for a while despite the fact that they're grounded. Celeste and Briar, the twins, scurry to the formal sitting room to play 'tea party' while Noah remains firmly at my side. He's only four and the baby of the family and likes to stay by me.... But Maddy has a surprise for him in the kitchen, apparently, and he's lured away by a maid with the promise of cookies and milk.

Maddy leads us into the formal sitting room, glancing at the girls playing with their tea set in the corner while Isaac leans over them, mumbling something about how the game would be better if coffee were on the menu, but then he sees us and gives us a short, flat smile.

My senses are going haywire. I have a feeling we're about to be told something bad–another war on the horizon or whatnot.

But when we're seated across from them on one of Maddy's fine fabric couches, Isaac sighs, smiling tenderly at his mate. "We've decided something," he says, turning back to me and Sydney. "Something that directly affects the two of you."

Sydney straightens. My hand finds his, our fingers knitting together. I imagine what Isaac might say next–that Sydney's being shipped off to fight in some skirmish with his forces again. That my services are needed for espionage.

But Maddy smiles at her husband, her dark blue eyes soft and shining with love and excitement. She looks at Sydney, saying, "You know how much we love Maatua and the time we've spent there. I feel like it's a family tradition now to plan to retire on the island and... I'm ready. I'm ready to step into a new pair of shoes, so to speak, and just be Grandma, not Luna Queen."

Sydney isn't breathing. I clutch his hand as Isaac says, "We've decided to step down, to step away from our throne and pass it on to you, Sydney."

Sydney takes a breath, but it's shallow. We knew this was coming but not this soon. Isaac was born to be Alpha King. He's just like Sydney and Blake. Stoic and serious. He's been an exceptional ruler that spirited Crescent Falls into a new age of peace and prosperity with our neighbors in Eastonia.

I honestly thought he'd rule until he died, but my eyes slide to Maddy, and I realize how wrong I'd been.

Just like Maddox and Isla, they've decided to slow down, to spend what time they have left–which could be decades–together.

It's exactly the conversation they've had and the reasoning behind their decision. Still, my head is spinning, and I'm still holding my mate's hand as I watch Maddy and Isaac happily discuss their plans, and ours, for the upcoming summer.

"The coronation will be held this fall," Maddy says excitedly, leaning against Isaac. "And Blake, as the heir, would be acknowledged as the royal prince, of course. That would be a ceremony in itself."

Sydney and I both go rigid at the mention of Blake. I already know we're going to have to fight him tooth and claw into a suit, but it's more than that.

Sydney, thankfully, is the one to say, "Blake will most likely be in Moonrise this summer, and possibly into the fall. But he'll... he'll be at the coronation, of course."

"Why is he going to Moonrise?" Isaac asks.

"For training," I say, hiding my feelings about it. Shipping my son away to the magical kingdom of my birth makes me feel a little sick to my stomach despite the fact he'll be surrounded by family while he's there... for what could be months, or years, depending on whether he can control his powers or needs more training as he matures.

The future I knew was coming suddenly barrels toward me, and I'm not prepared in the slightest.

Ever since the war a decade ago, I've been enjoying our slow, easy life. Our days are the same–structured and simple. I've had the luxury of watching our children grow up. They got to stay kids for longer than I did. Hell, Liam still plays with toys at thirteen when I was in hiding, trying to balance out my powers and pretend I was someone I wasn't.

Now, everything is going to change.

Sydney and I don't mention the bomb that was just dropped on us until later that night, tucked in our room and getting ready for bed. Sydney comes out of the bathroom in a T-shirt and sweatpants, checking his phone before slipping it onto a charger while I sit at my vanity and brush my hair until it shines.

"We'll have to move, won't we?" I ask into the silence.

"Yeah, we will. To the castle. It'll be ours and..." he trails off, looking down at his hands. "I thought I'd feel differently, I guess. I almost don't feel ready."

"It's because of the kids," I tell him, turning to look at him instead of his reflection. "I don't want to pull the girls out of school in Shadowcrest. I could drive them, I guess, seeing as I'll likely be giving up my job to take over Maddy's duties."

"And my job at the firm," he says under his breath, sinking onto the edge of the bed. I walk to him, sitting beside him and laying my head on his shoulder. He leans into my touch, drawing lazy circles on my arm with his thumb as we hold each other.

"You know... I thought, during the war when everything looked like we were going to lose... I thought it was such a shame that I wouldn't be able to see you as queen."

"That's what you were thinking?"

He nods, smiling a bit. "And now I'm wondering why I feel like this is happening too soon."

"It's up to them. They want to step down so you can rule. Otherwise, we might never see the throne." I laugh.

"I'm as shocked as you are that my dad is giving it up this easily, but I know Mom wants a break. She just wants to dote on the grandkids. I get it. She has so many of them now."

"I lost count ages ago," I smile.

"How do you think Blake is going to take it?" he asks lightly.

"I hope he takes it well... but he does need to train. I was wrong to doubt him. I think he's struggling with the powers that are emerging and... Moonrise is the best place for him."

Sydney presses a kiss to the top of my head. I close my eyes, wondering what our future as the Alpha King and Luna Queen of Crescent Falls will look like.

39

THE OUTCAST

Kenna

"STAY CLOSE, OKAY?" I SHOUT AS THE GIRLS HURRY AHEAD OF ME through the woven, interlocking streets of Moonrise. It's insane how much things have changed in the last decade. I tuck my phone in my purse; change number one. Yes, Eastonia has cell-phone service after decades of back and forth, but we've finally come out of the stone-age and into modernity, which includes change number two.

Brie yanks Maeve out of the way when a car comes barreling down the street, bumping over the cobblestone road. I lift a hand, waving at the careless driver. This area of the city is supposed to be pedestrian only, but not everyone follows the rules.

"Mom, we're going to be late!" Brie scolds, gripping Maeve's forearm. "Quit dragging your feet! You're going to scuff your shoes!"

"Then I'll get new ones," eleven-year-old Maeve grins, rolling her sea-green eyes.

The castle rises above us as the girls bicker back and forth. Brie, fifteen and so beautiful it hurts to look at her sometimes, throws me a look every once in a while that drips with annoyance, but I'm honestly not in a hurry. Not at all.

Brie's dark brown hair tumbles down her back as we walk through the main gate of the castle grounds, which is heavily guarded at all times. With the new road system between Eastonia and Crescent Falls came an influx of visitors and new residents, and while Eastonia remains peaceful, crime has risen in recent years, but that's to be expected when a city booms in size.

Moonrise is the capital of Eastonia–the gathering place of all magical kinds.

And today, I'm leaving one of my children here for what could be the rest of her life.

I bite back tears as my girls hurry up the steps. Maeve skips every other step, much to Brie's annoyance. Maeve and Brie are complete opposites. Maeve is playful but tends to fly by the seat of her pants, throwing caution to the wind.

Brie is... a rock. Solid in conviction and sense. She's the reason Maeve was able to have a childhood in Veiled Valley without needing to worry about her powers getting in the way. She raised Maeve as much as Evander and I did, and I know that right now, she's hurting as badly as I am...

But Brie isn't tenderhearted like me. It's impossible to know what she's feeling on any given day. Stoic, brave, and unfazed, she leads her little sister into the castle while I follow behind and let her take the lead.

"You'd better start being nice to me," Maeve teases, wiggling her fingers at Brie. "When I learn magic, the first thing I'm going to do is turn you into a toad!"

"You wouldn't dare," Brie shrugs, tucking her hands in the pockets of her jeans. "I can't braid your hair if I'm a toad, anyway."

Maeve halts in her tracks, her shoulders going rigid as she turns to me, then back to Brie. "Who's going to braid my hair now, then?"

"One of the maids," I say, walking past them up the main stairs. "Or any friends you make at school."

"You have to be nice to make friends," Brie adds, following close behind.

Maeve huffs, mumbling under her breath as we climb the stairs and cross into the private wing of the massive castle where I grew up and where the girls have spent so much time during their short lives.

We've been living in Veiled Valley exclusively for the past decade. I love it there. I love being the Alpha. I love having a warm home to share with my mate and our family… but our children are growing up. Aris, fourteen, has only another two years at home before he goes to Moonrise for training in the wolf arts. Brie will be graduating school soon and moving onto college in Veiled Valley, where she plans to study history and law.

And Maeve… she'll be here, training to become queen.

My throat tightens, making it impossible to swallow. The girls dart ahead of me down the hallway when my dad steps out of his office and opens his arms wide to catch them in a hug.

"Is Mom in her office?" I ask in passing, but Dad shakes his head.

"She's upstairs, the formal sitting room."

I keep moving while the girls stay behind with my dad. I feel like the world is moving in slow motion as I near the upper quarters of the castle—the rooms we named by the color of their wallpaper. I pass the private apartments where my cousins stay when they visit, and by the time I reach the sitting room bathed in butter yellow with warm cream finishes, my chest is tight, and I'm sure my expression matches the overwhelming feeling that time has moved far more quickly than I'd hoped.

Mom's sitting on a couch with Amanda, my mother-in-law and the wife of Granger, Ryatt's Beta. Amanda rushes to me, giving me a quick hug before asking where the girls are and then hurries away to dote on her granddaughters.

"Do you want some tea? It's the ginger kind from the Deadlands that you like," Mom asks, motioning toward a tray on the coffee table.

I sit in an armchair across from her and nod, watching as she pours the steaming amber liquid into a dainty tea cup and hands it to me. I pray my hands don't shake, but they do.

"Where's Evander?" she asks, looking toward the entrance of the room.

"He's with Aris at the training ground. Aris wanted a tour of the arena and barracks, of course. He says he can't possibly wait another two years to start his training."

"Well, two years will fly by, I'm sure. Starting him early wouldn't be a problem, you know. He's more than welcome to stay here, like Maeve."

I chew my lower lip before taking a sip of tea to calm my nerves. "He's been training his Shadowsynger gifts with me, and that's been fine. He could use the two years to hone those gifts before moving onto his wolf powers."

Mom's jade green eyes meet mine, scanning for any cracks in my dismal emotional armor. Unlike my eldest daughter, I wear my heart on my sleeve, and I've never been able to hide what I feel. It's my greatest weakness.

"Kenna," she breathes. "It's going to be okay. The fact we made it eleven years without Maeve accidentally killing someone is a miracle."

"I know," I reply, on the verge of breaking down completely. A decade ago, I'd been heavily considering leaving Maeve with my parents here in Moonrise full time. Maeve's powers were enormous–too much for her little body to handle, especially as a baby.

She's been learning how to contain her powers her entire life... but now she's going to learn to use them, and I am terrified she'll get hurt–or hurt someone else.

"You're doing the right thing for her," Mom says softly, giving me a weak smile. "You've always done the right thing for her."

"I've done my best," I whisper, taking another sip of tea. "I really have. Maeve is... she's a lot. Not just her powers, but her personality. She's the opposite of Brie, and Brie has been so–so good all her life."

"How is Brie doing with this?"

I sigh, setting my cup done. "She's fine. You know Brie is always fine. She'll never say she's not."

"Maeve and Brie are very close," Mom cuts in, shaking her head.

"When Maeve ascends my throne, it might be in her best interest to have Brie as–as perhaps a second in command, an advisor."

"She's already planning on it," I admit, turning my cup in a circle just to do something with my hands. "She plans on studying history and law, like I've said before. I just wish–I wish she'd tell me if it's truly what she wanted to do. I feel like everything she does is to make us happy, and I–gods, Mom–I wish she'd act out. Sneak out, kiss boys, steal wine from the kitchen, you know."

"You never did those things." Mom laughs, but I cut her a look.

"You did."

"Well, I was a very different kind of person, and I also grew up in Crescent Falls, so there's that." She pours me another cup of tea, the strange scars on her hairline a glossy white against her skin. Her eyes meet mine, soft and understanding. "You've done an amazing job with these kids, Kenna. Maeve is going to be fine. Aris will calm down and grow up; it takes boys longer to do that. Your father didn't start maturing until his forties, honestly."

I smile despite the ache in my chest.

"And Brie will find herself."

I shake my head, biting back my own guilt at the mention of her name. "She knows she's not like us. She knows she's adopted, of course. We never kept that from her, but... she doesn't have powers like we do. Even Evander is advanced when it comes to shifting–can shift into multiple forms–but Brie is a shifter, through and through. This shift in our family dynamic with Maeve leaving for school and Aris on the cusp of his own journey... Brie has been different. Quieter than usual. More serious."

Mom watches me, her smile fading.

"Brie actually mentioned," I begin, taking a sharp breath, "the need to start... looking into possible matches for marriage."

Mom laughs, "She's fifteen!"

"I know," I sigh, shaking my head. "But her argument is honestly quite sound, if you think about it. She's a princess. She's the eldest daughter of the Alpha of Veiled Valley and the granddaughter of the Queen of Eastonia. She says she has to find a match in someone with similar rank–an Alpha, for sure, or the heir of one. I told her it didn't matter to me, but she argued against it."

"Because she feels like her worth is in her rank?"

"It's an outdated notion, but yes. She doesn't have powers like us. I think she feels like she doesn't fit in with our family, and I hate that."

"She'll grow out of that feeling," Mom tries to say, but I don't believe it.

"She does everything she can to prove her worth to us even though we've never asked that of her. Evander is in pieces about it. He'd rather her go into a convent and be a priestess than marrying someone just because she feels the need to be matched with an Alpha. I can't take it, Mom. These kids are… killing me."

"Well, that's motherhood."

"When you were growing up," I interrupt, leaning forward, "did Grandpa and Grandma expect you to marry an Alpha just because you were a princess?"

"Grandpa? Yes, probably. But I think they were just shocked I survived my teenage years," she says with a smirk. "Isaac was actually the one who demanded that of me when he rose to the throne, and our parents moved to Maatua. It's a reputation thing. I was the sister of the king–who I ended up with was a direct reflection on our family."

"Exactly. That's how Brie feels about it, and I can't convince her otherwise."

"Then what will you do when the time comes? When she's grown and looking for a mate?"

"Support her? I don't know."

"And if her mate is a low-born soldier?" she asks.

I meet my mom's eyes. "She'd reject him. She'd reject him because, in her mind, she's only worthy of having us as a family if she contributes… even if that means marrying someone she doesn't like only for his title. How do I change her mind, Mom?"

"I don't think you can," Mom replies honestly. "But maybe, one day, her mate can."

40

I NEED AN ALPHA

"He can't be that bad, Brie," Maeve hisses as she clutches the crook of my arm, leading us down one of the winding staircases in our castle in Veiled Valley. Sconces flare to life on their own accord, lighting our way. "Mom said he's been dying to meet you, anyway. He's a warrior, you know. They're always *so* handsome."

I purse my lips as she tightens her grip. "You're entertained at my expense."

"You don't get to complain. You're doing this to yourself!" Maeve throws her head back in a beautiful laugh that echoes down the corridor. Everything my little sister does is beautiful because she's stunning. Beautiful of the drop-dead gorgeous variety. She's also only eighteen, and I doubt she fully grasps what this meeting with the Alpha of Rainway, a nearby pack in the mountains bordering Veiled Valley, and his warrior son means.

Mom and Dad wouldn't marry me off. I know that for a fact... but it doesn't mean that Mom isn't going to try to help me find my mate.

Not that I'm in a rush or anything. I'm only twenty-two, but Mom's a romantic, and I'm… *adopted.*

Maeve tugs me to a stop in an alcove with a full length mirror. The magic that makes the castle come alive swirls around our ankles before pulling back the curtains in the alcove to let in the warm afternoon sunlight.

"Oh, this is just gorgeous," Maeve croons as she adjusts the fabric on my deep purple gown. It shimmers in the sunlight–tight around my waist and ample breasts but falling loose around my hips before cascading to the ground.

She pulls a few pins free so my hair falls loose down my back in light-brown, spiral curls.

"There. You're ready."

I stare at my reflection as she fidgets with the skirt of my gown again. Even though I'm the elder sister, she's several inches taller than me. Her hair is rich, dark brown, and her eyes are the color of polished sea-glass as she meets my eyes in the mirror's reflection. She squeezes my shoulders, smiling, but her eyes are slightly sad. "I could… sneak you out?"

I smirk, looking down at my shoes. "It's fine. I'll be fine." I've been fine the last ten times I've worn a dress like this and paraded myself in front of Alphas and their powerful sons. It's Mom I'm worried about.

Another rush of air swirls around our ankles.

"We're going!" Maeve groans, reaching up to flick the scone above her head. "I swear, the older we get, the more bossy the castle becomes!"

I don't fight the smile tugging on the sides of my mouth as she takes my arm and hurries me down the corridor. The castle groans around us like it's annoyed it took us so long to get ready. I often wonder if the castle wants me to find my mate–or, at least, a husband–as much as my mother does because it gets rather excited when events like this spring up.

Maeve knits her fingers through mine as we reach the side doors leading into the formal dining room, which we rarely use as a family, but I can already smell the food and wine and feel the slight heat coming from what I assume are dozens of candles the castle arranged throughout the room to give the place a more romantic ambiance.

"You need to chill," I say to the magic rippling all around us. "It's not that serious."

As if in answer, the doors fly open, revealing my mother looking slightly flushed and an elderly man swishing a glass of wine.

I take a deep breath. Maeve watches me inhale, then exhale, and takes the first step into the room.

"Oh, there she is," Mom says, her silver eyes shining with relief and a hint of annoyance as she briefly glances at Maeve, who's smiling like a cat. "Alpha Fredrick, these are my daughters." She steps to the side, extending her hand in our direction. "Princess Brie and Princess Maeve of Veiled Valley."

Alpha Fredrick gives us each a polite bow before straightening, but his gaze lingers on me for a moment. I notice how he refuses to look at Maeve all together, but I'm used to that. So is she, actually, because people have been weary of her since birth.

Maeve wastes no time swaying toward the refreshment table and pouring herself a glass of wine, ignoring the daggers mom's shooting in her direction. I purse my lips to stop from laughing as Maeve sways past us again, white wine in hand, knowing full well Mom doesn't like her drinking at the young age of nineteen but isn't about to fuss with company standing mere feet away.

I do notice, however, the insane amount of food and drinks laid out and the fact that Alpha Frederick is here... alone.

I glance around, but we're the only people in the dining hall. "Alpha Frederick," I begin, giving him a practiced smile. "I was under the assumption you wanted me to meet your son, your heir, Michael."

"Yes, of course, but he's indisposed at the moment. We've had some bandits near our southern border in the past weeks, and he decided to stay behind in the event we came under attack."

Mom raises her brows. "I didn't know. Is it serious?"

"No, Alpha Kenna," he says with a slight bob of his head. "Our pack is able to handle it. It's one of the... unfortunate developments that came with your father's road projects, I'm sorry to say. But we're a hardy, well trained pack. Our warriors are top of the line." His gaze sweeps back to me. "We've needed someone strong to help lead our pack when the time comes for my son to take over in my stead."

"Ah," I say, smiling despite the discomfort raging through my body. "Well, I understand that completely. Your son isn't mated, then?"

"No, and he's well into his thirties."

"Oh," I reply, unsure what else to say. I'm sure some would look at this situation and wonder why my parents would be okay with this in the slightest. I'm essentially on auction, being paraded like something to buy. It wasn't like this a year ago, when I turned twenty-one. I'd been allowed to travel, to go to the mating balls and festivals all across Eastonia and Crescent Falls.

But... I'm a royal. I don't date. I'm not using one of those fancy apps that help match people with their prospective mates. I have expectations about my future partner, and so does my family. I will marry someone of high rank, of high standing. I will be a Luna one day because my family is extremely influential and powerful.

The only problem is that I'm *not*.

"So, I must ask," Alpha Frederick says, turning to my mother. "What are her gifts?"

Mom's smile flatters. "I'm sorry?"

"Her powers," he urges, his eyes flicking to my face before turning back to my mom. "What can we expect from her future bloodline?"

I chew my lower lip as Mom gapes. Maeve, eavesdropping on the other side of the room, arches her brow when I meet her eyes.

This is the reason I'm not having any luck finding my mate, or even a boyfriend, for Goddess' sake.

"I'm a shifter," I say. "Is that not powerful enough for you, Alpha?"

"Yes, but what else are you?"

He wants to know if I can turn into a shadow like my mother, or shoot fire and light from my fingers like my sister, or read minds and manipulate time like my aunts and uncles.

"I can shift. That's it. Is that not enough for you, Alpha?" The bite in my voice is obvious. So much so that Mom actually flinches like she hasn't heard this very conversation time, and time, again.

The castle, eavesdropping just like my sister, blows out every single candle. Alpha Frederick gapes, glancing at my mom, then turning to look at Maeve, likely wondering which of them used their powers to extinguish the flames.

I step back and curtsy before turning my body toward the door, extending my hand. "It was lovely meeting you, Alpha Frederick."

He chews his lower lip before scurrying out of the dining hall. The doors close on a phantom wind and the candles immediately reignite.

Mom turns to me, shaking her head. "Brie, I don't want to do this anymore."

"We have to," I say, pinching a piece of invisible lint off my dress and flicking it away.

"We don't." She turns and walks toward Maeve, saying, "In fact, this is over. I hate this, Brie." She snatches the wine out of Maeve's hand, ignoring her exaggerated whine. "You're not a breeder being sent to auction. You're my daughter—and a princess."

"I'm also normal," I rasp, pouring myself a glass of wine to ease the ache spreading through my chest.

Silence hugs the room for several heart beats, and I know I've struck a nerve.

My parents are wonderful. They love me—have loved me from the moment they met me twenty-two years ago. It was never a secret I was adopted and why, but I grew up in a family who have powers. Immense, unbelievable powers.

I am the odd one out in my generation, and now everyone knows it.

"I've already talked to your father, and we've decided maybe it's best you spend some time in Crescent Falls this summer."

"I want to go to Crescent Falls, too!" Maeve rushes me, skidding to stop at my side and leans in. "Please, Mom!"

"You'll be in Moonrise with your grandparents for training,

remember?" Mom picks up a grape and pops it into her mouth, chewing slowly.

"I'm staying here," I say, shaking my head. "I don't want to go to Crescent Falls, and I have no reason to go."

"If your mate is there—"

"He's not, and even if he were, he'd likely be just as turned off by the fact I'm nothing but a shifter, and I can add nothing to his *bloodline.*"

"Brie, that's not what's important."

"But it is," I say as calmly as possible, pacing across the room. "This is what I have to do. Marry an Alpha. I'm a princess. I'm also power-less. I don't have the luxury of time, like Maeve and Aris do. Like you did. If I don't find my mate, I need to settle, and… I will."

I want to fit in somewhere. I want to be somewhere I'm not just the powerless princess. I need to make a match that honors my family after all they've done for me. I need an Alpha. I am more than my birth. I am more than the orphan I could have been.

"You're breaking my heart," Mom says, but her words are absorbed by the doors to the dining room opening and dozens of heavy foot-steps charging in our direction.

Maeve whirls us toward the door just as Dad comes into view, dressed in his usual all black attire. His dark blond hair is peppered with white, but his dark green eyes are soft as he takes us in, giving us an uncharacter-istic smile. Maeve rushes into his arms while I hang back with Mom. She takes my hand, leaning in to whisper, "We'll talk about this later."

Aris steps into the room beside Dad, throwing me a cocky grin before clapping me on the shoulder. "Miss me?"

"Never," I tease, smiling in earnest as he steps past me toward the refreshments.

But at least a dozen warriors—all in black Ghost-issued uniforms, follow, stopping to bow or nod in hello to the royals in the center of the room.

Dad presses a kiss to Mom's temple before saying, "We'll be in and out. The Ghosts will be staying in the barracks."

"I figured you'd be hungry, so I had a late lunch laid out for everyone…"

Their voices fade as a strange feeling sets my senses on fire. My heartbeat roars in my ears, my vision going slightly hazy as I turn as if in slow motion.

Aris walks over to me, biting into a sandwich, but whatever he's saying to me as he reaches my side falls on deaf ears. A tall, dark haired man stands near the refreshment table with his arms crossed, his head bowed as one of his Ghost buddies chats at him. He nods along, his face totally expressionless.

"And then Dad said you're still making Mom set you up on dates with Alphas, and I said I'm sure I can set you up with someone if you're that serious–"

Aris's voice drowns out, turning to just… noise. The man lifts his head and goes perfectly, utterly still before slowly looking in my direction.

His hazel eyes turn nearly black as his pupils expand, his gaze locked on mine.

Time stands still.

"Oh," Aris says beside me, chuckling. "Oh, shit. Brie, you probably haven't seen him in years. Logan, come over here–"

Logan. Logan… the kid Aviva and Ryan took in like seventeen years ago? Surely not. The last time I saw him, I was thirteen or fourteen spending the summer in Moonrise, and he'd been one of the trainers Aris couldn't stop talking about when he went through warrior training.

I watch Logan's tongue dart out, sweeping across his lip. My heart pounds out of rhythm. I can't catch my breath and everything in the room feels like it's spinning, and I can't… breathe….

"Brie?" Maeve reaches my side, clutching my arm.

"I don't feel well," I rush out, reaching down to tug on the fabric clutching my waist which is suddenly too tight.

Maeve glances at Aris before turning me toward the door, but out of the corner of my eye I see Logan, who I'm still trying to place in my memory, taking a single step in my direction, his hands curling into fists at his sides.

Thank you for reading! Book 13 will be out in May, 2025!

ALSO BY BELLA MOONDRAGON

The Alpha King's Breeder series:

Bought by the Alpha: The Alpha King's Breeder Book 1

Loved by the Alpha: The Alpha King's Breeder Book 2

Lost by the Alpha: The Alpha King's Breeder Book 3

Luna of the Alpha: The Alpha King's Breeder Book 4

Legacy of the Alpha: The Alpha Kings's Breeder Book 5

Daughter of the Alpha: The Alpha King's Breeder Book 6

Descendants of the Alpha: The Alpha King's Breeder Book 7

Shadow of the Alpha: The Alpha King's Breeder Book 8

Son of the Alpha: The Alpha King's Breeder Book 9

Spare of the Alpha: The Alpha King's Breeder Book 10

Claimed by the Alpha: The Alpha King's Breeder Book 11

Atonement for the Alpha King: The Alpha King's Breeder Book 12

Rejected by the Alpha: The Alpha King's Breeder Book 13

The Luna's Vampire Prince series:

The Culling

The Kingdom

The Conquered

Pregnant With Four Alphas' Babies

Chosen As the Breeder

Mated to Four Alphas

Threats Against the Breeder

At War for the Breeder

The Stolen Breeder

Four Alphas, Four Babies

Becoming the Luna Queen

Descendants of the Breeder

Desired by the Devil series

Whispers of the Devil

Banter of the Devil

Murmurs of the Devil

The Mafia Kings series

Indebted to the Mafia King

<u>Loved by the Mafia King</u>

Claimed by the Mafia King

Secrets of the Mafia King

Burned by the Mafia King

Kidnapped by the Mafia King (coming soon!)

Dark Stalker Romance series

Tempted by Sin

Fated by Sin

Secret Billionaires series

Finding the Secret Billionaire by Olivia Bhelle Kildare

Falling for My Secret Billionaire by Bella Moondragon

Driven by the Secret Billionaire by ID Johnson

Wolf Shifter Alpha Kings series

Ravens and Ruins

Sundrops and Shadows

Snowflakes and Sabotage (Preorder now!)

The Vampire King's Feeder series

Claiming the Alpha's Daughter

Loving the Alpha's Daughter

Finding the Alpha's Daughter

Writing as B. Moon

The Boy Who Died

Sign up for Bella's newsletter here.

Or get a free novella from The Alpha King's Breeder series when you sign up here:
The Beta and the Maid

Follow Bella on Facebook here.

Follow Bella on Bookbub here.